SOUR GRAPES

SOUR GRAPES

Marilyn Todd

This first world edition published in Great Britain 2005 by
SEVERN HOUSE PUBLISHERS LTD of
9–15 High Street, Sutton, Surrey SM1 1DF.
This first world edition published in the USA 2006 by
SEVERN HOUSE PUBLISHERS INC of
595 Madison Avenue, New York, N.Y. 10022.

British Library Cataloguing in Publication Data

Todd,   Marilyn
    Sour grapes
    1.   Claudia Seferius (Fictitious character) - Fiction
    2.   Murder - Investigation - Italy - Tuscany - Fiction
    3.   Tuscany (Italy) - Fiction
    4.   Rome - History - Empire, 30 B.C. – 284 A.D. - Fiction
    5.   Detective and mystery stories
    I.   Title
    823.9'14 [F]

    ISBN-10 : 0-7278-6317-7 (cased)
                     0-7278-9158-8 (paper)

Typeset by Palimpsest Book Production Ltd.,
Polmont, Stirlingshire, Scotland.
Printed and bound in Great Britain by
MPG Books Ltd., Bodmin, Cornwall.

If there's a better way to grovel to the in-laws, I don't know it . . . so this book's for Bob!

One

L ow, grey clouds had fused with the hills, turning the landscape to lead. Gone were the lush vines that terraced the slopes. Gone were the olive groves that swept down the valley. Gone were the pastures for sheep. All that remained was a keen wind that whistled, and a nearby rumble of thunder.

Bent forward into the gale, a torch of flaming pitch in the one hand, a stick of stout laurel in the other, the old woman shouted his name. She waited. Listened. But once again, it was only the whine of the wind that answered her call and, as she pressed on up the steep mountain path, the first drops of rain started to fall.

Could it be thieves? Aye, the lambing season was a dangerous time. Wolves would devour every last one, given the chance, though not all wolves had four legs. This time of year thieves were all over, so it could, you know. It could well be thieves, and they wouldn't care that they'd stole from folk who owned just a handful of sheep. The poor were easy targets. You can't steal from a rich man's estate.

'Tages? Tages, can you hear me, boy?'

As she lifted the torch to guide her way, a crack of lightning lit up the beeches and chestnuts. Branches thrashed, silver with menace, then thunder boomed right overhead and suddenly the whole forest was creaking – groaning – moaning – in unison.

'*Tages?*'

Twilight darkened to black, rain lashed at the landscape, chilling the air and turning the trail oily with mud. Across the valley, rheumy eyes watched the lights of Mercurium twinkling out a grid of warmth and reassurance through the

1

storm, but Etha didn't waver. She'd raised this boy from a babe, loved him in spite of his birth killing her daughter. He was all the old woman had.

'Sweet Nortia, who holds our fortunes, I beseech thee.' Setting her stick to one side, she laid a hand on the earth in which the goddess made her abode. 'Vetha, who controlleth the seasons.' She held out her hand to catch the rain. 'Mighty Tins, who sendeth the thunderbolts and Uni, Queen of the Cosmos, hear me.' Earth, water, fire and air. 'Keep this boy safe, I beg of ye – and if it pleases ye that the Herald of Death visit tonight, let him visit upon me, not Tages. Tages is a good boy. An honest boy . . .'

She was unable to carry on for the lump in her throat, and, stumbling over the roots as thorns pulled at her skirt, the cold in her bones went unnoticed. Even when a blast of wind doused her torch, Etha didn't turn back, and though her fringed shawl flapped sodden at her breast, the old woman continued to climb.

'Where you are, Tages?'

It had to be thieves. What else could it be? He was a smart lad, and at seventeen he was skilled with the slingshot, so sure it was some dirty thief that had sneaked up on him. She paused for a moment to rest on her laurel stick. That would be all right, then. Thieves don't kill. Not for one or two lambs. She'd find him any minute, aye, that she would, with a bump on the head and a right tale to tell . . .

Wouldn't she?

As Etha called her grandson's name into the night, the wind echoed her pain.

Two

'**D**on't be ridiculous.'

Claudia pushed her stepdaughter out of the road, where the girl was single-handedly causing a jam of donkeys, handcarts, wheelbarrows and sheep. Not that Claudia had any particular aversion to gridlock. But the ears of that mule suggested it wasn't going to take much more of the driver's switch stinging its rump, and guess who was closest if it decided to kick?

'Your grandmother can't possibly be mooning over some man—'

'I didn't say *mooning*.' Flavia had to shout over the bleating of lambs. 'I said she was in *love*. It's serious.'

'There you go, then.' Claudia steered the girl down a side street lined with balconies that were fragrant with potted hyacinths and narcissus. 'I always said the old bag was soft in the head and this proves it. Now for heaven's sake, pick your feet up or the ceremony will be over before we've reached the wretched bridge.'

Dear Diana, this girl would come last in a snail race, she thought, hooking left at the goldsmith's, and it wasn't as though Flavia was the only lumpy, frumpy, dumpy creature on the marriage market. Rome was teeming with girls every bit as sullen, and they were being snapped up faster than a lizard catches flies. Ducking between the pepper warehouse and a marble store, she thanked Fortune that her late husband had had the good grace to foster Flavia on to his sister when his daughter was born. Inheriting Gaius's entire estate was one thing. Being stuck with this dozy dollop quite another.

'I don't know why we're bothering with this stupid ceremony.'

Typical Flavia. Gripe, gripe, gripe. Moan, moan, moan. Devoted to the great god, Me.

'Because consigning twenty-seven sacred effigies into the Tiber is a solemn religious occasion,' Claudia replied briskly. 'It's high time you stopped thinking of yourself all the time and started thinking of your duty to Rome.'

Or in this case, three hundred sesterces and, as she hastened her pace down the Aventine, Claudia reflected that there was no point in having double standards if you can't live up to both. That bookmaker on Tuscan Street had been taking bets as far back as last Sunday as to which of the *Argei* would be first past the next pier downriver. It was something to do with the current, she supposed, but Twelve had never failed her in the past.

'Now do stop slouching,' she said, yanking Flavia's shoulders back. 'You're giving hunchbacks a bad name.'

Ahead of them, the river shone silver in the afternoon sun, the reflections of its tree-lined banks rippling gently in the wake of the barges, though the plod of the oxen that pulled them was drowned by the crowds streaming down to the Sublician Bridge.

'I suppose you'd better tell me about your grandmother's latest act of folly,' Claudia said, elbowing her way through the crush for a better view.

Terrible thing, senility, she thought, and Larentia's problems were escalating fast. But how on earth do you reason with a mother-in-law who's got it into her head that there's a jinx going round and, fearful of catching it, takes herself off to the hills on the principle that if fir trees can filter germs and prevent people from catching a cold, why can't they stop someone from catching bad luck? Unfortunately, Larentia's faculties weren't fading so fast that she returned home any less waspish, but when a straight-talking, straightforward, cantankerous old battle-axe announces that she's installing a sorceress called Candace to cast spells to protect her, Claudia felt it would be like kicking a puppy to throw the charlatan out.

'Who do we need to apologize to for your grandmother's unwanted attentions?' she asked, as the Vestal Virgins lined up against the parapet.

4

A flute began to play, and twenty female acolytes dressed in white were joined by the Priestess of Jupiter, bringing the tally of celebrants to twenty-seven. With great solemnity, each was handed a small white effigy, little doughboys who had been baked hard and dusted in flour, and who were now set to propitiate Old Man Tiber. Claudia concentrated hard on Number Twelve as the effigies were released. Swim, three hundred sesterces, swim . . .

'They're not unwanted,' Flavia said, her perpetually turned-down mouth turning down even further. 'Some old fogey called Darius has asked her to marry him.'

Fifteen, Eighteen and Twenty-Two smashed on impact, Three, Five and Ten washed up on the bank, while numbers Twenty-Three to Twenty-Seven had already sunk to the bottom.

'Nonsense.'

Claudia's knuckles gripped the wooden rail. Two, Four and Seven were stuck in an eddy, Six and Eight were turning to mush. Come on Number Twelve! You can make it!

'Who on earth would want to marry your grandmother? She has no money.'

Claudia had inherited every copper quadran of her husband's estate and frankly the old bag was lucky to get an allowance. It had been open warfare from the day Gaius introduced his pretty, witty trophy wife to his mother – the only difference was, wars usually end.

'Who cares?' Flavia shrugged. 'Darius is rolling.'

Nineteen, Twenty and Twenty-One were caught in the weeds. It was the mid-runners, as usual, swirling downstream, although Number One might yet pull a surprise from the left.

'Then good luck to them,' Claudia said as Sixteen and Seventeen bumped heads and span off in separate directions. Down to six little effigies left in the running, one of them worth three hundred sesterces.

'Luck has nothing to do with it, according to Candace.' Flavia was more interested in chewing her nails than watching the race. 'It was the spirits that brought the two love birds together, she says, and she says my father's given the wedding his seal of approval, as well.'

Twelve gods on Olympus, it has to be lucky. *Come on, come on, Number Twelve!*

'Flavia, sweetheart, your father's been in his grave for three years. He can't possibly give the marriage his blessing.'

A swirl in the current put paid to Number Nine. Five little doughboys remained.

'Oh, yes, he can! Candace has spoken to him. She walks the wind and communes with the dead, and she's even let me talk to Papa myself. He's terribly well, honestly, and very happy where he is.'

Number One, the outsider, hit a dead cow floating down. It was neck and neck between Eleven, Twelve, Thirteen and Fourteen.

'And where exactly *is* your father, did he say?'

Only someone in the last throes of senility couldn't see through this Candace fraud. Correction. Only someone in the last throes of senility and a sulky teenage brat!

'Never thought to ask, but he sends you his love.'

'Does he indeed?'

Things were looking good. Eleven had sunk, while Fourteen snagged in the current and was starting to come back upstream.

'You know, Flavia, I think I might just go up to Mercurium and have a cosy chat with your father myself.'

Communing with the dead, my eye, and besides, it was high time Claudia looked in on those Tuscan vineyards. She was, after all, a wine merchant. Wouldn't hurt to see where the stuff came from, she supposed . . . And now it was just Twelve and Thirteen neck and neck. Yes, definitely something to do with the current.

'If you think I'm coming with you, you're mistaken. It's boring.'

'Nonsense, you'll have your father to talk to.'

'You only want me up there so you can palm me off on some dreary old fart in the country, where I'd just *die*.'

'Trust me,' Claudia assured her. 'That's not what I have planned, and since your foster mother's stuck in Naples looking after her sick cousin, you're in my care and what I say goes . . . *Bugger*.'

Thirteen had sailed straight under the bridge, and where was Number Twelve? Splattered all over the bloody pier, that's where it was, having crashed at the very last turn. Claudia felt a hole well up inside where three hundred sesterces should have been as the remnants of her effigy were devoured by six hungry ducks. How was she supposed to pay off her creditors now?

'You've gone green,' Flavia observed cheerfully. 'Is it something you ate?'

'No, that's just the taste of dreams being swallowed.'

Dreams of not being permanently in debt. Dreams of not having to constantly look over her shoulder. Dreams of freeing the shackles once and for all . . .

One by one, the crowd began to disperse, until only step-mother and stepdaughter remained peering into the thick, muddy waters. Oh, well. Claudia's fortunes might be dashed on the piers and the soothsayer might well be a fraud, but thanks to Doddering Darius, Larentia was one burden Claudia would no longer have to shoulder – and shortly, Fortune willing, the weight of financing her stepdaughter and funding the girl's sponges of foster parents would also be lifted from her.

'Flavia, there's something I need to talk to you about.'

'If it's about picking my nose in public, Aunt Julia's already worn her tonsils down on that one.'

'Yes. Well. We'll discuss that endearing habit another time.' Claudia took hold of the girl's hand, because this was no time to have the silly cow run off. 'The thing is, we – that is, your foster parents and I – have found the perfect husband for you, um, darling. His name is . . .' Wait, it would come to her. 'His name . . . Anyway, the point is, he's a wonderful boy.'

Bit gangly perhaps, and maybe his front teeth did cross a tad, though quite honestly it was hardly noticeable unless he laughed. But the law was the law. If a woman was of child-bearing age, she was obliged to marry and bear children and the State was unequivocal. Choose a husband yourself or have one appointed for you, and despite being the daughter of a prestigious wine merchant, Flavia was rapidly running

7

out of options. Every time the family identified a suitable candidate, she'd fob him off until it reached the point where her maidenhood was the only thing that kept suitors knocking on her door. For once, virginity could not be underestimated.

'He's honest, reliable, not at all the type to sleep around, drink or gamble, and everyone agrees that he'll make you an admirable husband.'

'Nope.'

'He's wealthy, his parents are extremely nice people, you'd have your own house here in Rome, where your babies can be reared in comfort with the help of the very finest physicians—'

'No, no, no, no, and in case you're not getting the message, *no.*'

'All right, it mightn't be a match made in heaven, but – ha, ha, ha – even in those marriages the day-to-day maintenance is done here on earth.'

'Don't care.' Flavia snatched her little fat hand back. 'I'm not having Honest-and-Admirable's babies and that's final.' She crossed her arms over her chest to prove the point. 'I'm having Orson's.'

'Are you, indeed. And who's Orson?'

'Honestly!' Flavia rolled her eyes contemptuously. 'He's the boy who made me pregnant, of course.'

Three

The sun was sinking as Claudia blazed a path through the crowds that had gathered for their evening entertainment in the Forum. If some money-grubbing, fortune-seeking, low-born, no-good scoundrel thought that by siring a baby out of wedlock he could worm his way into the Seferius fortune, he was bloody well mistaken, she thought, skirting the sacred lotus tree, where a Sabean Arab in fringed robes offered rides on a mange-ridden camel. For one thing, by the time she'd taken a gelding knife to the conniving son-of-a-bitch, there'd be no more siring, and for another . . . She marched through the troop of Sarmatian dancers balancing in full fish-scale armour and barely heard the clatter of metal on the flagstones. For another, there *was* no fortune.

From the moment Gaius embarked upon that ferry ride across the River Styx, the Guild of Wine Merchants had swooped, and for a man who they claimed was their friend, they had a funny way of showing it. The funeral feast was still spread and Claudia was swamped with bids, some kindly offering to take the millstone from her neck as a favour, others trying to wheedle the business from her through proposals of marriage. Oh, yes? He might have been fat, he might have been old, and his breath might well have felled a forest of oaks, but Gaius Seferius gave his life to those vines. Surely, the vines owed him something in return? As it happened, the return for vintage wine worked out to four per cent higher than its closest business rival, olive oil, a profit which Claudia was more than happy to distribute among jewellers, dressmakers, horse races and the like, had the Guild of Wine Merchants left her in peace. Trouble was, the bastards wouldn't let go.

Once they realized the widow was digging her heels in,

it became a war of attrition in which dirtier and dirtier tactics were employed to get their hands on Gaius's business. Credit where it was due, they proved every bit as creative in their campaign as they were unscrupulous, with the result that, when you take into account the costs of retaliating with maintaining an estate in Tuscany, a big house in Rome, not to mention the aforesaid jewellers, dressmakers, bookmakers and the like, assets soon became debts. It was true, she thought, fighting her way through the crush of fire-eaters, acrobats and poets. The best way to make a small fortune is to start with a large one. Orson was on to a loser.

Away from the Forum, the streets quickly narrowed. Basilicas and temples gave way to six-storey tenements, and in no time the seductive tones of orators were drowned by the ringing of hammers as metalworkers beat out everything from swords to ploughshares to pastry cutters by torchlight. From the upper storeys, babies bawled and dogs bayed, while in the workshops below, chisels, planes and saws rasped out sideboards, ladders, writing tablets and hay rakes, as cobblers sat astride their iron lasts. Looms clacked, and the smoke from tavern ovens mingled with the dust from the stonecutter's and picked up flakes of hemp from the rope-maker's premises. Lifting her skirts to avoid the refuse piling up in the gutters, Claudia understood his ambition to escape.

When you're born in the gutter, the desire to better yourself never wavers – though for men, at least, the route is more open. Indeed, Gaius had been a shining example. The son of a common road builder, he'd slogged night and day for what he believed in, until eventually he'd worked his way up to become one of the most respected wine merchants in Rome. Indeed, by the time he died, the name Seferius had become a byword for quality, and Gaius had been promoted to the prestigious rank of Equestrian by none other than the Emperor himself. In fact, the only thing Gaius Seferius had been lacking in his hard-won prosperity was the inevitable trophy wife to flaunt before his competitors, a gap the eighteen-year-old Claudia had been more than happy to fill. Admittedly, Gaius wouldn't have married her had he known that, having been orphaned and penniless at the age of fourteen, her only means of survival had been through dancing (for want of a better word) in a northern tavern for sailors, but a deal was a deal. They'd both stuck by their side of the bargain and it was simply fortunate for her, if not for him, that the Ferryman had come to Gaius before his allotted time. Which made her even more determined, as she turned into the dark twisting alley where Flavia's admirer had his carpentry workshop, that there would be no sneaking in the back door as far as Claudia's stepdaughter was concerned. If this Orson fellow wanted to better himself and live high on the hog, that was fine. Just find another damned pig.

'Hello?' She had to shout over the whirr of the apprentice's hand drill. 'Is the owner around?'

The apprentice, a thick lump of a boy with thighs like a bolster, laid his drill down. 'He be out.' He wiped the sawdust off his hands on his tunic. 'Can Oi help?'

'Only if you're a gravedigger, because I have three burly bodyguards outside this door, each of them armed with a shovel, and when I find the bastard who messed with my stepdaughter I intend to put them all together.'

'Oi see.' The boy frowned. 'And for this you be looking for Master Paulus?'

'Paulus? Hell no, it's Orson's hide I'm looking to nail to my wall.'

'Oi'm Orson.'

There was a crashing sound, as prejudices shattered into tiny pieces.

'*You?*'

Fortune-hunters she could handle. No matter how slippery, no matter how smooth, they were no match for Claudia Seferius. But this boy! How old was he? Seventeen at the most, with hair straight and thick, just like him, and eyes pale and dim, ditto.

'Why on earth did you own up?' She could see the back door and it was open.

'Oi'm not ashamed of me feelings for Flavia, miss . . . Oi mean, marm. She be a sweet girl and Oi'm right fond of her, and without wishing to brag, Oi believe she's right fond of me, too.'

11

'Too fond. The girl's pregnant.'

'She never is!' Orson drew himself up to his full, lumpy height. 'Oi'd not dishonour my Flavia out of wedlock and that's the truth of it, marm. Now Oi ain't saying we haven't kissed and cuddled a bit, coz we have, but Oi haven't overstepped no line seedwise, pardon my being so frank, so Oi don't know where she got that idea from. Well. Not unless . . .' He coloured to his sandy roots. 'A couple of times Oi, um . . .' He wrung his big, lumpy hands. 'But a girl can't get pregnant from that.'

Claudia sighed. That was the trouble living with an aunt who never allowed her own husband into the bedroom, she supposed. The facts of life become totally muddled, but praise be to Hymen, Flavia was still a virgin. There was a gleam of light in the darkness yet.

'Very well, Orson, this is what we do next. You write Flavia a note—'

'Sorry, marm. For one thing, Oi'm not lettered, and for another, Oi ain't going to give my Flavia up, not when Oi cares for her and Oi know she cares for me.'

Dammit, she'd spent the last hour bribing, beguiling and bullying Flavia into ending this ridiculous affair without success. Now we have an apprentice with scruples! Claudia perched on the edge of his workbench.

'You enjoy working with wood, don't you, Orson?'

'Aye.'

'Well, suppose someone were to set you up with your own business?'

Several seconds passed in which she wondered whether he'd actually heard her. Then he swallowed.

'Oi might not serve up no banquets at my table, but so long as my larder has enough in it to fatten a mouse, then Oi'm happy, and it's not that Oi ain't grateful for your offer, marm, but Oi don't have the experience to be running a shop of me own, and before you say you'd get people in to run it for me, that ain't the point, is it?'

Damn. She twisted round, smiled prettily and began swinging her leg.

'Experience, you say?' She picked up the abacus he had

been making. Ran her finger round along the exquisite grooving. 'Maybe I'm wrong here, Orson, but it strikes me that you're doing a professional's job for an apprentice's wages.'

'Reckon Oi probably am, aye.'

'You don't resent that?'

'As Oi see it, there's no going to Hades in a gilt litter chair.'

'Tell that to Flavia. Do you really think she'll be happy, living in a garret?'

Orson ran his tongue round his thick lips. 'No, marm, that Oi don't. But that's for her to decide, don't you think? Not the likes of you and me.'

Integrity as well as scruples. Claudia jumped down from the bench.

'Very well, Orson, *this* is what we do next.' She brushed the sawdust from her skirts. 'While I write Paulus a note, explaining how I've bought out your apprenticeship –' She tried not to think how much it would cost, but set against Flavia's virginity, it was worth every gold piece '– you pack your bags.'

For the first time, Orson looked worried. 'What for?'

'Because you're coming to Tuscany with me.'

'Oi am?' If anything, the boy looked even more anxious. 'You ain't just luring me outside to three men armed with shovels?'

'No, Orson, as much as it pains me, I'm not.'

There was a saying, she recalled, that when poverty walks in the door, love flies out the window. There was never any question of Flavia experiencing such a heartache, but equally there was no point in marrying her off against her will while she still had this ugly lug in her blood. Elopement and adultery were no grounds for a wedding! On the other hand, thrust these young lovers together and it's just a question of who backs off first. And how fast.

When Porsenna the Etruscan founded Mercurium during the height of his kingdom's military power, he would have stood on the hilltop and scanned pretty much the same panorama that the townspeople overlooked five long centuries later.

The Roman villas, glistening white with local stone, would not have been there, of course, nor the straight metalled roads bustling with legionaries, merchants, strolling players and despatch runners, but otherwise Porsenna would have surveyed the same rolling hillsides verdant with olives and vines, the same pasturelands dotted with sheep, and the same waving fields of wheat that fused with forests rich in timber and game in the distance. What's more, every last vista would have been suffused with the same golden glow that was such a feature of this glorious landscape.

Nine tenths of Porsenna's kingdom consisted of hills rising to mountains, from which a thousand streams sprung that merged and compounded until they formed a huge patchwork of rivers that kept his land fertile and green. In some places, water even spouted from the rock hotter than a first-rate bath and bursting with health-giving minerals. But from thermal spa to gently bubbling spring, rushing streams to slow-flowing river, all the waters were holy. To the King, as indeed with every Etruscan, the gods manifested themselves in every aspect of nature, so from the humblest vole to the most magnificent cypress, from fragrant wild sage to the swiftest of hawks, people knew that the gods moved among mortals and employed augurs to interpret their holy will.

Reeds were especially sacred. The reeds whispered the words of the gods and carried them off on the wind, and although the augurs came to decipher the whisperings, the reeds steadfastly clung to their secret.

But now, as the sun climbed high in the sky and warmed the waters in which their roots had taken hold, one particular patch prepared to divulge at least one of its mysteries.

High in the poplars, a flycatcher trilled, and a cuckoo called over the hedgerows. Fish darted in and out of the shallows, unaware of the heron's shadow that stalked them, while spring lambs gambolled across flower-filled meadows.

Deep in the reed beds, the water shimmered and rippled.

After three days' submersion, the gases inside gently raised the body to the surface.

And a seventeen-year-old youth set out on his final journey downstream.

14

Four

As the cart clip-clopped through the arched stone gateway, Claudia was aware of something different that she just couldn't put her finger on about the villa. At first, she assumed it was the mid-May sunshine bouncing off the walls, making them somehow lighter, brighter, full of radiance. But that was nonsense. The sun was in the wrong direction. Any enhancement to the redness of the roof tiles would come later in the day. So what, then?

Dismounting amid a flurry of slaves rushing out with everything from goblets of elderflower tea to slake her thirst to ox-hair brushes to sweep the dust off her robe, she wondered if it was a trick of the memory. After all, she wasn't the most regular of visitors . . . but no. The north wing still comprised the slave and estate workers' quarters, the forge still belched out coils of smoke, and the windows of the little bath house still diffused light through their panes of green glass. Claudia picked up the cage containing a growling, howling, hackle-backed demon and marched off round the peristyle to the only room she'd ever shared with her husband.

'*Hrrrowwwww.*'

'Yes, I know, poppet.' She flipped the latch on the cage and Drusilla, her blue-eyed, cross-eyed, dark Egyptian cat, shot out as though someone had set fire to her tail. 'I don't want to be here, either.' Nothing but hills, trees and vines; Hades offered better prospects for light entertainment. 'But with this Candace creature charging the most exorbitant prices to convince my mother-in-law that it's perfectly normal to commune with her dead son, what option do we have?'

'*Rrrrrrowwl.*'

Unconvinced, Drusilla took consolation in the plate of

ham and cold chicken laid out for her mistress. Claudia waited until the cat had finished, then plumped down on the only couch she'd ever shared with Gaius – and how well she remembered clinging to her own side of the mattress.

'Yes, that's another thing. This mattress.' She gave it a good hard prod and lost her finger. 'It's not only new;, unless I miss my guess it's swansdown.'

'*Brrrp?*'

Drusilla's ears pricked forward. Swansdown? The indignity of travel instantly forgotten, she jumped on to the bed, nestled into the centre by the pillows and began washing her whiskers.

'Good grief!' Claudia jumped up. 'That's it!'

No wonder the place gleamed and looked so different! Everything had been renovated top to bottom, inside as well as out.

'You're not allowed in here, you know.' A small face peered round the door to the peristyle. It was pale and freckled, and framed by a cap of gold hair. 'I'm Amanda, and this room's out of bounds, and if you don't leave at once, Indigo and me will tell.'

'Very well, Amanda.' She watched a small gleam of triumph light up tiny blue eyes. 'You and . . . um, Indigo go tell.'

The freckles merged into one humungous brown blob when she frowned. 'But we don't *like* telling tales, do we, Indigo?' She cupped her hands and whispered into thin air. 'Anyway, Indigo says you're supposed to go when you're told. Can we come in?' She didn't wait to be asked, but ushered her imaginary companion in first. 'Ooh, is this your cat?'

'*Reeeow!*'

'Not very friendly, is she?'

'Not very,' but the child hadn't backed off and Claudia decided Amanda was probably used to being snarled at.

'I say, is this your luggage?' The girl knelt down and unhooked the clip on one of the chests. 'I suppose you're a guest, then, so you won't have to leave, only you must be a pretty important one, if they've given you this room.' Tiny fingers prodded about in the clothes. 'But you want to be

16

careful,' she warned in a wide-eyed whisper. 'Mummy says this is the old *witch's* room.'

'Oh, Mummy said that, did she? Well, I would really like to meet your Mummy, Amanda.'

'No, you wouldn't.' The girl dragged a scarlet tunic shot with gold out of the chest and held it under her chin. 'Nobody likes Mummy, that's why me and Indigo have to keep moving on. What do you think? Too bright?'

'No, I—'

'Indigo says it's too bright.' She tossed it on to a chair. 'What about this one?'

'Peacock blue matches your eyes.'

'That's *exactly* what Indigo says.' Amanda pulled the robe over her head and belted it with a silver hair ribbon she picked out of the trunk. 'How do I look?'

'Ravishing.'

'Really?' Tiny eyes turned into dinner plates.

'If you don't believe me, look!' Claudia held up a mirror, in which the child twirled excitedly.

Bored with this girlie stuff, Drusilla wandered off in search of mice to torment, because time might have passed, but she hadn't forgotten where they'd made their holes.

'Indigo wants to know how long you're staying,' Amanda said, rummaging for a pair of emerald-green sandals.

'Tell Indigo she's very nosey.'

'Oh, she knows that, and she's rude and has terrible manners as well. Last night, she ate a whole plate of almond cakes all by herself and then she burped, but guess what? It was me that got a spank. Is this too much rouge?'

'You mean I still have some left in the pot?'

'I'm going to be a hairdresser when I grow up. What about you?'

'I am grown up.'

'No, silly, I meant what do you do? Or are you too *important* to do anything? Mummy said the witch – that's whose room you'll be sleeping in – Mummy says she's a gold-digging cow, but I don't see how, do you? Cows have horns, but you never see them digging with them.' She smeared a wonky red line over her lips. 'I suppose that's why she's a witch, though. When you're a witch, you can do anything you like, even dig for gold with your horns, although I'd have thought a spade would be better.'

'Where *is* your Mummy, Amanda?'

'I don't know,' she sighed, 'but you can bet that next time I'm in trouble, she'll be right behind me. Come along, Indigo.'

Amanda beckoned her invisible friend to join her, scooped the long robe over her arms then slopped off into the peristyle, tossing her little fair head like the princess she was.

Waving goodbye to Her Highness, her friend and her peacock-blue tunic, Claudia set off to make an inspection of the renovations. Was there no end to the work? Newly whitewashed walls. New tiles on the roof. The wall from the dining hall had been knocked out and replaced with folding doors that opened on to – you've guessed – a newly paved terrace that overlooked the whole estate. Nor was that the end of the list. The old well in the courtyard had been turned into an open pool complete with fountain. Brightly coloured friezes lined the walls of the portico in place of hazy geometrics. The gardens were unrecognizable beneath a new planting of plane trees, cypress, peach and cherry, oleander, box and myrtle.

'Your mother-in-law has made many improvements,' murmured a voice in Claudia's ear.

The voice was deep, rich and warm. Like melted honey drizzled on fig cakes. The sort of voice, no doubt, the dead enjoy communing with.

'I am Candace. But then –' she smiled an equally deep, rich, warm smile which somehow never quite made the journey to her eyes '– I suspect you guessed that.'

So this was what sorceresses looked like? Taller than the average male, with dark, watchful eyes and legs that came up to her armpits, this woman had 'feline' written all over her. Her skin was as smooth and shiny as the ebony that covered her homelands and every bit as black (not Mummy, then), and to highlight her beauty, she'd chosen a gown of fuchsia pink edged with silver and purple. But it wasn't her height, nor her skin, nor even the bold colours of her robe that made Claudia's eyes pop. Black and springy, her hair was cropped short like a soldier's, its scandalous style emphasized by Candace's swan neck, yet there was nothing masculine about this woman. Nothing mannish at all.

'She intends to install a sundial surrounded by roses,' the sorceress continued, 'and add a fishpond down by the paddock.'

'I'm surprised you haven't talked her into putting in a boating lake.'

'Your mother-in-law does not strike me as the type of woman one could talk into anything . . . '

How true, but that was in the old days. Before dementia kicked at her shins.

'And in any case, it is neither my interest nor concern what renovations she does or does not make. Larentia employs me to cast spells, not act as her decorator.'

Technically, since Larentia had no monies of her own, it was Claudia who was employing her, but she let the point pass. 'Are they working?' she asked innocently.

'All my spells work.'

The edge to Candace's voice was unexpected and Claudia resisted the urge to smile. So then, not quite the confident little cat she made out? Adopting a hopeful expression and wringing her hands as though embarrassed at asking, she hesitantly enquired whether Candace could help *her* some time . . . you know, when it was convenient. Her husband, she murmured. Larentia had spoken with him at length, as had Flavia . . .

'Of course, my dear, but of course,' the sorceress purred, because no self-respecting con artist is going to let an opportunity like that slip by them in a hurry. 'Suppose we say tonight, after dinner?'

'Won't it be too dark?'

When Candace smiled her slow, feline smile, Claudia's skin started to crawl. 'The dead live in the darkness, my dear. They will not come when it's light.' Black hands covered white in a well-rehearsed act of sympathy. 'How you must miss your soul mate, my child.'

Child? The woman could not have been more than thirty herself.

19

'Candace, you have no idea,' Claudia replied sadly, remembering Gaius's fat, shiny body and foul-smelling breath. 'I am just grateful to be blessed with so many wonderful memories.'

Most of them glittering merrily away in his moneybox, as she recalled.

'Tonight, then,' Candace crooned. 'Tonight husband and wife will be reunited, you have my promise on that.'

Claudia tilted her head in a gesture of coyness. 'I think you are more than a sorceress who casts protective spells,' she said with a simper. 'Look what you've done for Larentia and Darius.'

'Your mother-in-law did not ask me to cast spells for her heart. It is the winged spirits who brought them together on the winds of freedom and fate. The triumph is not mine to take credit for.' Candace leaned forward and transfixed her with her eyes. 'The forces of the supernatural surround each of us, my child. I am merely their instrument.'

As she turned away, the scent of her lingered for a long time in the open portico. Incense. Arabian incense, to be precise. Which struck Claudia as an odd sort of choice. And as she stood with her back to one of the columns, she noticed a young couple down by the wood store. Both dark and hawk-like, with deep olive skins, they performed backward stretches and made bridges of their spines in perfectly synchronized movements. From time to time, they broke off from their gymnastics to converse with foreheads almost touching. Lovers, so close that they mirrored one another's actions? She did not think so. Their noses, their jaw lines, the kinks in their hair. These things were too similar . . .

'Knew you'd be up here sooner or later, poking your nose where it doesn't belong.'

'Ah, Larentia! Lovely to see you again, too.'

And what a surprise it turned out to be. Far from the modest country woman Claudia remembered, her mother-in-law's hair had been skilfully dyed, with fine golden fillets woven right through it, a task that would have taken quite literally hours. Her gown was fashionably pleated and flattering, and dear me, was that rouge on her lips?

'If it's the money you're worried about, don't be. Darius has covered the cost of every single item, right down to new bread ovens in the kitchen.'

A tingle of alarm ran down Claudia's spine. 'He's moving in?'

That would explain his buttering up of the mother of a wealthy wine merchant, his generous acts of renovation, his worming his way into her heart. No doubt the old boy saw Larentia as the perfect inheritance for his children and grand-children, and she couldn't wait to see his reaction when it was pointed out to him that, actually old chap, your bride-to-be owns nothing, not even the clothes she stands up in.

'Move in here?' Larentia snorted. 'Certainly not! Darius is a horse-breeder from the south, with a stud farm ten times the size of this place, and that's where he's taking me once we're wed. And since he's had nothing but coughs since he arrived, he insists the climate will be better for my health, as well.'

Claudia chewed her lip. Horse-breeders live and breathe pedigrees, which meant Doddering Darius would already be apprised of Larentia's financial status, and he seemed more concerned with prolonging her life than shortening it. Claudia's thoughts turned to Orson and Flavia. The way they'd gripped each other's fat, lumpy hands all the way up here from Rome, gazing deep into one other's eyes, regard-less of the cart's jolts and jostles. Could it be that Larentia, a woman who could melt glass with one glare and slept upside down in a cave, wasn't senile at all, but had genuinely found love in her twilight years? At sixty-eight, though, she'd be keenly aware of her mortality, at the speed with which time slips away. Could that explain why she'd brought in this Candace? To give her an emotional cushion?

'There's nothing wrong with your health,' she pointed out. In fact, her mother-in-law was radiant and blooming, and looked a full decade younger.

'Then I'll live even longer.' Larentia twisted up her mouth in resignation. 'Suppose you'd better come in.'

Very generous, considering it wasn't her house. But then, much as one would like to, one can't go tossing unwanted mothers-in-law into the middens. Even the most venomous ones.

'No doubt you'll be wanting to give my fiancé the once-over.' Larentia sniffed. 'Might as well get that over and done with, too.'

'Dodd— Darius is here now?'

'The sooner I get his feet under my table,' Larentia cackled, 'the sooner I get 'em under my mattress! Oh, for heaven's sake, girl, snap your jaw shut. You look just like Flavia did when I said the same thing to her.'

And to think Claudia had castigated the girl!

'What?' Larentia scowled. 'Don't you think old people get consumed by the same urges as you youngsters? Course we do, and when you see my Darius, you'll understand why. Quite the stud, if you pardon the pun.'

Claudia sucked in her cheeks as she followed Larentia towards the atrium. So far the week had been one shock on top of another, but the idea of two wizened bodies writhing in ecstasy in the afternoon sunlight, their toothless gums clacking together like castanets, a sound matched only by the creak of their knee joints, was just too hilarious to contemplate. Good luck to you, Larentia, you poisonous old bat. And power to Darius's doddering elbow!

'You wait here.' Larentia stopped abruptly in the doorway. 'Not another step, understood? I need this threshold purified first.'

Claudia looked round, but the command was for her, not some slave she'd imagined, but by the time she'd turned back to protest, Larentia was speeding down the corridor on feet that were moving twice as fast as someone half her age. Claudia stuck her tongue out at the retreating figure. Heaven knows what gods Larentia imagined her to be offending by stepping over them, but she gave the threshold a bloody good kick anyway. A male voice chuckled as it stepped out from behind a marble pillar.

'I fear Larentia's been taken prisoner by local superstition,' he said, and his voice had enough gravel in it to pave the Forum. 'However, I won't tell, if you won't.'

Claudia studied him as he bowed. Early fifties and whilst

not exactly a sculptor's dream with his pepper-and-salt hair cut Caesar-style to cover his baldness, he wasn't gargoyle material either. Lean and tanned, with corded muscles that bulged out the long sleeves of his tunic, his eyes were as hard as granite, and instantly Claudia relaxed. Perfect. Another family member suspicious of their parent's motives! Presumably the eldest son concerned about his inheritance, but either way, someone she could do business with.

'Superstition be damned,' she replied. 'The old trout has never forgiven me for marrying her son at an age when he should have known better. I'm Claudia,' she added. 'Larentia's favourite person in the whole wide world.'

'I know,' he said, with a slight cough. 'I'm Darius.'

Five

A s the constellation of the dragon clawed its way slowly over the horizon, Marcus Cornelius Orbilio attempted to define the word ambition. It could, he supposed, be deemed any personal aim or aspiration, however small or unimportant – the desire to learn to swim, for example. To travel, write a poem, or even, for cack-handed hacks like himself, thread a needle. At the other extreme, it translated as obsession. A fixation with hunting down the biggest boar, being the best baker in the city, catching that elusive brown trout before your competitor hooked it. Then again, he thought, ambition could be construed as the pinnacle of personal achievement, the way a charioteer might set his sights on passing the winning post in the Circus Maximus to beat the record, say, or an athlete training for that once-in-a-lifetime Olympic crown.

'Here's that report you sent for, sir.'

Orbilio thanked the scribe, red-eyed from squinting too long over his smoky oil lamp, but left the scroll unopened on his desk as he supposed that ambition could also be classified as the desire to change society, regardless of the consequences. Revolutionaries, as he knew only too well, were every bit as driven as politicians, which – he sighed and twisted in his chair – was yet another facet of the word. It was that fervent, some might say fanatical, desire for fame, for power, honour, wealth, call it what you will, but which encompassed all the trappings by which certain types of people measured success.

'Oh, and this is the information you requested on the murder victim,' the scribe added wearily. 'Will that be it for tonight, sir?'

24

'It will, Milo. Have an enjoyable evening.'

'Thank you, I will. Although if you don't mind my saying so, it wouldn't hurt you to take some time off. "All work and no play," as my great-granddaddy used to say, "makes for one more funeral a day."'

'In that case, I shall take great care to cheat the undertaker,' Orbilio promised, but even as he spoke, there was no question of him slowing down.

During last year's visit to Gaul, the Governor of Aquitania had been so impressed with the way Marcus had handled that paedophile investigation that he'd offered him a job running his own branch of the Security Police in Gaul. For all the post's kudos, however, he didn't accept straight away, and it was not that he was too young or too ill-prepared for the job, which unfortunately went without saying. As always in life, there are personal complications and his came in the form of a wildcat with dark flashing eyes, rebellious curls and a tongue that could flay skin from a stone.

'Claudia Seferius.' He whispered her name into the night. 'Claudia, Claudia, Claudia. What is it about you?'

Would you believe, he'd actually followed that woman all the way to Aquitania from Rome? Trailed three hundred miles over land, river and sea, just to make an ass of himself? He rubbed his throbbing forehead. When, oh when, will we men learn? He exhaled slowly and realized this was what he'd been coming round to from the beginning, because love was the ultimate definition of ambition. Indefinable, intangible, as elusive as smoke, he questioned its very existence. Sure, there were phases people went through. Searing hot lust, tender affection, he was fully aware of those things. But the churning and yearning that gnawed at his liver? The burning that tore at his guts? Hell no, that wasn't love, so he accepted the Governor's offer. The Aquitanian climate was a hundred times better than Rome, averaging two thousand hours of sunshine a year, and since new trade routes had given a huge boost to their economy, the Gauls had proved excellent allies. Unfortunately . . .

Tearing his eyes from the dragon's twinkling scales, Orbilio lit another oil lamp and flexed his tired shoulders.

Unfortunately, crime doesn't shrivel with sunshine, murder least of all, and as Aquitania flourished, so too did the frauds and conspiracies. With a heavy sigh, Orbilio picked up the physician's report on the murder victim. Single deep stab wound to the stomach, which, though fatal, did not cause death. Foam found in the back of his throat indicated the poor sod had died as a result of drowning. For several minutes, Orbilio studied the parchment, making notes on the page, writing down questions, then reached for the first report that he'd requested.

Hunches, he believed, were the difference between his almost one-hundred per cent success record and the ratings of the other members of the team. It wasn't that he was cleverer than they were. Just that he'd been given an education and military experience that, as a patrician, the Roman class system denied his lower-born colleagues. Instinct, intuition, gut reaction, hunch, whatever you call it, it still boiled down to nothing more than years of insight and observation encapsulated in an instant, then having the nous to act on it.

He re-rolled the scroll then read through the physician's report for the umpteenth time. More than ever he was convinced that the chief suspect for this murder was innocent, and despite his personal interest in the case, the work of the Security Police isn't always about catching the bad guys. Sometimes it's about making sure a person isn't shoved in front of a bunch of hungry lions for a crime they didn't commit – and if you happen to catch the bad guys while you're about it, then that's a bonus.

Satisfied that he was far too busy to be lonely, Orbilio sharpened his quill.

In the beginning, the Five-Headed Serpent rose from the Darkness and coiled herself round the Chaos. Then, having laid the Egg of the World, she separated the land from the sea, the sea from the sky, and the sky she divided into four quadrants in accordance with the status of the gods. To the east dwelled the highest deities known unto man: Tins, Uni and Menvra. To the north lay the home of the gods of good fortune, such as Ani, who presided over new beginnings, and winged Turan, goddess of love. In the south the gods of the earth made their home: Fana, Horta and Fufluns. But it was in the west, in the dark caves beyond the sun, where the abode of the demons of death could be found.

Here, in these drear caverns at the edge of the Universe, sat wolf-headed Aita beside his Queen, their thrones flanked by the silver-haired God of Time who sharpened his sickle on the Stone of Adversity, and Vanth, who opened tombs with her bright silver key.

Around the gods, moving between them like shadows, were the demons who guarded the Underworld, and it was here that the Guardians of the Graves conspired in hushed whispers with the gods of witchcraft and spells. Here, too, the Herald of Death conferred softly with Night before slipping on his winged sandals, and with snakes for hair and the beak of a vulture, the Goddess of Immortality stared into the Pool of Prophesy while Seraphs measured the span of human life with sand that trickled through a holed jug.

Amongst them all strode a young man wearing a wreath of laurel in his dark wavy hair, and holding a yew bow in his hand. On his back hung a quiver of arrows tipped with gold, for gold was sure, gold was certain, but most of all gold didn't rot.

The name of this young man was Veive.

Veive was the God of Revenge.

Notching another arrow into his bow, he took aim.

Six

'Since you didn't bother to tell me you were coming,' Larentia said, collaring Claudia in the atrium, 'you can hardly complain when I've invited a group of friends round for dinner.'

'Are you spelling friends with or without the "r"?'

'Don't get smart with me.' Larentia pushed her thin nose into her daughter-in-law's face. 'You only married my son to get your claws on his money. Oh, yes. I saw right through you, from the moment Gaius introduced us, you devious, gold-digging bitch!'

'Both transparent and devious at the same time. How clever I am, Larentia, but I do wish you wouldn't keep flattering me. You know it goes straight to my head.'

'Your backchat and smiles don't fool me, girl. Think I don't know why you came up to the villa? The old bag's gone senile, that's what you thought, but look around, daughter-in-law. Do you see weevils on any of these vines? Has the bailiff reported any signs of rust or blight? Are the slaves still as strong and healthy? Have the draught beasts caught the mange? Has any of the food in the cellars spoiled and gone rotten?'

'No, no, probably, I don't think so, to answer your questions in order – though as to that fifth one, you might want to double check the wine store, because what you've been drinking has turned straight to vinegar.'

'My tongue might be tart, but it's small fry compared with the tart my son married . . . Ah, Eunice.' Acid became honey in the blink of an eye. 'How are you, my dear? You look ravishing.'

'Ravishing is as ravished does, darling,' the newcomer said with a wink. 'It's the best form of exercise I know.'

Clearly this "exercise" was doing her good. Eunice must be knocking sixty, Claudia mused, yet her jaw line was taut, her skin clear, and her eyes shone with mischief and health. Even her movements were youthful and lithe, and the only trace of her true age – the inevitable brittle, grey hair – had been concealed beneath a flattering wig.

'I'll leave you two to chat,' Larentia said, casting a sly glance at her daughter-in-law. 'Oh, did I mention? Eunice has recently married again.'

'Don't get me wrong, darling,' Eunice said, linking her arm with Claudia's and taking a slow turn round a courtyard lit by a thousand oil lamps and bursting with flowers at every level, from spikes of acanthus surrounded by narcissus in tubs, to columbines and mignonette tumbling from baskets that hung from brackets and hooks. All of which, according to Larentia, had been paid for by Darius, including flowerbeds overflowing with verbena, delphinium, storks bill and alliums, while hollyhocks imported all the way from Damascus lounged indolently against the pillars. 'I had an absolutely wonderful life with my late husband, who gave me two marvellous sons, three lovely daughters, a hatful of grandchildren and, praise to Minerva, my very first great-grandchild last month. But!'

When she leaned closer, Claudia detected a faint smell of wine and roses, a combination that, even after such a short acquaintance, she knew was far from accidental.

'I'm not one of those Celtish tribes who believes in re-incarnation. As far as I'm concerned, we have one life and it's short. Pluck the cherry from the tree while it's ripe is my motto, and my particular cherry's called Lars.'

She indicated the man paying his respects to Flavia across the way, whose Etruscan heritage of swarthy skin, stocky build and rather over-long nose was made more pronounced by the flickering lamps. Far from classically handsome, Lars was however not without sex appeal, and his face suggested he smiled a lot. Although, looking at him, lowborn for all his fine clothes, Claudia suspected Lars had a lot to smile about.

'Some cherry.'

'Thirty-seven last week,' Eunice said proudly, 'and thank Jupiter the family's finally come to terms with the arrangement. Why, only last month my eldest daughter came to visit.'

'You moved to Mercurium to be with your husband?' Somehow Claudia imagined it would be Lars following the money.

'What the hell, I thought, why *not* take a gamble? My little birds have flown the nest and have lives of their own. I'd only be an appendage in Rome. Thanks to Lars, I've a new life, new friends, a new style of living, and of course being happy gives you fewer wrinkles.'

Claudia could see that.

'Like I said, I don't regret a single day with my dear late husband, but since the State decrees that we women are incapable of looking after ourselves and need a man to make our decisions for us, it seems sensible to choose one over whom we have some influence, don't you agree?'

Eunice had no idea! 'Lars doesn't strike me as the sort who's easily manipulated.'

'Depends on your definition of influence, darling.' Eunice patted her wig and adjusted the choker of pearls that neatly obscured the crêpe-like lines round her throat. 'If I'd stayed in Rome, my eldest son would have assumed the role as head of the household, and I am not sure I've reached the point where I'm comfortable answering to my own son. Not when I'm still tempted to spank his bare bottom from time to time! Whereas Lars, who is, as you so rightly point out, very much his own man, was a masseur at the hot springs when I met him, and to put it bluntly, my dear, masseurs don't live this well.'

In the courtyard, moths diced with death among the hundreds of lamps to drink at the bounty of nectar.

'I bought a delightful townhouse in Mercurium with my dowry, which of course I get back if Lars and I should divorce, so I suppose it wasn't much of a risk. In return for not being a burden on my eldest son, I get a place of my own, a husband who's thirty-seven years old and a sex life I'd all but forgotten. Which reminds me – how's Flavia coping with love's new bloom?'

'If you can imagine a couple of flabby haddocks staring into each other's eyes and with about as much conversation, that's my stepdaughter and Orson.'

'Puppy fat, darling. It'll burn off once they find something to stimulate their interests.'

'That's exactly what worries me.'

Eunice watched her with a wry smile. 'I suppose it's occurred to you that you might have made a mistake, throwing them into each other's arms? That, far from driving your turtledoves apart, it might well turn out to be a case of "till death do them part"?'

'I may have faults, Eunice, but being wrong isn't one of them.'

'Personally, I think people worry too much about class,' Eunice said, nibbling on a handful of nuts. 'What's status compared to happiness, I say, because look at Lars and me. Three years down the line, we're as happy as the day we first met.'

Yes, but *two* younger men and *two* older women in the *same* town in the *same* circumstances at the *same* time . . .?

I bought a delightful townhouse in Mercurium with my dowry, which of course I get back if Lars and I should divorce.

But what happens should Eunice die? Lars would inherit the lot, and suddenly there was a smell of fish in the air which had nothing to do with the salmon being skinned in the kitchens.

Drifting away from the courtyard to a quiet corner of the garden where the light from the lamps couldn't penetrate, Claudia settled herself beneath one of the newly planted plane trees and rested her chin on her knees. It was night now, but in daylight all you could see from this spot were neat rows of vines hanging dutifully from their crossbars and the stately elm trees that supported them stretching into infinity. The buds on the vines had only just sprung into leaf, but according to her bailiff, it was still too early to prune. He was waiting until the last chance of frost had passed, something that was monitored, apparently, by the next full lunar cycle known locally as the red-headed moon.

31

Red-headed moon.

Claudia rolled the words round on her tongue. Funny how different people call things by different names. To her, it was merely a moon that waxed full at the back end of May. To those involved in wine production, however, this moon was the difference between a harvest or a famine on the vine.

Same thing, different viewpoints.

To her, the dodges she'd had to resort to, to keep the Guild of Wine Merchants at bay, were simply survival tactics. Whereas, to the Security Police, forgery, fraud, tax evasion and those other little things which were far too petty to mention, constituted a criminal offence. The Security Police were quite wrong. Claudia had every intention of repaying her creditors once funds started flowing, and heaven knows the Empire's moneybox wasn't creaking on its hinges for want of a few paltry back taxes. Indeed, the State coffers were quite capable of waiting another year, if not two, and no doubt would have been perfectly content to do so, had it not been for a certain patrician.

Marcus Cornelius Orbilio.

Three more words to roll around on her tongue, except these left a sour taste in their wake. Like rocks that split open beneath the plough to reveal the skeletons of creatures long-dead, Marcus Cornelius had the word 'ambition' fossilized in his bones. Young, tall and unnecessarily handsome, he employed centuries of inbred charm to snare any prey he couldn't ambush through more orthodox methods. Indeed, Claudia had almost fallen into his trap herself. Back in Aquitania, she'd been *this* close to making a fool of herself and she thanked every Immortal up on Olympus that he and that ridiculous floppy fringe of his – that mop of dark wavy hair, his impossibly bronzed skin and deep rich baritone – were setting up their own branch of the Security Police in Gaul. Good luck and good riddance, quite frankly. Already his features were erased from her memory, including that faint smell of sandalwood that always seemed to surround him.

Across the dark Tuscan landscape, a barn owl swooped silently over the vines like a ghost. Ah, yes, ghosts.

Who was this wind walker who went to great pains to

ensure no bad luck befell Larentia? She shifted position. Indeed, who suggested to her in the first place that an epidemic was going round? It took Claudia about ten seconds to establish that Larentia was no more senile than she was, so who would her mother-in-law trust enough to swallow such garbage? Candace? If so, how on earth did she convince her that bad luck was contagious? Aromas of honey-roasted lamb filtered out from the kitchens, but Claudia's mouth didn't water.

And what of Darius? What of this man whose voice had trodden the path to Hell? For once she was able to rule out the Guild, because why court Larentia? It would have been easier, and drawn far less attention, to woo Claudia direct, but why had Darius paid for these renovations? If he had no intention of living here after his marriage, why cover the cost of works on somebody else's estate, especially works that were ornamental rather than critical? Whether he was the horse-breeder he claimed or a fortune-sniffing rat, he'd have gone through Larentia's finances with a flea comb. He'd know every last detail of Gaius's will, be well aware that the widow inherited every penny.

'The *bastard*!'

Watching the three-quarter moon slip behind the hills, she suddenly understood why Darius had made a play for Larentia and not her. And knew that nothing on earth would stop him from marrying the old bag.

Roman law was ambiguous on many issues, but as Eunice so rightly pointed out, the subject of women wasn't one of them. Regardless of status, they were under the protection of men from the moment they were born. First they were their father's chattels, then their husband's, and finally, if widowed, they became either a son's or the closest male family member's. In Larentia's case, she was officially under the protection of her son-in-law, Marcellus, Flavia's foster father. But Marcellus was weak. He was also impoverished. Ever since Gaius's death, the family had relied on Claudia for support, which meant that on the face of it, Larentia's marriage to Darius would simply transfer that responsibility, taking Larentia off Claudia's hands.

But in a world where women are the property of men, Darius could argue that Claudia, as his wife's widowed daughter-in-law, was his responsibility as well. Bang goes her inheritance, as the head of the family takes over through the back door, something that would be impossible if he'd knocked on the front.

'Over my dead body,' she hissed. 'Over my dead body, you bastard.'

'You want to be careful using phrases like that.' Soft as a shadow, Darius stepped out from behind one of the peach trees and his teeth shone white as he smiled. 'Someone might be tempted to take you at your word.'

'I say, Terrence! Terrence, darling, do come and meet Claudia.' Eunice lowered her voice and whispered in Claudia's ear. 'He is *the* most eligible bachelor. His father was in silver or gold or something, so he's absolutely filthy rich, owns most of Tuscany and at least half of Umbria, and he throws the most lavish bashes you could ever hope to attend.'

'Pay no attention,' Terrence laughed. 'It's only half of Tuscany and a quarter of Umbria, and the only gold my father saw was through his role as a banker. But Eunice is right on one point. I'm a sucker for extravagant entertainment, and for that reason, if nothing else, I hope you'll join in my celebrations for the Lamb Festival, though I should warn you. The whole town is invited and by the time it finally winds down, what started off as cute little lambs have usually grown into ropey old muttons. Mercurium likes to have a good time.'

'A debonair party-throwing landowner, who's still unmarried in his thirties,' Claudia murmured, as a slave topped up her wine.

'The law has an abundance of loopholes, providing one knows where to look.' Green eyes appraised Claudia's glistening tiara, the emeralds at her throat, the gold earrings shaped like chariots, then slowly followed the soft curves of her dusky pink robe.

'And one certainly seems to know where to look,' she said sweetly.

One eyebrow twitched amused acknowledgement. 'Claudia, I think you and I should get together for—'

'Terrence!' A young woman with the same sandy-coloured hair and enormous round eyes came rushing up. 'Terrence, have you heard?'

'My sister,' he said, and though his smile never wavered, there was a distinct edge to his voice. 'Thalia, this is Claudia.'

'Oh.' Thalia's pale skin suffused in a rush of pink. 'I'm so sorry. How rude of me to barge in.' She curtsied in apology. 'Only Larentia didn't mention you'd be here – I mean, that's not to say she said you weren't welcome – I mean, of course you'd be, it's your house . . .'

'That's a delightful pendant you're wearing,' Claudia gushed. Anything to put the poor girl out of her misery.

'You think so?' Far from lifting her spirits, Thalia's lower lip started to tremble. 'My husband bought it for me. I'm wearing it tonight because—'

'Her late husband,' Terrence corrected. 'Died of an apoplexy last year. Thalia, what was it you wanted to tell me?'

'Did I? Yes of course, I remember now.' Her eyes widened to saucers. 'Oh, Terrence, it's terrible. That body that washed up on your land the other day? I mean, you do remember that poor boy, don't you?'

'One does not easily forget bloated, fish-nibbled corpses beached on one's pastures. What about it?'

His testiness merely added to her awkwardness, and Thalia hopped from foot to foot as she wrung her skeletal hands. 'Well, it seems it wasn't Tages the shepherd, after all.' She turned to Claudia. 'Tages is the boy who went missing in that violent storm last weekend. He's old Etha's grandson, and she's raised him ever since his mother died giving birth—'

'Thalia, would you please come to the point.'

'Sorry.' She ran a nervous tongue round her lips. 'The thing is, Terrence, Etha was called to identify her grandson, only it wasn't Tages at all.'

'Thank you, we'd gathered that.'

Thalia shot Claudia a flustered smile and mouthed the

word 'sorry' again. Claudia suspected it was a word she mouthed a lot.

'Anyway.' Thalia gulped. 'It was Rosenna who eventually identified the corpse as that of her brother, Lichas. Oh, Terrence, isn't this simply dreadful? I mean, those poor children in Mercurium. Where are they going to get toys from, now the toy-maker's dead? And who would *do* such a thing? He was such a nice boy, that Lichas. Who'd want to stab him like that?'

'I don't suppose anyone *wants* to stab anyone, Thalia. Look, why don't you go and tell all this to Eunice, there's a good girl? You know how she loves a good gossip.' He turned the full light of his attention back to Claudia. 'Where were we?' he asked smoothly.

'As I recall, you were on the point of explaining why you, rich, successful and not unattractive, were still unmarried in your mid-thirties.' Claudia shot him a radiant smile as she planted her goblet in his free hand. 'But Thalia saved you the trouble, because now I quite understand.'

Of all the improvements Larentia had made to the villa, the folding doors in the dining hall were the most impressive. Gaius Seferius had never underestimated the importance of entertaining clients in the growth of his business, and to that end had indulged the room with the same sumptuous marbles and exquisite mosaics that covered his townhouse in Rome. Indeed, it boasted the same overhead contraption to shower fragrant petals on to diners between courses. Those couches that weren't solid silver were of finely carved satinwood. The cushions were universally damask.

But for all its luxury, the hall at the villa could not compare to the spaciousness of its city equivalent, because at heart the villa remained a working farm. But by knocking out the exterior wall and replacing it with a concertina of woodwork, the room suddenly doubled in size as it spilled on to the terrace (perfect on warm late-spring evenings like this), bringing a sense of light and capaciousness to festivities that had been hitherto lacking.

Claudia speared a piece of crispy roast veal and concluded

that Gaius might well have come up with such an idea in time, but his mother? The wife of a road builder who rarely left Tuscany? Larentia was parochial in outlook, parsimonious by nature, and since the hall wasn't used from one year to another now that her son lay in his grave, such expenditure would not have crossed her mind. Once again, Claudia wondered why Darius had bothered.

Watching him winkle a snail out of its garlicky shell, she did not accept Larentia's explanation that from friendship love had grown – at least, not on his part – and she wondered how cold a heart needed to be in order to string an old woman along. Her glance moved to Larentia, laughing (yes, laughing) with Terrence and Eunice on the opposite couch as she wolfed down fattened goose liver, stuffed partridge and suckling pig. She noted once again the radiant glow to Larentia's face, the artful way she'd applied cosmetics, the new interest in fashion and hair, and for only the second time in her life felt a pang of genuine sympathy for her mother-in-law.

'. . . three years old and drops dead in the harness. *Pfft.*' Larentia snapped her fingers. 'Just like that.'

'Donkeys are plentiful around these parts, darling.' Eunice patted her hand. 'I'm sure the miller will find a replacement without any trouble.'

'I'm sure he will,' Larentia retorted, 'but that's not the point. You know his brother's wife walked out on him the day before, don't you? Took the children to Rome to stay with her mother, and how's the poor man going to visit them there? I ask you, he's a smith. Smiths can't leave their forges. Mark my words, bad luck begets bad luck. Candace?'

The black sorceress looked over from where she was conversing with Thalia. 'Larentia?'

'Next time you're in town, would you cast a spell for that poor miller?'

'Poor is the word,' Candace drawled. 'In my experience, millers are unable to afford my protection.'

Who could, Claudia thought? The woman was dripping with gold tonight, in the form of bracelets, armbands, earrings and pendants, tiaras, brooches and anklets. When she moved, she sounded like a rat-catcher's bells.

'I'll pay,' Larentia said, before realizing that her purse-strings were tied by the person reclining on the couch opposite, and that that person was not leaping in with offers to finance a charlatan's whimsies.

'My treat,' Darius cut in swiftly.

Candace cast him a long, slow, feline look. 'I am not a performing pony,' she replied at length, straightening her serpent-shaped armband. 'I target every ounce of energy on Larentia, who knows only too well how walking with the spirits drains me.' An unusually chastened Larentia nodded as the sorceress leaned towards her. 'Do you really wish me to transfer those energies,' she asked quietly, 'and dilute the spells that protect you?'

'No, I don't, and it was stupid of me to ask. People have to take responsibility for their own lives,' Larentia announced. 'The miller should have picked a better ass.'

'So should his sister-in-law,' Eunice said, and everyone laughed.

But as the remnants of the main course were wheeled out and fruits and sweetmeats brought in, Claudia noticed once again the watchful look in Candace's eye, and how Darius managed to bunch his facial muscles into a smile when he chuckled, even though the expression inside was as hard as a stone.

'I think it's fair to say Rex isn't coming tonight,' Larentia sighed, 'although I think he could at least have had the decency to send a note of apology.'

Claudia sank her teeth into a juicy red cherry and wondered who the devil was Rex.

'Trust me,' Terrence said, 'if that man hasn't sent a message, he's simply running late.'

'I thought generals were supposed to be on time.'

'Maybe that's one of the benefits of retirement?' Darius suggested, suppressing a soft cough. 'No longer bound to the great imperial clock.'

'And he does have to ride over from the far side of Mercurium,' Lars pointed out in his soft Etruscan brogue. 'His horse might have thrown a shoe.'

'His loss,' Larentia snapped, and Claudia was glad to see

the dragon's spleen was still working. 'The opportunity to commune with lost loved ones doesn't knock every day and he won't be butting in after we've started. Once Candace has summoned the spirits, that's it.'

Claudia glanced at the sorceress, reaching for a wine cake with long, elegant fingers. *Tonight,* she had crooned earlier in the peristyle. *Tonight husband and wife will be reunited, you have my promise on that,* the velvety tone of her voice suggesting a close and intimate encounter pledged on the spur of the moment. Huh! Tonight's 'walking on winds' had been planned long in advance, with half of Tuscany participating! But so long as the spider lures its fly, the end no doubt justified the means, and Claudia could only admire the spider's skill.

'Perhaps Rex is tied up with repairs to his estate?' Thalia suggested. She turned to Claudia. 'We had a terrible storm at the weekend—'

'You've already told her that,' Terrence said.

'Have I? Sorry.'

'That was the night Tages the shepherd boy went missing, wasn't it?' Claudia asked, ignoring him. 'Has he turned up yet?'

'No,' Thalia said, 'and his poor grandmother's out of her mind with worry. Of course, when I say out of her mind, I don't mean possessed like the goldbeater's uncle they have to keep chained—'

'Good god, woman, you sound like a fishwife,' Terrence hissed under his breath. 'For heaven's sake, can't you find an interesting subject to discuss, instead of dredging up gossip?'

'Talking of repairs,' Eunice breezed, 'did you hear? The wind tore the roof clean off the Temple of Juno in the night.'

'There was no wind,' Larentia pointed out.

Eunice shrugged. 'Be that as it may, darling, the whole inner sanctum was stripped bare, leaving poor Juno gazing up at the stars. Can you imagine! You know how bitterly she resents Hercules being up there!'

'No woman likes to see a bastard son take preference over her own offspring,' Terrence pointed out. 'Especially when he's rewarded with his own constellation—'

'Sorry I'm late, everyone,' a military voice boomed from the atrium. 'Brought you a few cheeses, Larentia. Trust that compensates.'

'More than, thank you,' Larentia called back, explaining to the rest of the company that the sheep on Rex's pastures produced the finest pecorino in Tuscany. 'He claims it's the herbs that grow wild in his meadows. I believe it's because he personally drills his lambs from the moment they're born, and I swear they never go *baa*, only *yessir*.'

Larentia cracking jokes? Dear Diana, whatever next!

'Got caught up in that wretched kerfuffle in Mercurium,' Rex explained, bustling in. Bull-necked, beetle-browed and jowly, he was every inch the retired soldier. 'Scandalous, what. Absolute bloody disgrace.'

'What is?' Darius asked, squeezing up to make room on his couch for the general.

Rex kicked off his sandals and joined him. 'Jupiter's bollocks, I thought everyone'd heard by now; it's all over town.' He paused to take a long draught of wine. 'When the tiler went up to start on repairs at the temple, he discovered that Juno's statue had been daubed red like a bloody Etruscan.' He tipped his head toward Lars. 'No offence, old man.'

'None taken,' Lars said.

'Only kids mucking about, I know, but the sooner Rome sorts out this ridiculous Fufluns business, the better – again, no offence, Lars. Which reminds me, Larentia. Hope you don't mind, but I've invited my young nephew along later. Been staying with me for a few days. Asked if he might tag along.'

'Whofluns?' Claudia asked, but Rex had galloped off on a different tack, something to do with skinning hooligans alive, she believed, and nailing their scalps to the basilica walls. It was left to Lars to explain.

'Fufluns,' he said, in his soft rolling brogue. 'Since the might of the Etruscan military was superseded – and isn't it amazing how few folk remember that we once controlled Rome, not the other way round? Aye, well. So much of our heritage has been absorbed, bastardized or copied by Rome

40

that it's not surprising our history disappears in the process.'

'Except for Fufluns?'

When he leaned towards her, she caught a faint whiff of his musky unguent. 'You take our Menvra, put her in a grand hall of marble and call her Minerva. You take our god of purification and name your month of February after him. And you just kidnap Fortuna and Vesta without even pretending to go through the motions.' He clucked his tongue. 'Make no mistake, though. We Etruscans aren't welded to temples of wood that rot in the winter, and we're not obsessed with the blowing of trumpets when we're used to hearing the drums. Between you and me, there's many things we're very happy to let slide.' Without thinking, his fingers went to the amulet that hung from a thong round his neck. 'But when we lift our eyes to our hillsides and see them covered with the vineyards laid out by our ancestors, we draw a line.'

Ah. 'Fufluns is your god of wine.'

'Wine features strongly in his divinity, aye,' Lars said, refilling her goblet. 'Except Fufluns represents much, much more. He's one of the earth gods who make their abode in the south, and as such Fufluns embodies vitality, fertility, merriment, joy and all the other earthly pleasures that can be obtained from the careful nurturing of the vine.'

Claudia raised her glass. 'I'm all for keeping happiness sacred.'

'So are the folk of Mercurium, which makes the sacrilege at the Temple of Juno doubly distressing, since we're approaching the full moon, when the Brides of Fufluns dance in front of their idol.'

All credit to Rex, Claudia thought, in sticking up for local principles, though surely he had the whole thing back to front? 'If this was hooligans on the rampage, wouldn't they have desecrated *your* god's statue rather than one of their own?'

'Absolutely.' Lars nodded emphatically. 'The defacement of Juno was made to look like an act of wanton vandalism to hasten the integration of Fufluns into mainstream Roman religion.' He sighed. 'No doubt we'll be calling him Bacchus before long, and gone'll be the goatskins and horns that he wears now, but until that day dawns, I'm afraid nothing's going to stop us daubing ourselves with red cochineal and paying the most robust homage we can muster to our fine liquid heritage, and in that respect, we have Terrence to thank.'

'How so?'

'Tell her, Terrence,' he called over. 'Tell her how the temple of Fufluns sits on your land, and how ye could have pushed for Romanization any time that you liked and taken the glory among your peers.'

'My family lineage traces back to Romulus and Remus.' Terrence shrugged modestly. 'We have enough glory and, compared to the number of locals who stream over my land to worship a god who embodies all earthly pleasures, one feels a metalled path is in order, rather than change. Or modernization, as Rome likes to call it.'

If there had been humble pie on the table, Claudia would have swallowed it whole. Terrence, she was forced to admit, wouldn't be the first brother who'd found his baby sister irritating and didn't bother to hide it.

'Aye, and we unmodernized types thank you for it. The Bridal Dance is an important part of our calendar,' Lars added. 'Perhaps *the* most important event hereabouts, given that most of our other temples have gone Roman. Aha.' He nodded towards Candace. 'Curtain up.'

Entranced by this new perspective on the Etruscans as much as her re-assessment of Terrence, Claudia had failed to notice that the tables had been cleared and braziers positioned carefully around the room. It was only when slaves began closing the folding doors that she realized Candace was about to fulfil her promise and bring Gaius Seferius back into his own dining room a full three years after his bones had been cremated.

'I call for silence,' Candace intoned, as she began to light brazier after brazier of incense – no wonder she reeked of the stuff. 'Sit forward, closer please . . .' Furniture scraped over the mosaic as couches were drawn together. 'And link hands.'

Slipping inside the circle, she picked up the long curved

42

blade that had been placed across a bronze bowl on the table beside a slender bronze rod, then pushed up the flounce of her sleeve to expose the length of her forearm.

'When shades arrive at the edge of the Underworld, they are made to drink from the Pool of Forgetfulness,' she explained in a slow, honeyed monotone. 'All memory of life with us is erased, leaving them free then to sail to the Isle of the Blessed untroubled by grief or by pain.'

She raised the knife. The curved blade glinted in the light.

'Only libations of blood can reawaken their human sensations. My blood, for it is I who must walk the winds that blow over the Elysian Fields, taking care that my feet touch no part of the ground, lest I be thrown into the River of the Damned. Silence, now!'

Slowly she ran the tip of the blade down her forearm. Blood drizzled down her elbow to drip into the little bronze bowl, and once a small pool had collected, she reached for a cloth and pressed it against the cut. When the bleeding had stopped, she picked up the thin bronze rod and tapped its tip on the floor, as though testing its sound.

'The dead inhabit a world of darkness and quiet,' she whispered, extinguishing the oil lamps with her unique combination of solemnity and grace. 'If we want them to return to us, we must recreate an environment where they feel comfortable, though for us, this environment is cold.'

As the light dimmed, the temperature dropped, and Claudia felt a slight rush of air from behind as the door from the atrium opened.

'There you are, m'boy!' Rex bellowed, as the last flame died in the room. 'Thought you were going to miss all the fun.'

'Not a chance,' a baritone drawled, and as he squeezed on to the couch next to Claudia, she smelled sandalwood over the choking incense as a strong hand slipped comfortably into hers.

'Marcus Cornelius Orbilio,' she hissed through the blackness, 'why the hell aren't you in Gaul?'

'That's odd,' he rasped back. 'I thought the whole point of tonight's exercise was to bring hell up to us.'

43

'Quiet,' Candace snapped, 'or the dead will not walk. Harpist! Play your music, if you will.'

It was a measure of her surprise that Claudia hadn't even noticed a harpist in the room.

Although, come to think of it, she would have preferred a harpoon.

The dagger that had taken the toy-maker's life hung snug inside its scabbard. The knife was not judgmental. Made of steel, it did not differentiate between self-defence and cold-blooded murder, the heat of battle or the skinning of coneys, all of which it had known in its time, along with other applications too exhaustive to list. However, the smith who had forged this magnificent weapon had imbued it with a spirit all of its own. This was normal. Since man first hammered out his first killing machine over the fire, he had been blessed by the gods and endowed with an aim straight and true. The dagger was no exception. Providing it performed well – a feat that could only be achieved with the aid of expert honing and care – who, or what, it was used for was irrelevant.

And the weapon had had plenty of use.

Lichas the young toy-maker was not the first person to die at the point of its blade, nor was the hand that had wielded the dagger unpractised. There was no question of this weapon not seeing the light of day ever again.

So it hung, snug, inside its scabbard. And waited.

Far away in the lands to the west, in that shadowy world between the dead and the living, Veive, God of Revenge, lifted another gold-tipped arrow from his quiver and fitted it into his bow.

Seven

'Come,' Candace drawled. 'Draw closer, my friends, for it is cold.' The sound of her chafing arms could be heard in the darkness, even over the jangling of her jewellery. 'But I ask you to ignore the chill in the air and to concentrate on the music. Listen only to the strings of the harp. Feel the restful beat of the rhythm.'

The audience duly obeyed.

'The music of the harp is the gateway to the Underworld,' she intoned in her dark velvet voice. 'Through this gateway we will pass together, entering the domain of the dead, walking where no living person has trod. Is there any amongst us who wishes not to enter this world?'

Claudia expected Thalia to back out, but either her brother had a strong grip or she had a genuine interest in staying, because nobody made any effort to move.

'Good,' Candace crooned. 'Because now I will begin the journey that takes me from this warm, physical plane to the cold winds that blow over the Fields of the Blessed.' She cleared her throat and the pitch of her voice deepened. 'O Vanth, Demon of Death, who has eyes on her wings and sees everything, hear me. Accept this gift of my blood –'

The unmistakable sound of liquid splashing on to the floor made Claudia's stomach clench.

' – to enrich the senses of those whom we summon.'

Three metallic raps tapped the mosaic, the same taps that she'd tested the bronze rod with earlier.

'O Leinth, who waits at the Gates of the Underworld and drinks of human tears, I call upon you also, that you might turn your featureless face to the stone.'

Three more raps of the bronze rod.

45

'By the Falcon of the Sun, by the Vultures of the Moon, I bid ye spirits let me enter.'

The knock that was returned didn't come from any slender bronze rod. It reverberated from the ceiling, from the walls, rose up through the floor. Knock. Knock. Knock.

'Enter, sorceress,' a voice echoed from everywhere and nowhere. 'Enter the Dark Kingdom and be welcome.'

At first Claudia was unaware of the smoke. It was only when Darius's dry cough erupted that she realized coils of grey had intruded through the blackness, to be joined by a smell of sulphur, odious and repulsive, that mingled with the incense then was gone.

'I am . . .' Candace's voice faltered. 'I am crossing the threshold,' she finished weakly, followed by the unambiguous thud of a body collapsing in a dead faint on the floor.

It was as though a winter wind blew down from the Alps. Claudia felt it round her neck, round her ankles, she felt it creep into her marrow, and now the smoke was back, curling, swirling, spiralling horizontally around the room. She could see nothing. Simply blackness and smoke, and the only sound was Darius's intermittent cough and the hypnotic strum of the harp. Time stood still. Nothing happened, then . . .

'Claudia, my dove,' a male voice chuckled. 'How the devil are you, my sweet?'

The breath caught in her throat. Only one man had ever called her his dove. 'G–Gaius?'

'Don't sound so worried, my pet. I've never left you, not for a minute.'

As if to prove it, she felt a soft brush against her arm.

'I am always watching over you,' he said tenderly, 'have no fear of that, and if it's of any comfort, I am *delighted* with the way you've handled the business. With the Guild of Wine Merchants snapping at your heels, it was never going to be easy, but I am proud of you, my little angel. I am proud of how you've handled my daughter's affairs and –' Claudia swore she felt a soft pat on the head '– I'm proud of the way you've taken care of my family.'

The cold intensified. She clasped her hands to stop them from shaking.

'And you, Mama.' A droll chuckle echoed from every corner of the hall. 'I'm proud of you, too. At your age, you minx! Have you two love birds set a date, yet?'

'Well, um, no . . .' Larentia sounded embarrassed.

'Then you should, Mama! You must! The Ferryman rowed me to Hades before my allotted span. Who's better placed than I to know how important it is to make the most of one's time on earth?'

'What do you say, Ren?' Darius asked through a throat full of gravel stones. 'Why not set a date right here and now?'

'I . . . er . . . '

'Why, Mama, someone else wishes to speak with you.'

'Renni,' a coarse voice croaked. 'How are yer, gel?'

'*Husband?*'

Claudia sensed, rather than saw, her mother-in-law shoot upright in her seat. Still the harpist's fingers continued to strum.

'Right first time, gel, but then you always was a good guesser. Missed yer, I must say. It's been bloody cold here without yer to warm me at night, but the boy's right, love. Grasp the nettle, while you've got strength to hold it.'

'But what about when . . . when, I . . . you know, cross over myself?'

'Things is different this side, yer'll see. There's no envy nor greed nor jealousy down here. We're one big happy family us, so don't yer go worrying yer pretty head about that. Enjoy yerself, gel. You deserve it.'

Other things followed. Rex talked to the wife he'd lost twenty years before, almost reducing the old soldier to tears. Lars had a quick word in Etruscan with a school friend who'd died in childhood. While Eunice steadfastly declined to speak to her cousin, claiming that the odious woman had refused to bother when she was alive, she could jolly well go hang herself now she was dead. Then Thalia piped up, wondering if she might make contact with her late husband as there was something important she wanted to tell him, but unfortunately the husband was unable to come through. The gateway, it seemed, was starting to close.

47

And once it did, it closed with a crash.

When the brazier in the east corner toppled out of its holder, everyone jumped and even the harpist missed his string. But before anyone had mustered enough breath to speak, a vase of cornflowers by the door smashed on to the floor. Someone gasped. Claudia thought it might have been her.

'Sweet Janus,' Eunice breathed, as sulphur engulfed the room.

'What's happening?' Thalia shrieked. 'What's going on?'

'Th–this . . . this has never . . .' Larentia's voice was unrecognizable under the fear.

Suddenly the jug of wine on one of the tables raised itself high in the air and hurled itself across the room, yet even before it hit the wall a stool overturned and figurines of ivory, onyx and silver began flying off their display.

Then it was gone.

The smoke, the cold, the smell of sulphur, suddenly they were gone, and the room lapsed back into a silence broken only by the drip-drip-drip of wine down the wall and the soft strings of the harp, though even their hypnotic cadence had been broken.

'Lights!' Rex was the first to speak. 'Someone light the bloody lamps, for gods' sake!'

Terrence, being closest to the door, fumbled his way across the room, cursing as his shin cracked against an overturned chair. Instantly, light from the atrium flooded the dining hall and slaves rushed forward to light the wicks, their open jaws betraying the destruction that confronted them. Glass, water, flowers, furniture, the desecration was everywhere. Still-rocking ornaments littered the mosaic. Wine drizzled like blood down the exquisite frescoes. Lumps of incense resin glued themselves to the woodwork.

Thalia's scream was like nails down a blackboard. 'Candace!'

Overtaken by events, the sorceress had been completely forgotten.

'Oh my god, Terrence! Look at the blood! Terrence, she's dead!'

'No, she's not.' Orbilio placed his finger on the pulse in

Candace's neck, and Claudia saw that it was only the blood she'd let splash on the floor that had seeped into her robes where she had fallen. Beneath the heavy embroidery and gold thread, the sorceress's breast rose and fell.

'Candace, speak to us.' Larentia leaned over and gently slapped the girl's cheeks. 'Candace!'

'Would ye look at that, now,' Lars exclaimed softly.

'Jupiter's bollocks!' Rex leaned over for a closer inspection. 'In all my years on the battlefield, I've never seen anything like it. It's healed. *The wound on her forearm has healed.*'

'Someone open the doors to the terrace,' Orbilio ordered, scooping her up in his arms. 'Quickly, please.'

Claudia was the closest and outside in the fresh air Candace's eyelashes began to flutter and her unfocussed eyes rolled as he set her down in a chair. Whatever words she muttered, the language was not Latin.

'Drink this.' Orbilio coaxed a few drops of water past her trembling lips.

'Did . . . did they come?' she asked thickly. 'The spirits. Did they come through?'

'They came through all right,' he assured her. 'Can you stand?'

'I . . . think so.'

She was wrong. The same legs that came right up to her armpits wobbled precariously when left to their own devices, and two muscular slaves were entrusted to escort the sorceress back to her room. In the dining hall, Larentia seemed mesmerized by the stains on the wall, Thalia was sobbing silently from the shock, and though Eunice comforted her by rubbing her shoulders, you could see from her white face that she was shaken herself, while the men stood with their feet planted squarely apart staring down at the floor, the walls, their own feet – anywhere, in fact, but at each other.

Out on the terrace, Orbilio took ten paces away from the house, clasped his hands behind his back and stared up at the star-studded sky.

'I have to hand it to you, Claudia Seferius. You lie, cheat and steal, you fiddle your taxes, you make fraudulent deals,

49

you forge signatures, documents and seals – plus you gamble, which is also against the law. But . . .'

He began to rock on his heels. Maybe he'd been shaken by tonight's events more than he let on, because in the light of the three-quarter moon it seemed as though his shoulders were shaking.

'But no one can ever accuse you of not throwing a bloody good party.'

Eight

A round the twisting streets of Mercurium, only the herald and the town cats were abroad. The herald enjoyed walking this tiny hilltop town at night. No beggars on the corners, no dogs or kids zigzagging in and out of his feet, no porters' poles to poke him in the eye. He could amble round the town at his own pace, even though by the time he'd called the hour at one end it was practically time to start calling the next at the other! This time of night, though, no one cared. Like country folk everywhere, they shuttered up their windows when darkness fell and rose again at dawn, and most of them, bless their hearts, slept like logs. You could hear half of 'em, especially that old pair on the corner of Pear Street and Hide Lane. Lord alive, there were some nights the herald could hardly hear his own bell for their snoring!

'Third hour of the night,' he intoned solemnly. 'Third hour of the night.'

On he strode, always taking the same route up the hill, checking on the goldsmith's and the shield-maker's, the vellum-dealer's and the spice-seller's, because even though they lived above their shops, they all slept soundly in their beds and so were happy to slip the herald a denarius each week to check the locks when he went past. Wine had made this town prosperous, he reflected happily. Wine and olive oil. Back in his great-great-grandfather's day, Mercurium was a walled hill fort like fifty others, a working town in days when meat was a luxury to be eaten once a week and most houses slept six to a room.

Not now! Mercurium had risen like its namesake, grown rich on the back of an increase in production from the olive groves and vines, their liquid output exported everywhere from Iberia to Damascus, Pannonia to Gaul. In reality, the herald had no idea where these places were. Further than from here to Rome, of course, but beyond that? It didn't matter. Wherever these exotic places were, they couldn't get enough of the liquid gold that was pressed out of these fruits and he was glad. It put fat goose on his table, brought fresh water to his street and educated his three kiddies as well.

'Fourth hour of the night.'

Aye, it was grand to walk streets that had been paved and guttered, and of course at night he could walk without impediment. Why, only yesterday the axle on the tavern-keeper's cart fell off, bumping amphorae of wine right down the hill, and he was bloody lucky only three of the buggers had broke. Not that you'd think it, listening to him! Lord alive, what language. Course, it stood to reason. Last week was it (or the week before), the poor sod got up in the morning same as usual and found his wine had turned to vinegar overnight. Now his axle broken, poor bloke. All the same, language like that, when there's lassies present!

On every block, he rang his bronze hand bell and called out the hour. 'Fourth hour of the night.' Every building he passed lay in darkness. Maybe he'd hit lucky and hear the squeak of a bat, or a moth would flutter close before his eyes, but usually it was just him and the odd tomcat, and that was the way that he liked it.

Approaching Saturn Street, he caught a chink of light through the shutters. He stopped. Watched the crack of amber for a while, but the light was not extinguished in the way it would, had someone needed the chamber pot, for example, or a drink in the night. The herald pursed his lips. Should he? Aye, why not? He rapped at the door, noting thick branches of cypress piled over the threshold. He waited. No answer. He rapped again.

'Rosenna?'

After half a minute, maybe more, the bar was eventually lifted and a swollen, tear-stained face appeared round the door, framed by a halo of tangled red curls. He smelled the dusty, dry air of wood and sawdust. Caught a glimpse of carved horses, jointed soldiers and a doll's house half finished.

'Rosenna, love, are you all right?'

'I'm fine. Honest, Herald, I'm all right. Just sitting with him, that's all.'

'I could send the wife round, if you're in need of company?'

'That's mighty sweet of you, but no. If it's all the same with you, I'd rather stay private in my grief.'

She closed the door and trudged back up the stairs. Love him, it was the herald who first told her that the body had been found.

'They think it's Tages the shepherd boy,' he'd said, 'but you might just want to take a peek,' because the herald was the only one who understood how worried she'd been.

'Your brother's just gone . . . you know . . . to the hot springs,' the townspeople kept telling her. 'Don't fuss.'

Don't fuss? A seventeen-year-old youth sets out to meet his lover one night and doesn't return, and they tell you *don't fuss?* Rosenna resumed her vigil beside her brother's bier. Would they have handed out the same advice, had it been a lass setting off in the storm? She wondered bitterly. Or a seventeen-year-old youth meeting with a female lover, not another man? Lichas's preferences might be common knowledge round here, but it didn't mean people accepted it! They liked him well enough, and when they bought their toys they'd pretend he were no different, when in truth it was Rosenna they felt sorry for, on account of the shame her brother visited upon her.

'Lichas, Lichas, what am I to do?'

The corpse on the bed made no reply, and Rosenna buried her head in her hands. The smell of jasmine in such a small chamber was making her retch, but there was no money in the box to pay for an embalmer, and in any case, three days in the river was three days too late for such services. She had to rely on oil of jasmine, camphor and a thick linen sheet, but she couldn't let him lie there alone in the State mortuary. Lichas had had his whole life ahead of him, a life that had been cut short with a sharp, stabbing dagger. The least Rosenna could do was keep vigil for her brother, burning torches at all four corners of his bier and laying cypress outside his door.

'All life is ordained,' the priest had told her, and no doubt he meant it as comfort. 'Man's destiny lies in the lap of the gods.'

Rosenna was having none of it. 'You can't teach us on the one hand that we're allotted seven times twelve years by the gods, then tell us that Satres can bring his sickle down any time he bloody well chooses!'

'You are angry, child,' the priest said. 'But destiny is destiny nonetheless, and the cycle of life to which you refer can only be achieved through dedication, sacrifice and prayer.'

'Lichas was seventeen!' she protested. 'If you're saying a person has to stuff all their sacrifice and prayers into their first two years of adulthood, why was it him and not me?'

'Child, we can only beseech the gods for postponement of the inevitable, and however much we read the sky and examine the livers of bulls, the gods only let us know what they want us to know. Their secrets are not always for human divulgence.'

Too exhausted to cry further, Rosenna picked up a painted wooden chariot and spun the wheels slowly.

'Wee orphaned Jemma's never gonna get that house for her dolls now,' she whispered quietly. 'And what of Tiro's crippled lad? How's he going to walk again without that contraption you were designing for him?'

It was typical of Rosenna to worry about the auctioneer's son, whose left foot was paralysed when he fell into the quarry, and not herself. At twenty-one, she had no fears for her own future. She'd get by, but Lichas . . . Now, Lichas had been marvellous. *I'll get that foot working, sonny, don't you fret.* She could almost hear her brother's voice. *I'll rig up a trolley that you can stand inside and push round. Between the two of us —* she even remembered the way he'd ruffled the lad's hair – *we'll have you right in no time.*

The upsurge of memories was too much and she was consumed once more by grief. Finally, when the spasm had passed and all that remained was an emptiness deep in her soul, she blew her nose, splashed her face with cold water and slumped back in her chair. There were some, she reflected sourly, who feared that any man who loved other men was a threat to their bairns. Huh! You canna help how you're born, any more than you can help having crossed eyes or a big nose. Lichas was a fine carver, he made loads of kids happy and there was nowt mucky about it!

You don't understand, sis.

His voice echoed back through the years when, even at thirteen, he knew he was different.

Folk'll always be prejudiced against something. In this case, it happens to be me.

That was why he took himself off to the hot springs now and then. There was a quiet corner, he said, where others of his persuasion could link up.

I'm among friends there.

Friends, aye – but also lovers, casual acquaintances who meant nothing or random encounters that satisfied a need . . . until that fateful trip in December.

It's Saturnalia coming up, he had said. *The hot springs attract a large number of visitors. There's a huge market for toys.*

And toy boys, she thought miserably.

Lichas returned home not only sold out, but happier than Rosenna had ever seen him.

I met someone, sis. His name's Hadrian and, would you believe, we've both lived in Mercurium our entire lives, yet never found each other until last week!

Hadrian. Rosenna rolled the name round on her tongue and the taste was bitter. Hadrian, who was a full seven years older than Lichas but a whole world away, with a rich family and a different set of attitudes and outlooks.

'He'll hurt you.'

Don't be daft, sis. How Lichas had danced round the room! *Hadrian loves me.*

'Maybe he does,' she'd retorted. 'Now. But what happens later? Lichas, trust me, this man can only hurt you.'

Beside his jasmine-sodden bier, wracking sobs overtook her once more. 'They won't listen,' she wailed, wringing her handkerchief. 'I've been to the City Prefect, the Tribune, the

Magistrates, the Quaestor. Holy Nox, I've been round anyone who's anyone in this town and told them who killed you, but not one of the bastards listened.'

At least, they pretended they hadn't.

'Bastards!' she said again. 'I hope the whole bloody lot rot in hell.'

It was his father. Hadrian's father had the clout to cover it up, because hadn't Rex been some general in their bloody army? And that was always the root of it, wasn't it? 'Them' and 'us'.

'Because we're Etruscans – commoners – we don't bloody count.'

What counted was money. Connections. Then you could cover up your son's murderous deeds and pass it off as a cheap homosexual quarrel.

'Well, *I* know,' she spat. 'I know who killed you, little brother, and I don't care what kind of high-flying patrician they've brought in to suppress the truth. That bastard Hadrian is going to pay.'

As it happened, that bastard Hadrian was already paying.

Nine

Dawn broke rosy and soft, bathing the vines in its warm rose-pink glow and turning the gnarled black stems to cochineal. Between the rows, hoopoes hopped, their black and white crests erect in courtship, while foxes slunk home and kestrels scythed the air in search of voles. High in the elms that supported the vines, dormice snuggled into a ball, while owls closed sleepy eyes beside their fluffy nestlings. Claudia envied the dormice their dreams. After the events of yesterday evening, she had not slept a wink and her shoulders were stiff from anxiety.

Bad luck begets back luck. (Larentia)

The forces of the supernatural surround each of us, my child. I am merely their instrument. (Candace)

Hard as she tried, Claudia had not been able to convince herself that the soft brush of a hand against her arm was imagination. *Claudia, my dove.* Or that gentle pat on her head. *I've never left you, not for a minute.*

Not only do the spirits hear in the dark. It would seem that they also can see . . .

Do you see weevils on any of these vines? Larentia had snapped. *Has the bailiff reported any signs of rust or blight?*

All my spells work, Candace said.

Strolling beneath the dangling branches, Claudia ran her fingers over the sprouting leaves and was once again struck by how hard these vines had to work. They didn't generate leaf until May, and in the six months before the leaves fell they had to deal with two sessions of hard pruning, flowers, get themselves pollinated and absorb sufficient moisture and sun to swell the grapes into juicy ripe bunches that could be trodden into juicy ripe wine. Oh, yes, they were tough little soldiers. To ensure their roots retained adequate moisture, it wasn't unknown for them to burrow a good sixty feet down – it's a wonder they didn't tickle the heads of the inhabitants of Hades. And isn't it funny how everything keeps coming back to the dead?

Claudia lifted her eyes to the horizon, where the first warming rays of Apollo were painting the sky the same hue as a kingfisher's breast and dabbing it with puffs of white cotton.

'Looking round,' a baritone murmured, 'you see what inspired the vibrancy and colour in Etruscan art and made them such a happy people.'

Dammit, this was another reason she hadn't slept one bloody wink.

'Can't imagine what they had to be happy about, Orbilio. There's sod all for miles except hills, fields and trees and a girl can hardly hear herself think for the racket.'

'I think you might find there's a technical term for that racket.' He pursed his lips and nodded solemnly. 'In the trade, it's known as birdsong.'

Correction, she thought, it was called naked ambition. You could hear it screaming through the air, pulsing up from the ground, proclaiming itself from the treetops, or why else throw her list of crimes back in her face? The truth was, the law had finally caught up with her and since she had no armour against this handsome patrician – bribes were pointless and any little-girl-lost approach would be futile – she might as well succumb to the inevitable. Then bribe and sweet-talk her jailers to freedom!

'So what next? Do you want to clap manacles round my hands and feet here and now?'

Dammit, this was no laughing matter.

'I appreciate the offer,' he spluttered, 'and there's nothing I'd like more – but don't you think we should at least have dinner first? Get to know one another a little better?'

How many times did she have to keep telling herself? He uses urbanity and charm as his bait.

'So.' He cleared the laughter from his throat, but the light that danced in his eye was more stubborn. 'Was last night's marital reunion all you'd hoped it would be?'

'Funnily enough, thank you, it was.'

'Hm.'

He followed as she continued to check the sprouting vines, their leaves as bright as freshly dyed linen, and as the sun climbed, the warble of finches and robins rose with it, while on the ground mice and shrews rustled among the thousands of wild flowers that flourished in this cultivated paradise to form a kaleidoscope of orange marigolds, red pheasant's eye, purple alkanet and lilac campanula.

'Impressive performance last night,' he murmured.

The forces of the supernatural surround each of us, my child. I am merely their instrument.

'Unfortunately, Candace wasn't faking.'

'No indeed. That distinctive sound her body made as it dropped to the floor? You can't feign something like that.'

'The traditional dead weight. Yes, I know.' Claudia nodded glumly, because up until the moment the lights went out in the dining hall, she'd been convinced that Candace was a hen who clucked loudly but laid no eggs. However, since Candace had taken no part in last night's proceedings . . . 'Thalia may have overreacted when the lights came back on, but I'm not sure I blame her.'

'Me neither. You saw the depth of Candace's breathing, the beads of sweat on her brow, the time it took to bring her round.'

And that was the problem. No charlatan can fake that kind of thick speech, much less those rolling eyes. That faint had been genuine. As had the smooth skin on the inside of her forearm. Not so much as a scratch . . .

'Friends of yours?' Marcus asked, squinting across to the paddock to where donkeys chomped on the dew-laden grass, rabbits chased each other in circles and two silhouettes performed elegant gymnastics.

'Candace's groom and maidservant,' Claudia explained. 'According to Larentia, they're Hebrew twins called Judith and Ezekiel that Candace picked up on her travels, and frankly they make my flesh creep.'

'Handsome couple.'

'Exactly. Well into their twenties, so why aren't they

married? And watch how they synchronize every movement, slowly, methodically repeating them until they're perfect.' Again, she was struck by how close their foreheads were when they stopped, and even at this distance she could almost hear their irritating whisper-whisper-whisper on the still morning air. 'They behave more like professional dancers than servants, and they don't mix with anyone else; they don't even *talk* to anyone else. Admit it, Marcus, that's odd.'

'Not necessarily.' He paused. Spiked his fingers through his thick mop of dark hair. 'Occasionally one hears about twins who grow exceptionally close, even inventing their own secret language. To you and me it's . . . well, unnatural I suppose is the word, but often this bonding comes about as the result of childhood trauma, and you have to remember that to them it's perfectly normal for two minds and bodies to act as one.'

'That's my point. If Judith and Ezekiel have two brains, two hearts, two sets of organs and limbs but only the one personality, imagine what that personality is capable of.'

'Now who's overreacting?'

She shrugged. 'Blame the . . . what did you call that thing?'

'Birdsong.'

'Yes, well, blame that if I'm overreacting, but I'm telling you I don't trust those two an inch.'

His shadow kept pace with hers as they reached the end of one line and turned down the next. 'Is Larentia really going to marry Darius?' he asked eventually.

'Apparently so.'

'What do you know about him?'

'Not a thing, but don't worry. That'll change soon enough.'

'It might change a bit faster with this.' He fished out a scroll from the depths of his patrician tunic. 'It arrived yesterday evening,' he said. 'One of the reasons why I was late, as a matter of fact, but there's no point in having a battery of informants and despatch riders at one's disposal without making use of them, and . . . well, since I was in the area, and what with your mother-in-law's relationship with Darius being quite a talking point locally and . . . er, because I happen to know you, I um, thought you might be interested in what we could dig up on our friend with the voice like a rusty horse razor.'

More fish stinking out the air, she thought. The Security Police had better things to dig for than a bit of hot gossip. Orbilio was up to something, the bastard.

Claudia took the scroll. 'How thoughtful.'

'I'm a thoughtful person.'

'Modest with it.'

'Modest Cornelius Orbilio was my nickname at school.'

'Thoughtful, modest, are there no end to your talents?'

'Wait till you see me at tiddlywinks.'

Claudia flipped open the scroll and read, then re-read and, just to make certain, read the report again, but the words on the page didn't alter. Blah, blah, blah, it boiled down to the bald fact that Darius Amarantus Tubero, patrician, forty-nine years of age, ex-this, ex-that, but currently a horse-breeder in Salernium, widowed twenty-two years but no heirs, was rolling in money.

'But he's exactly who he says he is!'

'You sound surprised.'

'In my experience, Orbilio, if something seems too good to be true, then it is.'

No breeder of racing flesh of his age, with reasonable looks and with gold pieces coming out of his ears, was so lost and so lonely that he couldn't find companionship with a more compatible partner, because Larentia's narrow existence and lack of education hardly made her an intellectual match and at twenty years his senior she wasn't going to fulfil him in bed, either.

'Maybe instead of worrying about Darius being who he claims to be,' Orbilio said as he followed the antics of a squirrel scampering between the overlapping branches, 'you might want to ask yourself how best to get round the problem of him assuming control of your estate once they tie the knot.'

'If there are any knots to be tied, it'll be a noose and I'll tie it, and quite honestly, Marcus, throttling Larentia will be an unqualified pleasure.'

His chuckle echoed round the valley. 'There you go again.

61

Inviting me to whisk out the imperial handcuffs when we barely know one another! Suppose we rectify that situation by having dinner tonight?'

'Splendid idea, Orbilio. I'll eat at my house and you can dine with Rex over at his.'

'I'll take that as a maybe, but with your wits that sharp, I can see you working out how Candace did it, what Darius's game is, what's behind the run of bad luck and why Lars married Eunice before the moon combs her lovely red hair. Oh, and I wouldn't put it past you to solve the political crisis in Mauritania while you're about it.'

'What political crisis in Mauritania?'

They walked on in silence, while, in the distance, the doves in the pigeon house flexed their collective wings over the villa, coils of blue wood smoke spiralled up from the forge, and steam rose like dragon's breath through the vents of the bath house. Slaves small as ants busied themselves with the morning tasks of laundry and food preparation, cows trotted out of the milking shed happy and mooing, and gardeners fetched pails to top up the troughs.

'So why aren't you in Gaul?' she asked, and it was interesting to see that he wasn't wearing a wedding band. Yet. The social pressures on such a post would be strong, and she wondered why it mattered that she was relieved. 'And don't give me any of that crap about being Rex's nephew, Orbilio, it won't wash.'

'Funnily enough I am, in a way. Rex was a close friend of my late father's, and I did used to call him Uncle on the few occasions I saw him when I was small. The thing is, Claudia . . .'

He stopped and leaned his weight against an elm. Tall and stately, it was one of several planted in perfect ranks and squares to take the supports for the heavy vines. Its military precision seemed appropriate for the subject in question.

'Hard to believe under all that bluster, but Rex was one of our finest generals. He led enormously successful campaigns in Galatia, Thrace and Iberia, and it was his masterful tactics that got the Fourteenth out of that mess on the Rhine, where they were surrounded by hostile tribes on all sides.'

'Dare I suggest that he shouldn't have got them into it in the first place?'

'Not his doing,' Orbilio said. 'The previous incumbent was ill. Dying of a tumour as it happens and doing the best that he could, but the bottom line was he led his men into an ambush and Rex got them out, with precious few casualties into the bargain. Over the course of his career, Rex won several crowns and he earned every last one.'

'But?'

'No buts. Here he is in Tuscany, with his olive groves and pastures, where he intended to grow old with his wife.'

'Except she died twenty years ago.' Claudia hadn't forgotten the lump in the old soldier's throat and the tenderness in his voice as her ghost spoke to him in the dining hall just last night.

'She did, and I suppose that it was because he was on campaign most of the time that Rex never married again.'

'I know it's expected of you aristocrats to keep remarrying every time you mislay a wife, but perhaps the founding of one dynasty was sufficient for Rex?'

Marcus chuckled. 'In some cases, perhaps, but not his. You see, his wife bore him five daughters but only one son, a boy called Hadrian, and trust me, Hadrian is not going to continue the ancestral line.'

'Is he ill?'

'Not exactly.' He folded his arms across his chest. 'Don't forget I've known Hadrian all my life. He's only three years younger than me, and whilst you'd never accuse us of being friends, I know him well enough, I think, to judge him incapable of killing Lichas.'

'The toy-maker?' Claudia goggled. 'The boy whose body was washed up on Terrence's land?'

'One and the same.'

'Why on earth would the son of a wealthy, respected general be the prime suspect in an impoverished woodcarver's murder?'

'Because they were lovers,' he said, 'and the same attitude

to homosexuality that applies in Rome applies to the whole of the Empire.'

'We live in a world where men are men and women are drudges. Yes, thank you, I'm already aware of that.'

'If you're a drudge, then I'm a drury.' Not much of a pun, but the best he could manage this hour of the morning. He prised himself away from the elm tree and ambled slowly beneath the overhead vines. 'Right now, public opinion sides with Lichas's sister, Rosenna, who's convinced Hadrian murdered her brother. Quite honestly, it's only a matter of time before the local authorities move in to arrest him, and the only way I can prevent that from happening is to find out who really killed Lichas.'

'Nepotism obviously taking priority over the scores of conspiracies fermenting merrily away in south-west Gaul.' Claudia plucked a sprig of mint and rubbed it between her fingers.

'The importance of false accusations can never be under-estimated,' he said sanctimoniously.

'Ooh, can you hear that, Marcus? That bellowing in the distance?'

'No,' he said, craning his neck to listen.

'Funny, but I could have sworn I heard bull. Carry on.'

Orbilio ran his hand round his jaw and wondered what the bloody hell he was supposed to say. Admit that he'd been missing her so bloody badly that he was prepared to risk his whole career just to see her? That during one of his regular trips to Rome, the news shot round the family like a fireball about Hadrian allegedly stabbing his lover and Marcus had snatched this as his chance to be close to her? That while he was here, it came to his ears about Larentia and her younger suitor and, worried Darius was a conman, investigated him on Claudia's behalf? He'd jump into a vat of boiling oil first.

'According to Rosenna,' he said tetchily, 'Lichas was an honest, helpful, earnest young man without an enemy in the world, who was deeply in love with his patrician boyfriend.'

'Like I said, if something sounds too good to be true, then it probably is.'

'You can't blame a grief-stricken girl for idealizing her

baby brother as he lies on his funeral bier. It's just ironic that the same pain that paints Lichas in such glorious colours also prompted her to blurt out that Hadrian, being so ashamed of the relationship that he only ever slipped away on the quiet, was planning to finish the affair, but when Lichas threatened public exposure, decided to silence his lover's mouth in the most decisive way possible.'

'Honest, helpful and earnest on one side of the coin. A blackmailing cad on the other.'

'People who have been hurt can often be both. We've all said and done things in the heat of the moment that we regret.'

'So why not Hadrian?'

'Claudia, you haven't met him or you wouldn't be suggesting it, but take it from me, that boy's so wet, you could wring him out with your bare hands. He has neither the guts or the strength to pierce a stomach wall with his dagger, then yank it out and drag a writhing, gurgling, terrified Lichas across the water meadows before pitching him into the river.' Marcus blew out his cheeks. 'The wound was undoubtedly fatal, but stomach wounds are messy, painful and slow. Lichas drowned in the end.'

A horrible, horrible way to die, and no wonder Rosenna was bitter.

'If there was a storm that night, wouldn't it have washed away any bloodstains? How do you know he wasn't killed by the river and simply fell in?'

'Imagine you were arranging to meet someone in that kind of weather. Wouldn't you choose a place where there's shelter? Exactly. And your trusty investigator found a pool of blood in the lee of a large yew below the hill in the bend in the river.'

No wonder they'd promoted him, Claudia thought. The man thinks of everything. Including forgery, tax evasion, fraud, theft . . .

'You know what strikes me as odd?' she said, picking up a handful of pebbles and tossing them one at a time at the wicker fence that enclosed the vineyard to prevent deer browsing on the tender new shoots. 'Everywhere you look at the moment, it's either toy boys, playboys, lady boys . . .' She paused in her aim. 'All *boys*, though, have you noticed? All boys.'

'Yes I have, and I'm thinking of one seventeen-year-old boy in particular,' he said grimly. 'One who is very much dead.'

'Really?' She hit the target with her very last pebble. 'Strangely enough, I was thinking of old Etha who went searching for her grandson the night of the storm. Tages was seventeen years old, as well.' Claudia turned her face to the hills. 'And that boy remains very much missing.'

Ten

Bad luck, Larentia called it. An epidemic of bad luck was sweeping the town, but praise be to Candace's spells, it had passed over her and spared the estate, the villa and its slaves. No blight, no rust, no vine weevil, she'd said, and she was certainly right about that. Claudia had examined every single leaflet and since that was what bailiffs were for – ensuring such plagues were kept at bay – she'd sent for him the minute Orbilio had ridden off.

And wasn't remotely surprised to hear the bailiff express astonishment (if not downright bewilderment) that the Mistress should even *mention* blight or rust, much less weevil. Everything was exactly as he'd detailed in his monthly reports, he'd insisted, adding that – ask anyone – weather conditions had been perfect for the vines this winter and spring, and throwing in a baffled scratch of his head for good measure. The Mistress mustn't fret, he assured her firmly. The customary precautions had been, and would continue to be, taken. Seferius wine would continue to uphold its prestige and reputation.

Claudia had returned to her room, changed into a robe of pale lilac linen and pinned up her hair. Either Candace's spells were so powerful that she'd ended up protecting half of Italy, or viticulture remained a skill, not a lottery!

'Clemens the driver says he's waiting to take you to Mercurium,' a small voice piped up.

'Clemens talks too much.'

'So do I.' Amanda made herself comfortable on the bed and began to unpick the tasselled fringe on the coverlet. 'Mummy says.'

'Mummy's right.'

'No, she's not. I heard her tell someone that the old witch arrived yesterday, but it's only you here, so what does *she* know?' Little blue eyes rolled upwards in disdain. 'Anyway, Indigo and I are going to Mercurium with you.'

'Are you?'

'Yes, we're all packed and we have enough cheese and sausage to last us to Rome.' She held up a package that wouldn't last a mouse to the end of the driveway.

'Rome, you say?'

'Indigo and I are going to live with my father, and though we don't know who he is yet, we know we'll find him in Rome. It's a very big place.'

'All the more reason not to find him, don't you think?'

A lot of cupped hands and whispering into thin air followed. At which point, Amanda announced with a sniff that Indigo said that was so *negative*, but could Claudia say whether Rome was as far as from here to Mercurium and back, or maybe a little bit less?

'Are you sure you want to run away today?' Claudia asked. Amanda had already abandoned the tassels in favour of a lump of black sausage. 'Wouldn't you rather wait, say, until after the Beating of the Bounds?'

'That's *ages* off.'

Twelve days probably was ages off when you're only six years old and running away from home with just a small chunk of pecorino cheese and a badly gnawed sausage.

'Yes it is, but in between we've got the Lamb Festival, the Parade of the Trumpets as well as the Dance of the Brides of Fufluns on the full moon, and you tell Indigo that the Beating of the Bounds is well worth waiting for. There's feasting and singing, you can dance, dress up in costume—'

'Children aren't allowed at the ceremonies.'

'Oh, but this is a holiday for everybody, Amanda. Children, grown-ups, poor people, animals—'

'*Animals*? You mean rats and snakes have a holiday, too?'

Claudia meant beasts of burden, but she supposed snakes deserved a day off now and then.

'And . . . we get to dress up, me and Indigo?'

'Like the Queen of Sheba with bells on.' Another robe down the drain!

Amanda wrinkled her nose then called a Council of War with her friend. 'All right, we'll wait till after the beater thing to run away, but only because we like lambs and the trumpet parade's fun, but Indigo says we're *still* coming with you this morning.'

Did she indeed?

'Very well.' Claudia dug a copper quadran out of her purse. 'Heads or tails?'

Childish freckles merged into a single brown mass of a frown. 'Huh?'

'There's only room for one person beside me in the cart,' Claudia said briskly. 'So the fairest thing is to flip a coin to see whether it's you or Indigo who gets the spare place.'

Several seconds passed while Amanda thought this through, and Claudia imagined it was the first time anyone had taken her make-believe friend seriously.

'We've decided we'll both *stay*,' Amanda declared at last, 'because we need to tell all the animals that they're going on holiday soon.' And off she skipped, leaving Claudia wondering why Mummy hadn't had a nervous breakdown. Bitch or not, the woman deserved at least one.

'I want to take a detour,' she told Clemens, once the cart was clear of the estate.

She was no physician, but epidemics don't go unchecked and last night's theatricals suggested a distinct escalation in whatever game was being played out here. Certainly, the show hadn't been staged for her benefit. Candace's communion with the dead had been planned well in advance – hell, she'd all but sold tickets! – and Claudia intended to find out why, and in particular *where* Larentia's obsession with bad luck fitted in.

'Pull up here,' she instructed the driver.

Until recently, this converted grain store had been used by a local paper merchant until fire had swept through, destroying his stock. Claudia studied the blackened walls and a courtyard that was already being reclaimed by weeds. Fires were common in Rome, the threat of it constant, and it was not unusual to see the night sky glowing orange as a tenement went up here, a warehouse caught fire there, especially in the winter, when portable stoves were all too easily overturned and burning logs jumped out of their baskets. More than one paper merchant in Rome had suffered the same fate. But twice? In six months?

'The brickworks next,' she told Clemens.

And as the mule clip-clopped along, she mulled over the profits to be made from construction, now that peace had settled over the Empire. With a whole generation having grown up without the spectre of civil war looming over them, one could not emphasize too strongly the effect this peace had had. The tombs that lined the main roads into cities were being filled with the bones of old men, not young warriors, and a massive influx of prisoners of war had brought about a prosperity the Empire had never experienced. Thanks to this slave labour, the land produced a glut of foodstuffs, which could then be exported, plus there was mineral wealth to be mined – again by slaves or convicted criminals – and industry was flourishing as never before. Warehouses, bath houses, shops and apartments sprang up like groundsel. Temples, basilicas, bridges and roads became the backbone of Augustus's new Empire, along with aqueducts, sewers, theatres and gates, race courses and triumphal arches, and it was the Emperor's boast that he inherited a city of brick and would leave it a city of marble. *In such an economic climate, how on earth can a brick-maker go bankrupt?*

Claudia stared at the business that had been snapped up for a pittance by one of the insolvent brick-maker's competitors. It wasn't as though he'd set up his works too far from Mercurium and overreached himself with transportation costs. and in any case it was a small-scale operation. Claudia counted forty, fifty slaves – no more – and, watching the bricks being tipped out of their moulds, reflected on Larentia's explanation that his kiln had been cursed by the gods, or why else would his fires keep going out?

Fire . . .

'Thank you, Clemens. That's all here.'

One man gets too many fires, while another gets too few . . .

Yet not all this so-called bad luck could be laid at the door of a capricious arsonist. There was the miller's donkey that dropped dead in its prime. The tavern-keeper whose wine turned to vinegar and whose axle then broke, costing him several gallons of wine. Listening to Larentia – and Claudia freely admitted that she'd got lost among the clouds of detail –she vaguely remembered somebody's well going sour, live-stock keeling over somewhere else, crops failing, and all sorts of personal difficulties erupting at once. Quarrels, death, divorce, and wasn't it the miller's brother's wife (dammit, why are these relationships always so complicated?) who'd walked out recently, taking the children with her to Rome? The brother was a blacksmith, Claudia recalled. And don't blacksmiths have forges?

With fires?

Bad luck . . . or simply bad character? There was no denying that a lot of bad things had happened round here, but coincidence? Uh-uh. The sun would have to rise in the west before Claudia accepted that. Sabotage was almost certainly behind the poisoned well, the spiked wine, the fires at the paper merchant's warehouse, the damping of the brick-maker's kilns. And just as it was a human hand, not a divine one, that was orchestrating these disasters, so it was a human hand that stabbed Lichas and dragged him – still twitching and gushing blood – across the field and calmly tipped him in the water.

Larentia might call it a run of bad luck.

Claudia called it unadulterated evil.

Now she needed to track this evil back to its lair, because Tages the shepherd boy still hadn't come home and she had personally endangered the life of another seventeen-year-old youth.

And if evil thought it was going to get its hands on young Orson, evil had another think coming.

In the dark, sulphurous caverns between the living and the dead, Veive strode upright and proud. His was no life to be spent gazing endlessly into the Waters of Prophesy or poring bent-backed over the Runes of Adversity among the sorcerers

71

and necromancers of the netherworld. Like Terror and Panic, twin sons of black-winged Night, and their sisters Discord, Deception and Strife, the God of Revenge was constantly on the move. Always alert, ever dispassionate, it was Veive's role to answer the calls of those who invoked him. To ensure that his aim was true.

'Forgive me for intruding.' With great reverence he approached the Goddess of Shadows, who guarded the Mirror of Life. 'But I wish to track the progress of my arrows.'

'There is no intrusion,' she whispered, and her voice was a thousand echoes as she unveiled the Mirror. 'You are always welcome in my house, dear friend. Tell me, what do you see?'

'I see fires. I see death. I see desecration,' he told her, and his heart neither rejoiced nor saddened, for it was not Veive's role to apportion sorrow and blame. It was for other gods to move among the reeds and take the shape of birds to impart their wisdom to mortals, just as it was their task (should it please them) to even out the distribution of health, wealth and happiness and administer justice.

'Is that all you see?' the goddess asked.

'No,' he replied truthfully. 'I see your sisters Ruin and Greed walking amongst the devastation, but equally I see Success, O Wise One.'

Every arrow that had been loosed from Veive's Bow of Vengeance had found its rightful target.

'But hark! My name is being invoked even while we speak. Forgive the brevity of this visit, O Wise One, but I fear I must leave. My work, it seems, is not finished.'

Beside him the Goddess of Shadows laughed softly. 'Our work is never finished, dear friend, but I bid you call again soon.' She closed the veil over the Mirror. 'You are always welcome in this house.'

Market day in the Roman Empire fell every eighth day, and in Mercurium the narrow, twisting streets were packed with sacks and stalls, trestles and trays selling everything from needles to fleeces to honey in little red-painted pots. There had been talk of building a proper marketplace at the foot of the hill between the basilica and the Temple of Saturn, but so far the plans remained nothing more than outlines on parchment. What was the point? The townspeople were never going to change their ways, and maybe it was the sense of community – jostling through lanes clogged with donkeys laden with panniers or carts piled high with fruit, hides and chickens – or simply a sense of security, being packed into so tight a space, but since their ancestors had raised the first walls round this town, this was how markets had been held and this was how markets would continue to be held.

Which made trade both effortless and impossible at the same time.

The same jugs of wine that enticed shoppers with their bouquet banged against elbows and stained clothes with their careless drips. The same wreaths that hung from ropes pegged across the street to lure matrons into decorating their homes tangled in their neatly coiffed hair. No forehead was safe against dangling poles, swinging baskets, protruding cauldrons or muslins and mugs. Reactions were universal. Some laughed at their misfortune, others groused, some cursed, some scolded, while there were always those on both sides of the commercial fence who thrived on exaggerating the damage. It drew attention and bolstered their sense of importance, they argued, little realizing that it had the opposite effect.

'Thimbles!'

'Goose eggs!'

'Who'll buy my tasty veal pies?'

Another time Claudia would have enjoyed browsing among the bolts of brightly coloured cottons that sat cheek by jowl beside cucumbers, mackerel and pitch as she nibbled on hot, flaky pastries washed down by dark Tuscan wine. Today, though, her mind was on murder and sabotage, and a man bent on taking over her business . . .

His motives didn't concern her. She'd known men who were richer than Croesus, who still wanted more money. Greed, covetousness, a mere itch they wanted scratching . . . who cared?

You might want to ask yourself how best to get round the

problem of him assuming control of your estate once they tie the knot.

She might also want to ask herself why the Security Police working a murder case in which a family friend was the chief suspect would concern himself with a man who was nothing more than a bit of hot gossip, but Orbilio had a point. If Larentia went ahead with her marriage to Darius (and at sixty-eight, this was her last chance for happiness, so why wouldn't she?), how could Claudia stop him taking power over her business?

Sauntering through the crush, patting piglets in their crates, examining some very odd-shaped roots in a basket and overhearing how the wheelwright's eldest had come down with a ringworm and kindly passed it round the whole family, she wondered where Candace fitted into the puzzle. Orbilio seemed confident that Claudia would work out how the sorceress pulled off that stunt yesterday evening, but she wasn't so sure, and whilst well within her right to turn her out of her house, she felt it was far better to keep an eye on this walker of winds and see where her ambles led.

Turning the corner at the basket-weaver's stall, Claudia felt a light tap on her shoulder. 'Terrence!'

'I was finalizing the arrangements for the Lamb extravaganza when I happened to notice you.' If he'd been rattled by last night's performance with Candace, he masked it well. 'Perhaps when you come to the party you could set aside a little time to talk privately?' he suggested. 'There's a little business matter I would like to discuss . . . Oh, for pity's sake, Thalia!'

'You . . . you don't like it?' His sister's pale face blenched even whiter as she smoothed the robe that hung over her arm. 'The dressmaker assured me that these pleats are the latest fashion, is . . . isn't that right, Claudia?'

'It's not the dressmaker's word that's at issue, Thalia. The Lamb Festival is supposed to be a celebration of new life, not a bloody wake.' Terrence rolled his eyes. 'What on earth made you buy grey, for gods' sake?' He turned to Claudia. 'I'm sorry, I'm going to have to sort this out while the dress-

74

maker still has time to run up a new gown. But remember what I said. Come early. Please.'

He grabbed Thalia's new robe and almost pushed his sister back in the shop. Thank Juno, Claudia had never had siblings! Pushing on through the market, she noticed a familiar Caesar-cut outside the silversmith's shop.

'If Larentia told you she's pregnant,' she quipped, 'she's hooked you under false pretences.'

Replacing the perfume flask he'd been admiring, Darius turned his eyes to her. 'Oh?' They were amber brown like quartz, she noticed. And every bit as hard. 'I thought that was her granddaughter's device.'

Claudia wondered what other family secrets Larentia had been pressed to divulge. 'Like any healthy teenage girl, Flavia is discovering life's rich tapestry,' she trilled back. 'It's simply unfortunate that she makes progress one stitch at a time.'

'Don't you think maturity will remain out of her reach, so long as you persist in shielding her from things such as last night's events?'

Claudia had forgotten how much gravel he kept down his throat. 'As a matter of fact, it was her choice not to attend Candace's summoning of the spirits.' Communing with her dead father was all very well, but . . . 'She and Orson opted for whispering sweet nothings under the stars instead.'

Darius's lips parted in what he must have presumed was a smile. 'Ain't love grand.'

'You should know.'

'I do.'

He started to cough, that same dry, unproductive cough that Claudia hoped was his conscience, and when the spasm was over, his voice was softer.

'I don't expect you to believe this, and you've every right to be sceptical, but I've grown very fond of Larentia during the past few months. I won't lie to you. She's not the love of my life and she knows it, but neither of us are in the first flush of youth and, since I have no family, companionship does have its merits.'

'As does a profitable wine business.'

'With all respect, Claudia, my stud farm turns three times

75

the profits your vineyards make, and even that income pales into insignificance when set against the rents and profits from my property investments and, as I am sure you know already, my not inconsiderable inheritance.'

At first, she mistook the rumble at the back of his throat for another cough.

'Holy heralds,' he said, shaking his head. 'In all my life I never imagined asking permission for my bride's hand in marriage to a girl young enough to be my own daughter.'

Claudia chewed her lip and thought there was only one way to get round the problem, and that was to discredit the bastard. 'Larentia *is* happy,' she said.

The laugh deepened. 'Did it hurt very much to say that?'

'Yes.'

'Good. Because now, perhaps, we can be friends.' He picked up a silver mirror. 'Do you think Ren would like this?'

'Darius, the woman's sixty-eight. She's not going to appreciate being shown her reflection by a man twenty years younger than she is.'

'See?' He exchanged the mirror for the silver perfume flask he'd been examining earlier and didn't haggle over the price. 'I knew we'd be friends.' He handed the bottle to Claudia with a bow. 'Please accept this as a token of my undying gratitude for being spared a hideous embarrassment.'

A genuine gesture? Or a trinket to bribe her round? Darius was proving difficult, she realized. The more she knew of him, the less she understood. This was not as straightforward as she had hoped. But then discrediting wealthy respectable breeders of horse flesh was never going to be easy.

Down one of the side streets, a creaking cart loaded with timber *graunched* painfully and Darius excused himself a moment to push his way through the produce and livestock to run after it. Curious, Claudia followed.

'You want to grease those bloody wheels!' Darius was shouting out to the driver.

'Oh, yeah.' The waggoner sneered. 'And what's it to you?'

'Me? Nothing. To the oxen, it makes a whole world of difference.'

The driver spat insolently into the gutter. 'Give me one good reason why I should worry about them, when they sure don't worry about me.'

'Because if nothing else, they'll live longer and save you money,' Darius snapped, adding 'poor buggers' to Claudia under his breath.

'Talking of living longer,' she said as they rejoined the swaying crowd, 'I notice you didn't ask to speak to any of your loved ones last night.'

'For one thing, I have no loved ones to call upon,' he said, raising his voice to make himself heard, 'and for another, I believe in keeping communications with the dead to a minimum.'

'You surprise me.'

'May I ask why?'

'The way you accept Larentia's confidence in Candace's spells. "Taken prisoner by local superstition", I believe you called it.'

Darius stopped and looped his thumbs into his belt. 'Acceptance isn't the same as approval,' and once again she thought, this was indeed a voice that had trod the path to Hell. 'But somehow Ren's got it into her head that this town has been jinxed, which is absolute bullshit. However, I have to respect that Larentia's buried one husband plus three out of four children, and that old age is also creeping up. She's bound to be . . . what's the word?'

'Suggestible?'

'Susceptible,' he corrected with a dry chuckle. 'If I may speak bluntly, Claudia, Candace is the main reason I'm pushing Ren to fix a date for the wedding. More and more, your mother-in-law is becoming dependent on that woman's visions and spells, and I'm not convinced that's a healthy development.'

'I doubt there's a woman yet who hasn't consulted some kind of fortune-teller, astrologer, soothsayer or quack when she's about to get married.'

'Are we men such ogres?' he asked, sidestepping a crate of grey hazel hens. 'Seriously, though.' He shook his head. 'Try as I might, I can't find out one damn thing about

Candace. Other than the fact that she's Kushite by birth, our lovely sorceress remains a mystery, and mysteries, my dear Claudia, trouble me greatly.'

Claudia wondered what his opinion was when it came to pots calling kettles black.

'Where did Larentia find her?' she asked.

'Ah, well, that'll teach me to go back home on business.' He gave a rueful cluck of the tongue. 'It was even my treat, you know, packing Ren off to the hot springs for a few days of luxury and pampering, because what happens? I check on my horses, I tie up a few deals and when I come back, she's addicted to spells, spirits and magic, and the quicker she's away from Candace's influence, the better. Without our lovely sorceress, Ren's a strong, funny woman – in fact, you and she have a lot in common.'

'I do not take that as a compliment.'

'I wish you would, because you're more alike than either of you think, and you like each other more than you care to admit. And I'll bet that's another bitter pill for you to swallow.'

'I don't take medicines, Darius. The cure is invariably worse than the problem, and if it's true that men marry women who remind them of their mothers, shoot me now.'

'See what I mean? Funny.' He broke off as another dry spasm wracked his chest.

'And while we're on the subject of medicines, are you taking anything for that cough?'

'Everything,' he sighed, dodging a porter balancing three sacks of grain. 'Horehound, coltsfoot, mullein. Janus, I'm a walking herbalist's half the time, which is another reason I'm pushing for an early wedding. Since I arrived in Mercurium, my throat and chest haven't let up and, Claudia, I care for your mother-in-law deeply, but you have no idea how my lungs yearn for their homeland.'

'Campania?'

His face brightened. 'Do you know it?'

Never been. 'Intimately. Particularly Naples, Capua and the peninsula out by Capri.'

'Stunning, isn't it? My farm's further south, on the plains

of Salernum, but Naples is handy for shipping the beasts in and out. Do you know anything about horses?'

'Only that my last one is still running.'

'Then it's not one of mine. I only breed winners, and you have no idea how satisfying it is, watching wobbly foals turn into sleek racers, although sadly the credit is not mine to claim. As you employ specialists to oversee your vines, I employ trainers who do all the hard work.'

'Could you spare one for Flavia?'

'Only if you want her lapping the posts of the Circus Maximus,' he retorted. 'But if you're worried about the girl, seriously, why don't you sign her up for the Dance of the Brides of Fufluns?'

'You've lost me.'

'I doubt that,' he rumbled. 'But come.'

Instead of following the flow of the market, Darius turned into a side street and followed the steep path to the summit of Mount Mercury. Like the seven hills of Rome, the air up here was cleaner and fresher, trees lined the squares – laurels, plane trees and cypress – and from their branches birds serenaded the white limestone fronts and blood-red roof tiles of the villas of the well heeled. Facing west, these sumptuous villas overlooked the soft rolling landscape and sat in perfect alignment for catching the refreshing sea breezes during the baking hot Etruscan summers. Claudia followed the point of Darius's index finger to a hill to the south that was fronted by a forest of salmon-pink columns.

'That's the Temple of Fufluns down there,' he said. 'Have a word with Tarchis the priest. See if he can't help Flavia to grow up.'

If he could, Claudia thought, it would be the only miracle to take place around here.

Including last night's shenanigans.

Eleven

When Augustus triumphed over Cleopatra and Mark Anthony, he united the Empire and promised his people an end to the carnage of war, but his peace came with a price tag. In return for safe highways, better living standards and grain in your granaries, he told the vanquished nations, you pay tax to Rome and abide by Roman law. It's all right, you can keep your customs, your clothes, your obscure religions, we don't mind. In fact, your culture enriches ours. But cross me, he warned, and your soil will be stained red with blood for a decade. Which path do you choose?

Too many lives had already been sacrificed, too much lost, for the tribes to challenge the might of the Romans. He knew full well that they'd bow to the inevitable, then try to squeeze as much as they could out of the deal – which was all very fine, but left Augustus with something of a dilemma. Given the peace that had settled over the Empire, what was he going to do with seventy legions, now that most of them had nothing to do?

Augustus was nothing if not shrewd. Rumours had abounded for years about how he'd offered himself as Julius Caesar's catamite to advance his own cause, and whether those rumours were founded or not, it was the nineteen-year-old Augustus who inherited the Divine Julius's crown. No one else! So the administering of territories stretching from the eastern shores of the Black Sea to the Oceans of Atlantis was nothing short of child's play for the Emperor. By replacing amateur conscripted farmers with a force of hard-core professional volunteers, the army's efficiency multiplied. Within two years he'd reduced seventy legions to fewer than thirty, allotting the redundant veterans generous

80

pensions as well as parcels of fertile land in the conquered territories to those that wanted them, while opportunities naturally flourished within his elite and restructured army.

The father of Publius Peregrinus Macedo might well have bought his son's original commission, but there was no disguising the lad's military genius. Nicknamed Rex on account of his imposing stature, he was the youngest legate to march into Gaul and the first to fully appreciate the importance of civilian support on campaign, the so-called 'Second Army' of carpenters, engineers, musicians and blacksmiths, orderlies, veterinarians and scribes.

Waiting in the general's office, Orbilio scanned the gleaming collection of weapons, armour and other trophies of war that obliterated most of Rex's walls and was flooded with memories of his own tribuneship. Hardly the happiest time of his life. The marriage he'd been contracted into prior to his first posting hadn't got off to the finest of starts, and being absent from home for the best part of two years did nothing to bolster the relationship. Add on his refusal to follow the proud ancestral tradition and take up law once his stint was up, opting for what his family considered to be some grubby, poorly paid post in a demeaning little backwater of the Administration, and it was no great surprise that his wife ran off with a sea captain from Lusitania, causing a scandal that still clung to him like a wet shirt. He peered at the battle-scarred helmets, the rows of pierced shields, an Egyptian corselet still stained with blood. No matter how hard or how often he tried to explain, not so much as one distant third cousin had grasped the fact that enforcing the law was infinitely more important that practising it, especially since the object of defence was to get the accused off and never mind that the bastard was guilty!

Testing the point of a Scythian arrowhead, Marcus prided himself on his work within the Security Police. The satisfaction of knowing that this assassination attempt had been foiled, that conspiracy had been thwarted, those rapists and murderers thrown to the lions. He might only be a small cog in the wheel, but that was the wheel that kept Rome safe and the Empire thriving, and no one could take that sense

81

of fulfilment away. He saw, in time, taking a seat in the Senate, like his father before him, and voting on issues that would change not just the law, but the whole structure of society. Make it better and stronger for generations to come. There was a sense of achievement in that, too.

But . . . He ran his finger over the red horsehair crest of an antique Spartan helmet. But at the same time there was something missing in his life, and that something was a woman. A wife. And that something also had a name.

Watching the tumble of curls bursting out of their ivory hairpins this morning, Marcus felt the same wrench in his gut that he always felt when he was with her. It wasn't love, of course, because love wouldn't keep a chap tossing and turning all through the night, then leave him aching and empty in the morning. Love was about holding hands in the moonlight and whispering sweet nothings in one another's ears, not chasing round the countryside risking your career on a girl who took life's corners on two wheels. Nevertheless . . . He examined his teeth in the shine of an ancient Mycenean breastplate. The Governor of Aquitania was pressuring him to set an example of Roman propriety by remarrying, while Claudia's estate was under threat if Darius married Larentia.

Expediency, that's all it was. She knew him enough to trust his word that she could continue to manage her own affairs without his interference. He'd have the appendage of respectability that the State required. Expediency. Yes, that's what it was. Expediency, pure and simple.

'Ah, Marcus!' Rex strode into the room with his customary briskness, and for all that he was clad in civilian clothes, he might just as well have been wearing his red legate's tunic, with his red woollen cloak swinging jauntily over his shoulder. 'Been admiring my collection, have you? That – ' he jabbed a stubby finger at a leather belt hanging empty in pride of place behind his desk '– was Agamemnon's own baldric. By your right shoulder hangs the girdle of Hippolyte the Amazon queen, and this,' he said proudly, 'this is the very sword with which Achilles despatched Hector beneath the walls of Troy!'

Orbilio was reminded of charlatans in Rome selling dead

snakes cut from Medusa's head or feathers shed from Pegasus's wings

'Hoping to add Hercules's olive-wood club very soon. Depends on whether my source can negotiate a fair price—'

'About Hadrian, sir.'

'Hadrian?' The old war horse filled two goblets to the brim with wine. 'Waste of time, m'boy. Appreciate you coming up here and all that, and happy to put you and your scribe up for as long as you want, but no need, no need. Local army chappies are quite capable of handling the investigation.'

'There are rumbles of a cover-up.'

'That'll be the sister's doing. Take no notice.' Rex indicated for Orbilio to take a seat on a high-backed upholstered chair with carved lion armrests. 'Keeps stirring the wrong pot, that's Rosenna's trouble. Won't face the truth.'

Orbilio placed his glass on the desk untouched. 'And what is the truth?'

'The truth, m'boy, is that Lichas was a nasty little shit, who deserved everything he got.'

The general downed his wine in one swallow and Marcus wondered idly whether anyone ever deserved to be stabbed and thrown into the river alive.

'Which makes it doubly unfortunate for Hadrian that he was the last person to see Lichas alive and has admitted quarrelling with him under the yew,' he said evenly.

'That admission was made in this room, dammit, when there were only the three of us present, and if you take that outside, both my son and I'll deny it and never mind I sat next to your father on a bench in the Senate, I'll have you denounced as a liar, understood?'

'No, sir, I don't understand.' Orbilio laced his fingers. 'Your son is *this* close to being arrested for Lichas's murder, and right now the only thing that's preventing him from being marched off in chains is the fact that you've leaned on the local judiciary. Rosenna knows it, the townspeople know it, and if I've any hope of clearing Hadrian's name, you have to let me interview him again—'

'Categorically not!' Rex pounded the desk with his fist. 'The boy's said too much as it is.'

'Are you worried he'll say more?'

Colour suffused the general's face, turning it a deep shade of purple. 'If I was still a legate, I'd have had you flogged for that remark.'

'If you'd still been a legate, I'd have been a tribune, and you could not have had a tribune flogged for *any* reason. Sir. Now let's not forget we're on the same side here—'

'What we shouldn't forget, sonny, is that I didn't invite you here and I didn't ask you to meddle in affairs that don't bloody concern you.' The old soldier regrouped. 'See here, m'boy. You came to Tuscany for all the right reasons, I realize that, and I appreciate the sacrifice you've made, too. Building a reputation for yourself in Aquitania and all that. But best get back while you've still got a job, eh?'

'Is that a threat?'

Rex's lips tightened and for several minutes the only sound in the office was that of him tapping his finger on his satin-wood desk. Orbilio let his gaze range across the various antiquaries. What was Rex hiding, he wondered?

'Sorry if I appear to be breaking your balls, but you see how it is, don't you?' The general harrumphed around in his chair. 'Just . . . just not *right*, this sort of thing.'

'Murder?'

Rex wasn't listening. 'Have fun, by all means. At his age, we all did. Sow your wild oats and if that includes hopping over the fence for a bit of a change, then so be it. But to make a vocation of it, dammit! Just ain't natural, and I'll cure that boy of his ridiculous notions if it's the last thing I do. Think I'll have a word with the Emperor, what. Ask for Hadrian to be put in charge of a cohort out on the Rhine. That'll make a man of him right enough, because there'll be none of this namby-pamby nancy-boy stuff, not on my watch, even if I have to beat it out of the lad myself.'

'I'm sure that'll do the trick.'

'Are you being funny?'

'No, sir.'

'That Lichas, he was one of 'em, y'know, and we all know how far they'll go to protect one of their own.'

'With all due respect, you can't lump homosexuals in a box and—'

'Not talking about bloody poofs! Commoners, Marcus. Riff-raff. You served abroad. You know what it's like, living among vanquished tribes. Can't trust 'em, can't turn your back on 'em, and forget this talk about the Etruscans being conquered so far back in time that they're fully integrated. Bollocks. It's them and us, always was, always will be, and it don't matter a damn what we've done for the ungrateful buggers, they still resent us.'

'One can see their point, though.'

The general pushed his jowly face towards his. 'I'll not have my son's reputation smeared through these preposterous allegations. If Hadrian says he didn't kill that snide little queer, that's the end of it, so you leave it, Marcus. Leave it alone or so help me you'll be pushing a quill for the rest of your sordid little career.'

Watching her brother's pyre burn, Rosenna experienced an unexpected sense of release. At last, she thought, Lichas was free of the indignity of lying there with his corpse ravaged by murder, by water, by savage wee teeth. At last, Lichas was free.

As the choir of four (it was all she could afford) sent him on his last journey with hymns, an acolyte sprinkled sacred water on the pyre as the priest raised his arms in supplication that the gates of the Fields of the Blessed would open and the newcomer find peace among his ancestors. There was no question of hiring wailing women or professional mourners for Lichas, but the modest funeral had not deterred the townspeople from paying their respects. The toy-maker had been a nice enough lad and his skills would be missed, but wasn't it wicked the way that patrician boy cut him down in his prime and was gonna get away with the murder? Discontent rumbled through the crowds like distant thunder and Rosenna's heart found comfort in the sound.

'There'll be no funeral meats,' she explained.

They understood. Lichas was young, he hadn't had time

to establish his business. Rosenna couldn't afford a funeral as well as a feast.

'You are bearing up well, child,' the priest murmured. 'Lichas would be proud of you.'

She smiled thinly, knowing he interpreted her pursed lips and fists clenched white as grief. This was undoubtedly true. But they were pursed and clenched in vengeance, as well.

Flames crackled and coils of incense spiralled upwards on the warm breeze. Rosenna hadn't actually lied about her financial situation. All she'd said was there'd be no funeral meats and left people to draw their own conclusions, whereas Lichas's toys had sold for a tidy profit. That was a lot of money she'd found in his chest. But not so much, unfortunately, that she could afford a funeral, a feast *and* bribing a slave in that bastard's household.

The choir continued to carry Lichas on his final voyage, calming the River Styx with their voices and steadying the Ferryman's oars.

The spy's news was bad. The worst possible, as it happened, as he'd listened in on the conversation between Rex and that high-flying crony of his from Rome. It was, as Rosenna had feared, a full-scale cover-up. Having admitted to quarrelling with Lichas at the spot where he was killed, Hadrian was one step away from confessing to the murder, something Rex had no intention of allowing him to do. According to the spy, the investigator from Rome was more than happy to drop the case, whilst Rex had personally spoken to the Emperor, who was arranging for Hadrian to be despatched to the Rhine, where the rumours about his precious boy wouldn't have surfaced.

Boy. The word made Rosenna sick. Holy Nox, Hadrian was twenty-five years old and at an age when most men of his class had been married for ten years and raised kids, having served two years in the army then either continued with a military career or taken up a post in the Administration. What had this Hadrian done? Become a leech on his father and society, that's what. A hanger-on without backbone or conscience, yet Rex still called him a *boy*. Rosenna pulled her long red hair loose as a gesture of mourning and sprinkled ashes over her head. Dammit, the cover-up made Rex as big a bastard as his murderous son, but nits grow into lice, she supposed. And both were equally easily exterminated.

After a while, the funeral pyre ceased to crackle and the flames no longer leapt higher than herself. The townspeople had dispersed; the choir, the acolyte, and even the priest had slipped away until it was just Rosenna and a pile of smouldering bones on a field surrounded by cypress and poplars.

Rosenna did not believe in clinging to the old ways. She understood why folk'd want to bury their dead in the City of Shades out in the country, but as far as she was concerned, times change and life moves with it. And how can they call themselves traditionalists, when the necropolises themselves had changed so drastically over the years? Once upon a time, tombs were tiny replica houses, to which the family brought food and other gifts that would nourish the deceased's spirit in its new residence. Then, through the flight patterns of birds and the clouds in the skies, the gods divulged more about the afterlife and tombs were excavated deep in the rock that the dead might be closer to Aita the Unseen, who ruled over the Underworld. Such sepulchres were a complex arrangement of chambers and corridors, passageways, columns and courtyards, but even that changed when the City of Shades was laid out in a pattern of properly recreated streets and plazas, so that the dead might feel more at home.

Except the dead were *not* at home, Rosenna thought bitterly, and better their ashes were buried in an urn close to the living, where flowers could be laid at regular intervals, than leave their souls to flit like bats in the void. Untended. Unloved. Ultimately forgotten . . .

A kite mewed high above and, down the long straight road that led to the Burning Field, a set of hooves echoed. The horse snickered as the rider pulled up and dismounted. His head was veiled, as men are obliged when paying respects at a funeral, so his face was deep in shadow, and the loose way he draped his cloak betrayed little about his build. After standing in swirling wood smoke for several hours, many of which had been spent sobbing, Rosenna's smarting eyes couldn't tell whether the rider was young or old, thin or stocky, Roman or Etruscan, though for the life of her she couldn't understand why a stranger should stand some distance from her brother's funeral and just stare. No words of comfort were offered to the bereaved. No token thrown upon the flames. Just a stranger. Staring from across the other side of the field. Without acknowledgement, the rider picked up the reins of his horse, flung himself into the saddle and galloped off, his mount's hooves kicking up clouds of dust on the road.

It was only once he'd ridden off that Rosenna noticed the couple.

Standing close together in the shade of an ancient cypress, their skin was an identical shade of olive, their hair an identical length, their noses identical in profile. The man wore a green tunic that mirrored the cypress, the girl's was a deep brooding blue, both embroidered with patterns that Rosenna had seen only once before and then on a Palestinian merchant. No words passed between the pair, yet they were communicating, Rosenna was sure of it. And as the sun slowly set and the last of the energy drained from Lichas's pyre, she was reminded of vultures standing over a body, waiting for the victim to die.

Shivering, she turned back to the fire, rubbing the goose pimples flat on her arms. When she looked back again, the couple were gone.

Standing in middle of the Burning Field as dusk settled over the landscape while she waited for the priest to return and sanctify her brother's remains before they were washed then locked away in their urn, Rosenna had never felt so alone.

Twelve

'Claudia! Darling!' Eunice embraced her as though she was family. 'So glad you joined me for dinner.'

She swept her into the atrium of one of the exclusive villas that Claudia had noticed when standing on the top of Mount Mercury beside Darius earlier. But, though of fine quality, the stone inside was porphyry rather than marble, and the trimmings were fashioned from ivory rather than gold. As the widow of a rich merchant, this would represent quite a climb down for Eunice. Whereas for a masseur from the hot springs, it must be luxury beyond his wildest dreams . . .

'I do so detest my own company; it's unspeakably dull, and with Lars off at another of his dreary Etruscan dos and Larentia still mooning over that man of hers, I was in danger of collapsing from acute isolation.'

'If anything, Eunice, you're more likely to collapse with a cute eye doctor,' Claudia laughed.

'Darling, you know me so well.'

Her throaty chuckle mingled with the lavender and pinks wafting their fragrance into the warm evening air, along with wallflowers, chamomile and aromatic crimson rock rose. Eunice was a sensual woman in every respect, Claudia reflected. Yet she was no more likely to be swayed by flattery or the slow touch of a man's hand than the forthright, no-nonsense Larentia.

'Now, tell me honestly. What do you think of the décor?'

Well, there was one thing about this atrium, Claudia thought. She wasn't likely to forget it in a hurry! Lars talked about Etruscan culture being assimilated by Rome, but in this house they met in a fist fight. On the outside, the villa was Roman from the tip of its roof tiles to the gleaming bronze knocker via the lion's-head rainwater spouts. On the inside, although the architecture was still very much Roman, with its pillars and pools, the red-painted walls were covered in Etruscan-style frescoes in which joyous families danced and dined, priests blessed painted fields and augurs divined the will of the gods from the skies and the behaviour of beasts.

'Honestly?' she asked, examining the four shrines that dominated the atrium. East was garlanded with laurel, the herb of prophesy, South with white-petalled, yellow-bearded Etruscan irises, while a small flame burned on North's shrine and verbascum was on West's as defence against sorcery. She studied the frescoes of Lars's gods and goddesses, in which some wore helmets and carried spears, others went naked and winged, while at least half had assumed animal features in one form or another. Vultures' heads, horses' ears, cloven hoofs, feathers . . . Right through the room, though, light mingled with dark, death with rebirth, air with water, healing with joy to create an effect that was sinister, exhilarating, uplifting and strange. 'Don't tell anyone,' she whispered to Eunice, 'but I like it.'

'Not too pagan?'

'I think it's safe to say your husband isn't letting go of his heritage, certainly. Who's this?' She pointed to a child rising out of a ploughed field with two snakes for legs. Beside him, priests seemed to be scribbling down the boy's every word.

'The son of Genius, who first decreed that all things on earth must be in accordance with the cosmos and let it be known to mortals that their every action is controlled by the gods.'

'I see. Genius tells us that we're nothing more than mindless puppets and so, being mindless puppets, we accept it.'

Eunice laughed. 'Either you've just pinpointed the reason why we Romans prefer our own system of worship or I haven't explained myself very clearly, but perhaps you start to see why the Etruscans place so much faith in the power of amulets, touchstones and rites.'

'Is that what this is?' Claudia nodded towards a giant phallus in the corner. 'A touchstone?'

'Please don't get me started on what that stands for, or I'll need a bucket of cold water thrown over me! The thing is, darling, fertility lies at the very heart of Lars's religion, which is why you see so many paintings of trees dripping with fruit and fields bent with ripe waving corn, and why half our own walls are covered with olive trees whose branches sweep the ground from the weight of the harvest and goblets overflowing with . . . Good gracious, where are my manners!' Eunice passed across a glass filled with wine and the two women chinked rims. 'To health, happiness and . . . Great heavens, darling! Are you all right?'

'This wine . . .' Claudia gasped for breath '. . . is very . . . strong.'

The glint in Eunice's eye danced, as she clapped her guest on the back. 'Another local custom I've thoroughly enjoyed taking to. Not watering Mercury's milk!' She summoned a slave and called for water, then blinked when Claudia tipped it straight into her goblet. 'And here's me thinking it might cure your cough,' she laughed.

'Water's perfect when taken in the right spirit, and this was the right spirit. The proof is that my cough has completely disappeared.' Claudia paused. 'Which is more than Darius's has.'

'Indeed, the poor man.'

Eunice ushered her into a cosy dining chamber laid out with platters of roast venison and pork alongside steaming spiced mushrooms, prawns, peppered parsnips and succulent new season asparagus.

'Our damp northern winter really got to his chest and the cough simply won't budge, though I've finally convinced him that a trip to the hot springs is just what he needs. If they can't cure the wretched thing there, nothing will. You're coming, of course?' Eunice broke a hot roll into small pieces with dreamlike abstraction. 'The waterfall's warmer than a hot bath, there are dozens of bubbly warm pools to wallow in, mud packs that'll take ten years off you at least, and even the river runs hot.'

The hot springs. Where Eunice met Lars, where Lichas met Hadrian, where Darius packed Larentia for a few days of pampering, and where Larentia hooked up with Candace.

'I'll be leaving claw marks in the rock as they drag me away.'

'Splendid, and do bring your young man with you. Young Marcus looks like he could use a spot of relaxation.'

'Orbilio is not my young man,' Claudia said through gritted teeth.

'Of course not, whatever you say,' Eunice replied cheerfully. 'Only remember that dashing young aristocrats don't stay single for long.'

'I think you'll find he's divorced and none to keen to repeat the experience.'

'Nonsense.' Eunice popped a morsel of venison into her mouth. 'Men hate being alone and you two—'

'Are from different classes,' she pointed out evenly. 'He's patrician, I'm—'

'There you go again!' The older woman shook her head. 'You will keep going on about class, when anyone with half an eye can see that Marcus Cornelius isn't the type to worry about nonsense like that. Which reminds me – I invited Terrence over to dinner tonight, but it seems he's tied up with whatever it is that rich landowners get tied up with, which means Thalia won't be allowed out either, which is ridiculous. He's far too over-protective with that girl, when what her nerves need is more social intercourse, not less. Did you know she even told me once that she'd killed her husband?'

Claudia reached for a pastry containing a thin strip of chicken marinated in wine, then coated with a paste of walnuts, honey and mushrooms before being rolled in its melt-in-the-mouth blanket. 'Maybe that's why Terrence keeps her on such a tight leash.'

'Stuff and nonsense.' Eunice dismissed the notion with a wave of her hand. 'I agree, it was an absolutely ghastly marriage. Hubby was a banker, much older than her, and they were constantly at each other's throats, with Thalia never able to remember what the quarrel was about, while he could never forget.'

The concept of Thalia at anybody's throat seemed decidedly at odds with the nervy, harassed creature Claudia had met, but if the girl had enough backbone to stick it out while Candace walked the winds above the Isles of the Blessed, there was obviously more to Terrence's sister than met the eye. But then, couldn't the same be said of everybody?

'But Hubby *is* dead,' she pointed out.

'Yes, but it was his heart, darling. Gave out at the hot springs while I was there, and like I said, he was old. Perfectly straightforward business.'

The hot springs again. Everything happens at those hot springs . . .

'Yet Thalia sat through the opening of the Gateway,' Claudia said, 'and even asked to speak to her husband.'

'I have to confess last night's experience shook me.' Eunice shuddered. 'Watching Candace slice her arm open, watching the blood drain into a bowl, then seeing her skin smooth and unscarred afterwards. I'll be honest, that's the real reason I didn't want to be alone this evening, but dear me, I'm a big girl, I'll get over it. How is Candace, that's what I want to know?'

'Spent the day recovering in bed, apparently.'

I target every ounce of energy on Larentia, who knows only too well how walking with the spirits drains me.

'I'm not surprised.' Eunice speared one of the parsnips. 'Have you any idea what angered them?'

'Who?'

'The spirits. I mean, everything was going swimmingly – well, if you can call talking to the dead a good thing – then crash! The whole room exploded and, I don't mind admitting, I've never been so frightened in my entire life.'

Could this be an act she was putting on for Claudia's benefit? Right now, everything pointed to Eunice being a victim of a money-grabbing gigolo, but this affair had more twists than the serpents in Medusa's hair.

'Did I ever tell you about that goats' wool merchant who came courting me before I married Lars? What a horror! Never saw the wretched man sober, but I'm sure you know the type. Never went to bed with an ugly woman, but certainly woke up with a lot '

Claudia laughed. 'Eunice, you are an incorrigible gossip.'

'Baloney. Secrets are merely things to be passed on to one person at a time. Now tell me honestly, darling.' Eunice sighed, as a plate of wine cakes and honeycombs was laid out for dessert. 'Isn't this a simply heavenly end to a simply heavenly day?'

Claudia could not in all conscience disagree.

Vorda stared at the deep pool in the river and watched the reflection of the waxing moon in its stillness. According to her mother, the pool was created when Nethuns, the river god, fought with Fraon, the snake-headed, blue-feathered demon who wanted this stream for his own. During the course of the battle, which lasted two hundred years, a huge bowl was gouged out of the riverbed, and whilst the sky gods didn't mind, the gods who lived in the earth couldn't sleep for the noise. So they intervened in the battle and partitioned the territory themselves.

The clear, flowing waters that burst through rocks high in the hills then slowed to feed the lush pasturelands, would be the realm of the river god. Fraon the demon had to be content with the deep bowl that filled up with water once the skirmish was over.

It was said that those who fell into Fraon's domain were sucked straight down to the Abode of the Dead, instead of passing through the Hall of Purification, where their souls could be cleansed and the heaviness of their hearts lifted. And because the bodies of those who fell in were not seen again, the Guardians of the Graves would have no place to stand, so their souls would be denied immortal protection.

Vorda's mother felt very strongly about such matters. Vorda's mother would have none of those wicked Roman ideas. There was only the One True Religion, and unless man obeyed the will of the gods, disease would visit the sinner, their limbs would become weakened, their spine twisted, they would go blind and lose the use of their tongue. Vorda's mother knew this for a fact, because when she was a young girl, she'd witnessed the gods' wrath descending on the poulterer's wife, who lived next door.

'Right as rain when she went to bed, but when she woke up the following morning, why, the whole of her left side had shrivelled up and died in the night.'

According to Vorda's mother, the poor woman dribbled and babbled from that moment on.

'Spoon-fed like a bairn till the day she expired, and let that be a warning to you.'

So as Vorda stood beside the pool, watching the reflection of the scudding clouds in its waters, she had no illusions when it came to divine retribution. When the augurs read the entrails and inspected the livers, she knew the sages to be right. Even though she was only thirteen summers old, she understood what it meant when magpies flew in a circle, why clouds in the north-west were bad omens, why she should swallow beans when a cow with a crooked horn stumbled in front of her.

'Human deeds must be consonant with the will of the gods,' the priests insisted. 'If we stray from the Code, lightning will strike and flatten our cities, the seas will rise and cast a flood over the land, and the earth will be shaken by whirlwinds.'

Vorda didn't want to be responsible for the destruction of the universe.

Whenever a half moon rose with a pale-blue halo, she'd place white stones round her bed for Zirna to shine down on and stop Vorda from riding the night mare. When an owl hooted thrice two times in succession, she'd pour a libation to Fana, to ensure the morning's bread would still rise. Every week without fail she'd leave offerings of grain beneath the alder for the smiling Goddess of Plenty.

But what happened tonight . . .

'The Dance of the Brides is a holy ritual,' her mother had told her, giving her cheek an affectionate pinch. 'You're privileged to be taking part, that you are, lass. You'll be doing the family proud on the red-headed moon.'

Proud? How could she feel pride in what happened tonight?

Listening to the grate of the crickets and the rasping of toads, Vorda strained for a sign from the gods. She strained and she waited, but no omens appeared. The sky held no portents, the earth offered no comfort, and why would they? Vorda had sinned.

No tears dribbled down her bloodless cheeks. She was too exhausted, too drained, for that.

Her mother would insist that what happened was the will of the gods. The priests would agree this was the will of the gods. Even the gods, speaking through the entrails of sacrifices and the clouds in the sky, would confirm this had been their divine will. *But in her heart, Vorda knew she had sinned.* She knew because she felt dirty and cold, and no amount of scrubbing could make her feel clean. She had tried. Heaven knows she had tried, and her skin was rubbed raw from the scouring, but the sense of pollution would not go away. She felt dirty and sullied, and whether this was her own transgression or the will of the gods, she wanted no part of it.

None at all.

Tying a rope round the stone that she'd rolled to the edge, Vorda picked up the rock and threw it into the pool. Her body did not make so much as a splash.

Thirteen

'**F**ace towels!'
   'Skin softeners!'
  'Gifts for the river god!'
This could have been Mercurium yesterday, such was the crush round the hot springs. The instant Claudia's gig passed through the archway, vendors in braided tunics and long pointy shoes descended like blowflies on a carcase, offering the new arrivals everything from hotel rooms to pancakes to castor-oil purges (guaranteed to work in less than two hours) and swamping them with ointments and amulets.

'Not sure I'd have come, if I'd realized you were bringing that witch along with you,' Rex muttered, pushing through the clamour to help Claudia dismount.

'She's my mother-in-law; I could hardly refuse.'

'Not Larentia. *Her.*'

He pointed to where Candace was shaking the creases from her embroidered robe and dazzling the eyes of the traders with the number of gold bands clamped to her skin. Never a smile, Claudia noticed. At least not one that ever made the journey up to her eyes. Always watchful and catlike. Was it because our lovely walker of winds was cold and calculating through to her marrow? Claudia followed her slow, feline glance in Darius's direction. Or was the sorceress simply cautious?

'You'd think the bitch would have realized she's caused enough trouble,' Rex was expounding.

Flanked by her Hebrew servants, Judith and Ezekiel, Candace swept off to the bath house as though she owned the establishment, and from the corner of her eye Claudia noticed that, although Darius was helping Larentia down from the gig with solicitous chitchat, his expression was harder than granite as his eyes followed the trio inside. So then, he hadn't missed that evaluating glance! But then everything happened at the hot springs, she reflected. Everything happened here . . .

'By trouble you mean . . .?'

'Raising the dead.' Rex's military bearing cleaved a path through the hawkers. 'Contacting the likes of our spouses is one thing, but where does it lead? Will we end up talking to shopkeepers next? Suppose she conjures up ghosts of men slain on the battlefield? What then, eh? Are we going to see headless Dacians prancing round? Let sleeping dogs lie, that's what I say, but not that witch. It's the only reason she's come to the thermal springs.'

'To allow the dead a mud bath and massage?'

His mouth twisted politely at Claudia's joke, but Rex's hobby horse was off on a gallop. 'They call this place Lavernium, meaning Underworld. See the river that gushes out of the rocks over there?'

Claudia could hardly miss it. Hot and steaming, it reeked of sulphur.

'Peasants used to think it was an entrance to Hades, and mark my words, that's what's brought that black-hearted witch out here today. She's looking to get in touch with the dead through that gateway, and you want to watch your back with her.' He wagged a forceful finger as he marched off. 'That bitch is trouble.'

'I, um, I'm afraid my father gets rather carried away sometimes.'

Claudia spun round and found herself looking into the face of a man who had the word 'weak' all but tattooed on his forehead. Fair hair turning to ginger didn't help, nor did pale eyelashes, a pallid complexion or the soft line to his chin, but many men had overcome such disadvantages and gone on to become consuls, magistrates, legates and kings.

'Are you in the habit of apologizing for your father?' she asked Hadrian.

Never complain and never explain was the imperial armed

force's motto. She imagined Rex would rather fall on his sword than have his son mop up after him.

'Well, I . . . er . . . I thought his observations were rather harsh,' Hadrian said, picking an imaginary hair off his spotlessly clean, zealously pressed, obsessively draped toga. 'In view of Candace's talents, I mean. It's, um, well, it's not everyone who can summon the spirits, is it?'

'Perhaps he's worried she'll summon Lichas.'

'Can she?' Something flickered across his pasty face which might have been hope. Or then again, might have been fear. 'Can she bring him back, do you think?'

'No, Hadrian, Candace can't bring the dead back.'

The predicament came in proving the point!

Pushing through the crush of healers and masseurs, it appeared that whether you suffered from dandruff or deafness, diarrhoea or delirium, there was a specialist here who could cure it. Lumbar pain? Bleeding gums? Tumour? Come inside my tent, dearie. And whether it was your nose that was running or an open leg ulcer, somebody somewhere had a poultice, a pill or a pessary that would put you back on your feet in a jiffy. Charlatans were on hand to prescribe weasel dung for your boils, wolf's fat for your haemorrhoids and spider's heads to help you get pregnant, while old crones sold mandrake and charms, aphrodisiacs and love potions alongside pompous astrologers who laid maps of the heavens over the pavement, the better to plot your future, my dear.

Rex was wrong. Claudia followed a path lined with willows and poplars towards the hot springs and thought, Lavernium wasn't the entrance to Hades. Lavernium was the gateway to immortality, and listening to these frauds one could almost believe that from here sprung the very fountain of youth.

Tapping her forefinger against her lip, she turned back. *I wonder . . .*

Three owl claws, two lion's teeth and one spider's head later, at least one piece of the puzzle had slotted into place, and as she approached the waterfall, she became aware that the laurels and rosemaries lining the bank had been planted deliberately so that their heady fragrance would overpower the sulphur to turn the valley into something that smelled more like the open sea than a deadly inferno. High in the sky buzzards circled, their cries drowned by the crash of the falls as the river smashed against the giant boulders in its path and splintered into a series of watercourses that plummeted down twenty feet of rock face in scores of racing warm torrents. Claudia picked her way down the wet, slippery steps using the rope handrail for support. Now and then, a tree had managed to root itself between the rocks and children used the overhanging branches as climbing frames from which to dangle fearless limbs in the surge. Below, anxious mothers prayed to the river god that he would spare their darlings from falling in and either breaking a bone or becoming trapped in the crevices and drowning, while beside them, carefree fathers splashed toddlers in the shallow saucers of rock and ducked the older children under the stream.

Kicking off her sandals, Claudia waded towards one of the rushing cascades and surrendered herself to its lush thermal waters. Darius was about the only man present who hadn't stripped to his loin cloth, but sat with his back to a rock while two attendants led Larentia into a swirling torrent and held her steady while the force massaged her arthritic hips.

'No offence, marm,' Orson said, splashing through the shallows to join Claudia under the waterfall, 'but Oi'll not be hanging about here, if you don't mind. Poncing about in healing springs might be fine for them that's used to it, but Oi need to be doing something constructive.'

'My dear Orson, what on earth makes you think I'd be offended?' Claudia lifted her head to let the torrent massage her face. 'Now do go back to your poncing, there's a love, because there's absolutely no question of you going home to the villa.'

'Not the villa, marm. Oi'm not particularly comfortable there . . .'

'Is the bed hard?'

'No . . .'

'Your room cold?'

'Course not.'

'Maybe the pillows are lumpy?'

'No, marm, it ain't that kind of uncomfy and Oi reckon you knows that.'

Claudia lowered her chin to its usual position, since that last jet seemed to run rather chilly.

'From the moment Oi stepped into your marble atrium, you knew Oi'd feel out of place. You're hoping that by sticking me and my Flavia together that she'll see me for the uneducated working man that Oi am, then she'll be ashamed of me and break it off.'

This time Claudia turned her whole face away. At first that was exactly what she'd hoped, but things had changed even in the short time since their arrival. Orson's acclimatization to luxury and abundance actually seemed further away, rather than closer.

'Dammit, Orson, can't you just bugger off and enjoy yourself for once?'

'Begging your pardon, marm, but Oi don't think you heard me right over the water. Oi *ain't* enjoying myself, and it's understandable, you not wanting the likes of me in your villa when you ain't there—'

'Orson, this has nothing to do with honesty—'

'Oi wasn't proposing to stay there anyroad. Me hands get jittery when they've got nothing to do, so Oi've asked at the toy-maker's if Oi can help out—'

'Lichas? For gods' sake, Orson, the boy was *murdered*!'

'Aye, and cause of that his sister's been left with a stack of unfinished projects and, me being a woodworker, Oi thought Oi might finish them off for her.'

'Well, that's very noble of you.' Now she had generosity of spirit to add to his list of fine qualities! 'But,' Claudia indicated to where Flavia was lying flat out in a shallow pool and being pummelled by a dozen foaming warm jets, 'in affiancing yourself to my stepdaughter, you have certain obligations – and moreover, until you are married, both you and Flavia fall under my guardianship and therefore you will both do as you're told.'

Pale blue eyes blinked. 'Oi, um, haven't actually asked Flavia to marry me yet.'

At long last Fortune provided Claudia with the edge she'd been looking for.

'What did you say?' It's not easy to look affronted when your clothes are dripping wet and your hair is plastered all over your face, but by drawing her shoulders back and lifting her chin, she made a pretty good stab. 'Good god, man, I've left you two unchaperoned for *how* long?' She threw in a shudder for good measure. 'Heaven only knows how far you've compromised my poor baby!'

'No, marm, there's been nothing—'

'Orson, you will make an honest woman of Flavia this instant, do you hear me?'

He shifted position and wrung his big hands. 'With all due respect, Oi'll propose to Flavia when Oi think the moment is right, not when you do, and . . . Here! Oi'm not under your guardianship.' Shrewdness tightened the plumpness of his face. For heavens' sake, where were three men with shovels when you needed them most? 'You're trying to box me into a corner, that's what you're doing. Forcing me hand when there's no need for it to be forced. Lord alive, you must think Oi'm daft.'

As a matter of fact, she thought Orson was anything but. She thought he was decent and honourable, mature beyond his years, a man who didn't suffer fools gladly and could be pushed only as far as he allowed himself to be pushed, which is why . . . Claudia drew a deep breath.

'My opinion is irrelevant, Orson. You will remain with my stepdaughter and that is final. Now kindly sod off and do your poncing elsewhere.'

For a moment, she thought he was going to say something. But he just pursed his lips and turned away, his bolster-like thighs pushing the warm waters aside like the oars of a warship.

'Why don't you tell him straight out that you want to keep an eye on him for his own safety?' a baritone rumbled.

Claudia spun round so fast that she lost her footing on the slippery stone, but an inch before her shins cracked against the jagged limestone, a pair of strong hands had her clasped round the waist. Even over the sulphurous waters, she swore she could smell sandalwood, and were his eyes always that dark, she wondered?

'I have no idea what you're waffling on about, Orbilio. And thank you, you may let go of me any time that you like.'

'Claudia, it's me. You don't have to pretend you're consigning Orson to compulsory pampering on Flavia's account for *my* benefit.'

'Don't flatter yourself that I do anything for your benefit, Marcus, and while we're about it, you might want to remember that you're still holding me round the waist.'

'You said I could let go any time I liked.'

'Change of rules. It's any time that *I* like.' She wriggled free and felt unaccountably exposed.

'Drat.' He grinned. 'But I'm not letting you off the hook that easily, Mistress Seferius. You want Orson around so you can watch over him, except you're too damned proud to show your feelings.'

'(A) I don't have any feelings, and (B) why on earth would I want to watch over that big ugly lug?'

'Because one seventeen-year-old youth is dead, another's still missing and you feel responsible for bringing a third into the equation.' He spiked his wet hair out of his eyes with his hands. 'If it helps, I don't believe for a moment that there's a monster abroad feeding off the flesh of seventeen-year-old boys. I think whoever killed Lichas had a strong personal motive—'

'What about the shepherd boy?'

'Are you asking, did Tages kill Lichas?' He rubbed his chin with the back of his hand. 'It seems an obvious conclusion, given his timely disappearance, except for the fact there's no motive.'

Upstream, reeds offered a safe haven to buntings raising their young and sunlight danced on the gently swirling waters.

'Perhaps you're not looking in the right place,' she suggested.

Downstream, hypochondriacs knotted together on the riverbank like migrating geese, swilling down the health-giving waters as though alkaloids were about to be rationed.

'Bearing in mind Mercurium's hard-line reputation, if a young shepherd boy was struggling with his sexuality, Hadrian might not be the only person who wanted to keep his secret a secret.'

'There's no suggestion Tages was anything other than heterosexual.'

'I think that's why they call it a secret, Orbilio. And remember that if Hadrian and Lichas had to trek right the way out here to meet like-minded souls, Tages might have as well.'

'What? Tages came to this town because he's *metro*sexual?'

Claudia waded back to the shore for her sandals. The more urbane, the more dangerous, she reminded herself. Never forget that.

Orbilio picked his way carefully over the shingle behind her. 'We seem to have drifted away from the point,' he said. 'We were talking about Orson, and I want you to know that it's . . . well, it's . . . perfectly natural to worry about people and . . .'

Strange, she thought. Not like him to struggle for words, and suddenly his eyes were everywhere except meeting hers.

'And . . . it's perfectly normal to let them know,' he finished awkwardly. 'Look, Claudia, what I'm trying to say—'

'Orbilio, you're in no position to lecture people on what's natural and normal. Not when you creep up on them beneath waterfalls.'

His smile was weak. 'If a national hero refuses to allow the Security Police to interview his son through the customary procedures, subterfuge becomes the Security Police's weapon of choice, and should this entail mingling among women clad in clinging wet robes, then, as a dedicated professional, I will not shirk my duty.'

She towelled her hair dry. 'Haven't you noticed? The rule here is the greater the obesity, the flimsier the garments.'

'Happily for your trusty investigator, there are at least a dozen oculists on hand to prevent him from going blind,' he quipped with an airy wave of the hand. 'Anyway, now that you've met Hadrian, have you *any* idea why Lichas would have fallen for someone so totally devoid of personality and looks?'

'None whatsoever, unless you count sensitivity, compassion, love of nature, the arts . . .'

'I'm waiting to hear the word money.'

Claudia stopped rubbing. 'Why?'

'Because Rex is a wealthy man and Hadrian is his sole heir. Because Rex doesn't want anyone sniffing around, even to the extent of confining his son to his room whenever I'm on the premises. And because Rex is so desperate for me to leave this case alone that he's given me an ultimatum. Drop the investigation or he'll have my balls.'

She chewed her lip. 'What did you say?'

'Told him straight, I don't have any.'

She laughed with him, though her mind was on a timid, motherless child overwhelmed by emotions beyond his control. Those clothes, she reflected. Those immaculate clothes . . . So white, so spotless, so fearfully well pressed. That didn't smack of a man who was happy inside his own skin, and she saw years of fragile self-esteem being systematically eroded to the point where he'd been left powerless to the point of incapable. Hadrian's clothes, she suspected, were the only aspect of his life over which he had any control.

'So you've come round to the idea that Hadrian killed Lichas, after all?'

Orbilio leaned down to tie his boots. 'Those haunted eyes had me fooled, I don't mind admitting, but Rosenna's adamant that Hadrian intended to break off their relationship because he feared public exposure.'

Public exposure? Claudia wondered. Or Rex's wrath? 'You're suggesting that Lichas, an impoverished toy-maker with his sights on the high life, threatened to blackmail his patrician lover and the situation backfired? Marcus, I haven't heard a single person suggest that boy had a mercenary bone in his body, and the purple hollows beneath Hadrian's eyes suggest he's hurting from grief, not a conscience.'

'Really? Well, if love's young dream was so bloody good, why's he avoiding me?'

105

'You said it yourself. He's never been able to stand up to his father.'

'No, but I'll bet it's not beyond him to go running to Daddy, still splattered with his lover's blood, and blurting out what he'd done. That's why Rex wants to keep the investigation local, Claudia. That way, he can slap a seal on this scandal that's so watertight, it'll probably mummify.' Orbilio pulled on a clean tunic and belted it at the waist. 'The very fact that Rex is threatening me suggests he's far more rattled than he lets on, and frankly there's only one reason I can think of why a wealthy, influential, retired war hero would be worried.'

Claudia pinned up her curls, fluffed her pleats into place and decided there was only one reason she could think of, too. 'A witness.'

'And guess who's been missing since the night Lichas died?'

Marcus tossed three copper quadrants to a hovering attendant in exchange for two spiced apple buns. The buns were warm in the middle, and the taste of cinnamon and cloves exploded on Claudia's tongue.

'I've walked those water meadows between the yew tree and the river twice now,' Orbilio said, 'and Tages' pastures overlook them in several places, plus there was a storm that night, remember? What if Tages was rounding up his sheep to prevent them from bolting when he heard Hadrian and Lichas shouting? His curiosity's aroused. He watches. Sees Hadrian stab him.'

'Pull the knife out, drag his lover still kicking and screaming into the river.' She licked a dribble of soft apple from her finger. 'Oh yes, I can just picture it.'

Hadrian might be capable of killing. We all are. He might well have tried to cover it up. We all would. But the boy was too weak to carry off something like murder. He'd have cracked at the very first grilling.

'Let me tell you what I think happened that night.' There was a distant look in Orbilio's eyes as he polished off the last of his bun. 'It's dark. It's raining. It's thunder, it's lightning, there's a gale flattening trees to the ground. The sort

106

of night when passions run wild. Hadrian meets with Lichas. He tells him he can't go on with this terrible subterfuge, his father's bound to find out if he keeps sneaking out and he won't bring dishonour to Rome's distinguished military champion. It's over, he says. Now who knows, maybe Lichas is a lover scorned, maybe he simply sees the good life slipping away, but either way he vows to carry out this threat and go public with Hadrian's sexuality. Hadrian panics. He probably doesn't mean to stab Lichas. He just wants to scare him enough to back off. But somehow his blade ends up in his lover's belly, so he runs back to Daddy and confesses the terrible thing he has done.'

'And you think Tages witnessed that?'

'I think he witnessed that and more,' Marcus said quietly. 'I think he saw Rex go down to the yew tree. I think he saw Rex pull the knife out and dispose of the body, something a battle-scarred warrior would have absolutely no qualms about doing.'

No need to waste effort in despatching a fatal blow. He'd have recognized instantly that his son's thrust was fatal, and considering Lichas was no more than a piece of filth in his eyes, the boy's screams would have cut no ice. For Rex, it was waste disposal pure and simple.

'That's why Hadrian's in pain,' Marcus said. 'Whether he intended to kill Lichas or not, between him and dear old Uncle Rexie they murdered that boy, and I'm pretty sure Tages witnessed the whole thing.'

'Then why hasn't he come forward?'

Orbilio packed his comb back in his satchel and tightened the leather strap. 'Rex is a senator with a glowing record in the field who has considerable influence in Mercurium. If a lowly shepherd boy suddenly accuses him of murder, what odds the accuser ends up with a knife in *his* ribs, the victim of bandits or thieves? It's far more likely that Tages is biding his time in a bid to do a spot of blackmailing of his own.'

'In which case, his ribs are in even more danger.'

'Agreed. So in the interest of ribcage protection, it behoves me to find as many holes in father's and son's stories as possible in order to substantiate Tages' testimony when he *does* eventually surface. Enjoy your mud bath!'

'Wait! Don't you want to hear how my investigations are going?'

'Nope.' He picked up his satchel and slung it over his shoulder. 'Loverboy's down for one of the spa's famous cures in two minutes and guess who just happens to have his name down for a session alongside? I can't afford to miss this chance. However . . .'

There it was again! That shifty look, his eyes darting this way and that, but never, not once, meeting hers. And what's with the hopping from foot to foot all of a sudden?

'About getting round the Darius thing . . . I, er, have a solution you might want to think about.'

Now he was rubbing his forehead and chewing his lip.

'No hurry,' he said. 'Take your time, but . . . well, have you considered a marriage of convenience?'

'According to a trawl through the fortune-tellers' tents, I'll be marrying an ambassador/banker/merchant from Rome/Athens/Spain any day, who will bestow upon me wealth and happiness beyond measure, not to mention three/six/eight children, all destined to live to a healthy old age.'

And to think there were still some cynics who claimed astrology wasn't a science.

'I'm sure you'll lead a wonderful life with all three handsome husbands,' he replied, only instead of laughing as she'd expected, it looked like he'd swallowed a rat that was gnawing away at his entrails. 'But until they come along, think about what I've said, Claudia.' He shot her a tortured look. 'You could do a lot worse, you know.'

Fourteen

The hell she could.

Claudia marched across the precinct of the Temple of Fufluns the following morning with her skirts billowing like a merchantman in full sail. Grey clouds had snuggled over the hilltops like a dirty blanket, while out across the valley – and a reminder that the temple sat in the middle of Terrence's land – armies of slaves pruned Terrence's willow hedges, dipped Terrence's protesting sheep in a bath full of dip and waged war on weeds and caterpillars that threatened to undo months of Terrence's careful nurturing. Thankfully, though, it was not the patchy smell of Terrence's sheep dip that prevailed in the windless air, just the exotic aroma of incense.

Dammit, Claudia thought, skirting the sacred pool rimmed with pomegranate trees beneath which vividly painted marble satyrs cavorted with intoxicated marble nymphs. I haven't come this far to toss everything away on some wet drip of a husband, and how very convenient for the Security Police to have her frauds, forgeries and tax evasions wrapped up at the same time! Another laurel crown to lay on the head of an ambitious young investigator. Another step closer to the Senate! As oblivious to the tall smoking tripods that lined the plaza as she was to the host of temple kittens chasing each other, Claudia thought *come into my parlour, said the spider to the fly.* She rolled her eyes. Honestly, Marcus Cornelius! Do I look like I have wings?

On the other hand, watching Larentia and Darius laughing and joking at the hot springs (and what is it with the old battle-axe cackling away these days?), Claudia didn't think it would be long before her mother-in-law set a date – and June was traditionally an auspicious month. That gave

109

Claudia six weeks at best, three at worst, to discredit that smarmy horse-breeder, so where better to start than by searching his room at the villa while he was ensconced at the hot springs?

'Are you sure you have to go back so soon?' he'd asked over a breakfast of rhubarb, fennel and lightly boiled chicory. 'We only arrived yesterday.'

'And already I'm feeling too healthy for my own good,' she retorted. 'Tempting though that yarrow tea is, Darius, duty calls.'

He rose from the couch. 'Then at least let me help.'

Why? So you can pick up some tips about viticulture to help you take over my business more smoothly? 'No, no, you keep up the good work with those cowslip and horse-radish syrups.'

'The physician swore he could hear an improvement in his cough just from yesterday.' Larentia reached for another liquorice root, blissfully unaware that it was turning her gums black. 'Said there was definitely less of a rattle.'

'That rattle wasn't my lungs, Ren, it was the crowd of doctors you had swarming all over me.' Darius sucked on a dark-green pastille that smelled as foul as it looked. 'It won't be any cough that kills me,' he told Claudia, with a rueful shake of the head. 'It'll be the crush of physicians that woman has set on me. At least let me escort you back to the villa.'

Taking control already, are we?

'I'll give you a ride if you like,' Lars said, striding into the dining hall and resting a hand on Eunice's shoulder. 'Sorry, pumpkin, but business calls me back to Mercurium.'

'You'll regret it,' Eunice warned, patting his hand, and even at breakfast she smelled of roses and wine. 'You'll come back from your trip, you two, frowning and frazzled – and I warn you, those of us who've been pampered to within an inch of our lives will have absolutely no sympathy.'

I can see you working out how Candace did it, what Darius's game is, what's behind the run of bad luck and why Lars married Eunice before the moon combs her lovely red hair . . .

Could she? Could she solve all four in as many days?

Seated beside him in the gig, Claudia became conscious of the Etruscan's musky scent as the mule clip-clopped up the hill, and noticed the way his muscles bulged as he fought with the reins on the tight turns.

'You have to wonder whether there's any part of the Empire Terrence looks out on from his windows that doesn't belong to him,' he observed cheerfully. 'With what he makes from Lavernium, he'll be minting his own bloody coins soon.'

'Terrence owns the hot springs as well?'

'That and every other hill you can see, and talking of the big man, whose side are you on? Are you in the Rexie and Terrence camp – and don't think I don't know they call me the Red Gigolo behind my back? Or do you agree with your mother-in-law that we're made for each other, my lady and me?'

As a matter of fact, Claudia wasn't in either.

'One can't deny Eunice looks well on marriage,' she said, oh and how tactful was that?

'As well she might,' he said. 'I picked up a whole batch of health tips when I worked at the hot springs. Is any man better placed to dose his wife with extra minerals of a day?'

Why Lars married Eunice . . .

'You . . . administer them yourself?'

'It's no great science,' he laughed. 'You pulverise herbs, turnips, lettuce and broccoli until you're left with the juice. Oh, don't twist your face, woman. With a pinch of mustard, it's practically palatable.'

'That's what they say about hemlock.' She smiled back, and by coincidence the poison was exactly the same consistency and colour. No doubt as Eunice sipped, she'd thank her husband for making her feel soothed and relaxed – until the point where she tried to move and found every muscle in her body was paralysed . . . 'I'm guessing it wasn't your love potion that fired Cupid's arrow?'

'A legionary would blush at the names Eunice calls me when I make her swallow the vile brew, but strange how I'm instantly forgiven when she looks in the mirror and sees clear skin shining back or bends down to adjust her sandal strap and realizes there's no stiffness in any of her joints. As for Cupid . . .' He broke off to pull the cart over and allow a wagon to pass. 'I'd give her regular massages at the springs . . . Look, will you stop spraining your face like you're a prude. We're Etruscans, girl. We're free spirits.'

'Who evidently don't believe in single-sex bath houses.'

'Men have bigger hands, stronger muscles. Oh, you can visit your fancy bath house in Rome and it'll smell grand, sure, and you'll enjoy your rub down well enough, but once a man's worked on those tension knots of yours, woman, you'll not know you're born.'

Eunice might be in danger in the longer term, she reflected, but she was surely in heaven while she was waiting.

'My lady lived in Rome in those days,' Lars said, 'so we'd not see each other that often. Then she rented a house here for the whole of the summer, invited me over to dinner and the friendship grew. To be honest, neither of us gave it a second thought until I went to kiss her goodnight on the cheek and caught her on the lips by mistake.'

'And that's it?'

'Aye.' He jiggled the reins and, when that didn't work, gave the mule a quick flick on the rump with the switch. 'I stayed the night and in the morning I realized that one man is no man, for one is no number. Never went home.'

Cue harps and rose petals . . . But did Darius put Lars up to it, or vice versa? And where the devil did Candace fit in?

'Thanks for the lift. Can I offer you wine and possibly a more substantial breakfast?'

'You're forgetting I spent two decades in that bloody spa,' he laughed, patting his stomach. 'Luckily for me, the head cook still has fond memories of my time there, for I swear it's the only place in the Empire where servant eats better than master.'

It probably was, but what kind of business would Lars have in Mercurium that was so urgent that it took him away from the hot springs almost before he'd arrived?

Inside her villa, slaves were industriously taking heather brooms to the floors, feather dusters to the ceilings and leather cloths to the marble. In the flurry of water being fetched

112

from the well, oil lamps topped up, cushions plumped, furniture waxed, geese plucked, rugs beaten and vegetables peeled, no one noticed the mistress slip inside Master Darius's room.

Compared to the big house in Rome, the villa was cramped. Of course, to the average citizen it was a palace, and quite frankly the entire apartment in the slums where Claudia grew up could have fitted inside the atrium and have room to spare. But the point was, space was at a premium in Gaius's villa. There were far fewer guest bedrooms for one thing, and by the time things like couches, tables, chairs and clothes chests had been added, there was very little floor space to spare. All the more surprising, then, that Darius's room made the average Spartan appear profligate.

It wasn't unusual among the very rich, Claudia reflected, and actually it was one of the first things she'd noticed. In the same way that Orbilio, whose lineage traced back to Apollo himself, wore his clothes in the manner of a man born to affluence but without any need to advertise the fact, Darius also draped himself in expensive linens with the same casual neglect and kept jewellery down to the essential seal ring. Quality and minimalism often went hand in hand with breeding. But to have no personal possessions at *all* beyond the essentials . . .?

'Have you lost something?' an irritatingly familiar little voice piped up as it clambered on to the bed. 'Indigo thinks Darius must have stolen something from you and that's why you're poking around in his chest. Is it?'

Claudia was desperately trying to think of a better explanation for being up to her elbows in an honoured guest's underwear when Amanda saved her the bother.

'Indigo says she hopes it's a ring or a necklace or maybe a gold brooch set with amethysts and rubies and pearls. Something *really* expensive that means soldiers will have to come and arrest him.'

'Indigo would like that, would she?'

'Very much.' Amanda yanked back the coverlet and embarked upon a forensic search of her own. 'I overheard Darius telling Mummy that Indigo was bad for me and Mummy should stop moving round and that would get rid of her, but I told Indigo not to worry, no one's going to get rid of her, because why should Mummy listen to what Darius tells her? She'll be moving on soon, we always do, but this time it won't matter, because Indigo and me are running away after the Animals Holiday to go live with my father in Rome, only you promise not to tell Mummy, won't you?'

'Cross my heart.'

Comb, razor, scissors, but not so much as a painted cameo to remind Darius of his late wife. In fact, no personal mementoes full stop.

'He hasn't stashed his loot in the bed,' Amanda said miserably, and Claudia thought whirlwinds couldn't have made a worse job of that coverlet. 'But Indigo says Darius is clever.'

'Indigo's right.'

'She says he hides things.' Little hands stuffed themselves between the mattress and the bed frame and began prodding. 'Ooh, is this your brooch?'

Claudia took the box from her, lifted the lid and sniffed the unmistakeable balm of Gilead.

'Lemme see, lemme see.' Amanda scrabbled across the bed on her knees, craning her head for a better look. 'Ooh, yummy, are they sweeties?'

'No, they're buds.' Dried buds to be precise. The most expensive dried buds in the world.

'Bo-r-ing.' Amanda slid off the bed and picked up Darius's razor. 'Why does Darius shave his head?' she asked, peering closely.

Claudia snatched it away and placed it out of her reach. 'He shaves his face, not his head.'

'He does so, too, and he rubs ointment from that jar on his chest.'

'That's oil of frankincense for his cough,' Claudia explained, replacing the box of buds in exactly the same place that Amanda had found it and straightening the coverlet. When she looked up, Amanda was happily gouging a lump out of the table with Darius's scissors.

'Can I sleep in your bed tonight?' she asked, as the scissors were whisked out of her hand.

'No.'

'I could play with your cat.'

'We're still finding body parts from the last person who tried.'

Amanda giggled. 'If I can't find my father in Rome, I'll come and live with you. You're funny, and you won't make me move on all the time.'

Claudia made a mental note to have a word with Mummy and find out what the hell Mummy was playing at, condemning her six-year-old daughter to constant upheaval when the only thing children need at that age is stability. Didn't the woman realize that, in creating an imaginary friend, Amanda wasn't just lonely, she was deeply unhappy? For heaven's sake, what kind of mother can't see that her daughter's invisible friend is nothing more than an embodiment of the girl's confidence? That the minute Amanda becomes absorbed and able to state her own mind, Indigo vanishes? Unfortunately, Mummy would have to wait, and as much as Claudia would have liked to poke around Candace's quarters, she'd need to hold off until inquisitive little eyes and loquacious little tongues weren't around to betray her. Plus the Hebrew twins mightn't mix, but news of the mistress snooping around in the slave quarters would certainly make it to their well-attuned ears.

Which was why she was here, marching across the precinct of the Temple of Fufluns, just as the first drops of rain began to fall.

Up close, the forest of columns that fronted the temple was taller, pinker and infinitely denser than she'd imagined when she stood beside Darius at the top of Mount Mercury squinting down over the valley. What she couldn't see from that distance, either, was that rather than being built on to the hillside, the shrine had been painstakingly gouged out of it in a series of deep and tortuous terraces, and that the columns were actually remnants of the original rock face. Fufluns, she remembered Lars saying, was one of the gods who lived in the earth.

As she climbed the steps, haunting music emanated from the very soul of the temple, beautiful tunes made by strings, flute and tambour, soothing yet at the same time uplifting.

115

The further she entered, the more lamps that burned, and wild herbs that had been woven into fragrant ropes garlanded every column, wafting out scents of fennel, oregano and thyme that mingled with the fragrant oils that burned in the lamps: mint, lemon balm and sweet clover. The same rich red paint covered these walls as covered those at Eunice's house. Lively, energetic frescoes depicting people dancing, eating, bedding one another with wild abandon, reminding all those who came here that Fufluns wasn't just the Etruscans' god of wine. He was the embodiment of all earthly pleasures.

And to prove it, votive offerings hung from every inch of the prayer rails that lined the steep steps, some asking for the return of a child's health, others put in requests for sophisticated love-making techniques, the majority pleading that the Roman method of watering wine wouldn't catch on. Bronze tubes dangled from the roof to catch the breeze and chime a gentle message from the gods. Prayer ribbons danced, and other offerings to Fufluns lay scattered seemingly at random. Here a bunch of carved wooden grapes, there a set of clay dolls, elsewhere inscribed tablets, food, candles, or cork masks that had also been painted with smiles.

'May I be of help to you, my lady?'

Unlike Roman priests, who dazzled their worshippers in white, Etruscan priests clothed themselves in long red robes, painted the exposed parts of their skin red and wore conical mitres upon their heads, which were also, strangely enough, red. Surrounded by so many soaring pink columns darkened by the unnatural light, he had simply blended into the backdrop.

'I was looking for Tarchis the priest, but I guess he's found me.'

'Truly he has.' He bent his right knee, rested his elbow upon it and placed a clenched fist against his forehead. 'Come forth and welcome in the House of Fufluns, Lady Claudia. May He embrace you in His inestimable peace.'

'You know me?'

Tarchis rose. 'I was acquainted with your husband,' he said in a voice that radiated confidence rather than authority, yet could not disguise the crackle of old age. 'I was a guest at his house many times and was deeply saddened by his passing. Apart from being a good friend, Gaius was instrumental in bringing prosperity to this town.' He smiled. 'A mixed blessing,' he added wryly.

Indeed. A rabid desire for wine and olive oil throughout a burgeoning Empire had generated wealth for Tuscany and improved standards of living in everything from housing to schooling to health. At the same time, though, as Lars had pointed out, Romanization had taken its toll, and where more noticeably than Etruscan religion? Take that old wooden temple on the Via Tuscana, for example, dedicated to the triumvirate of Uni, Tins and Menvra. Who in Mercurium bothered that, these days, they'd become three temples, not one, made of marble, not wood, linked by an art-lined stone portico? Who honestly cared that it was Juno, Jupiter and Minerva who were invoked? Providing their prayers were answered, that's all that mattered.

Unless, of course, you were a priest of the old ways . . .

'How may I serve you, Lady Claudia?'

'Do you remember my husband's daughter, Flavia?'

'Indeed, I do,' he replied warmly. 'Although I never met the child, I recall Gaius fostering her on to his childless sister shortly after the baby was born. A typically noble, selfless and generous gesture, I always thought, a widower who appreciated only too well how a girl needs a woman to raise her and sacrificed his own happiness . . . Oh, my dear, what a terrible cough!'

'It's the incense.'

Noble, selfless and generous her arse! As head of the household and free to do as he liked, Gaius dumped a child he didn't want on a sister he didn't like, whether Julia wanted her or not – and she hadn't. Her own marriage, which had been going through a bad patch at the time, promptly plunged to rock bottom and had remained there ever since, the damage irrevocably cemented by the whim of an autocrat and an imperial law that let him do it.

And Orbilio dared to suggest marriage of convenience as a means to thwart Darius?

117

Claudia cleared her throat. 'The thing is, Tarchis, I realize this might be an odd request, considering Flavia is a stranger to Fufluns, but . . .'

'You'd like her to perform the Bridal Dance?' The mitre nodded. 'Darius said you might be in contact.'

Oh, goody. Darius is his new best friend now – no wonder Tarchis wasn't exactly overcome with astonishment at seeing her. Sly bastard.

'And did Darius say that before I committed her to such an undertaking, I'd need to know more about it?' Unable to keep the edge out of her voice, she congratulated herself at stopping short of calling it a primitive pagan rite.

'He suggested that you would probably want to satisfy yourself that this was no vulgar instruction into the art of the bedchamber, yes, and indeed you are right to question the morality of our ways.'

His glance automatically flew to the walls, which seemed to be covered in art (most of it of the bedchamber), and most of it energetic, as well.

'However, the days of orgies in the Temple of Fufluns are long past. Today we seek only to initiate young women in the awareness of their bodies in the sense of femininity, elegance and grace, and thus every year on the night of the red-headed moon, thirteen virgins perform the Bridal Dance in front of the idol.'

'Which still makes it a sexy dance?'

'If dancing helps a few graceless pubescent girls – how can I put this? – familiarize themselves with certain aspects of adult life that they might not otherwise acquire, I don't see this can harm them. Sexual awareness is an important part of maturity, for when the heart of the bride is fulfilled, then the heart of the bridegroom is glad and the two halves of marriage become one.' His voice was solemn, but there was a twinkle in his rheumy eye that was no reflection of the flickering lights and Claudia thought that for a man who was forced to juggle two cultures, he was doing a pretty good job.

'Why thirteen?'

'One for each moon of the year, and each has her own

costume and characteristics to act out, for self-expression is a very important aspect of the ritual.'

'Which happens to eliminate teenage competition at the same time.'

'Gaius said you were shrewd,' he laughed. 'Now considering the red-headed moon waxes to maturity a mere four days hence, Flavia should commence instruction at once. And though she cannot hope to master every nuance in such a short time, Timi ought to be able to choreograph a simple routine for her to memorise.'

'Timi?'

'Our instructress. Come, I'll introduce you and she can explain what takes place and where, only men aren't allowed near the Bridal Chamber—'

'Tarchis, this is all very obliging.' She followed his cracking pace through the lamp-lit labyrinth. 'But don't you have your full complement of virgins?'

He stopped so abruptly that she cannoned into him. 'As it happens, Lady Claudia, we do not. Vorda, who was to be our little harvest moon this year, sacrificed herself to Fraon, the blue-feathered demon.' He spread his hands. 'Rivermen noticed her amulets piled on top of her neatly folded shawl next to the demon's pool at first light yesterday. When they dived in, they discovered her body tied to a rock.'

He dropped on to one knee and lowered his head.

'May the prayers of Aita make you strong as you stand before the Mirror of Truth, little Vorda. May the spells of Leinth protect you as you pass through the Halls of Purification, and may Efan ensure no road in the Underworld is blocked to your soul. Let the hearts of your ancestors rejoice at your coming.' He stood up and straightened a mitre that didn't need straightening. 'As death is certain, so is its hour, my lady. The gods allocated Vorda but thirteen summers—'

'You mean someone told her she was destined to die yesterday?'

'Who knows when the Herald of Death appears?' he replied smoothly.

Or in what form, Claudia thought as they continued along

119

the vaulted stone corridors. 'Was she having trouble at home? Anxious, perhaps, about her abilities to perform?'

'Her home life was strict, but not unusually so, and by all accounts Vorda was an accomplished pupil who was very much looking forward to performing the Bridal Dance. Indeed, it was all she chattered about.'

'And you don't think it peculiar when that same cheerful thirteen-year-old throws herself in the river?'

Their footsteps echoed six-fold on the stone floor, and whichever way they turned the music was neither louder nor softer, garlands of herbs drifted out their fragrance wherever they passed and the figures on the wall laughed, danced and feasted, because for all they were supposed to be alive, they were dead, and so was Vorda, and Vorda was nothing to them.

'The will of the gods is unalterable, my child. They speak to the augurs through every aspect of nature, and Their prophesies are absolute.'

How can you argue with that?

'That was another thing I wanted to talk to you about,' Claudia said, and at least this was one topic Darius wouldn't have broached. 'Vorda's death seems to be the latest in a string of misfortunes that have occurred recently. In fact, I've drawn up a list.'

It was all there. The paper merchant's warehouse. The brick-maker's kilns. The tavern-keeper's sour wine, his broken axle. She'd written down those couples that had divorced, listed whose livestock had keeled over, the donkey that dropped dead in the harness, the well that was probably poisoned, so-and-so's financial hardships – the lot. And as Tarchis took the parchment closer to the light in order to read, she noticed that he was a lot older than she'd taken him for. Seventy, eighty, possibly more. It was hard to say under that paint.

'This is very strange.' He took off his mitre and scratched his head. 'You say Crantor's crops failed, yet make no mention of his neighbours' fields being blighted, and how odd that it was the miller's donkey that died.'

'Odd how?'

'Crantor is the miller's brother and his son is the black-smith, the one whose beehive collapsed and whose wife left him and took their children to Rome. And look, here's another coincidence. The paper merchant's sister is married to the man whose cattle fell sick, and it's his mother whose well went sour, while his . . . *Holy Horta!*'

For an old man, he took off down the corridor like an Olympic sprinter, his robes flapping like some great red bat's wings as he flung open his office door. Without bothering to take a seat, Tarchis reached for a quill and began scratching away, connecting the names in great inky lines until the whole page became a criss-cross of grids.

'Misfortune be damned, Lady Claudia, this is *judgment.*' He thrust the parchment under her nose with the same forceful gesture. 'Thufltha has been unleashed.'

'Whofltha?'

'Do not mock the gods in my temple!' he thundered. 'Once invoked, His wrath is unstoppable. The gods have surely taken vengeance upon the wicked.'

A small, tight ball began to bounce around in her stomach. 'I don't understand.'

'Every bad thing that is listed can be traced to five men, and it is they who suffer the punishment of the gods—'

'Along with their families, it appears.'

'When injustice has been done, the gods wreak revenge, and I suppose the closest thing to Thufltha in your religion is the Furies. Winged avengers, who pursue those guilty of crimes against the family to the four corners of the earth, then punish them.'

'Including the innocent?'

'When Thufltha is summoned, Veive obeys.'

'Veive . . .?'

'Veive is the God of Revenge, and perhaps you have forgotten the story, my lady; perhaps you have not heard it.' Fiery eyes skewered hers as he bade her sit. 'Twelve years ago, in the fifth year of the Emperor's reign, the five men listed bore witness at the trial of Felix Musa here in Mercurium. The charge was treason, a charge Felix denied, but since the evidence was incontrovertible, he was

121

denounced as a traitor, stripped of his assets and sentenced to ten years' hard labour in the silver mines.'

'If the evidence is not in dispute, why would five upstanding pillars of the community need to be punished?'

'Why?' Tarchis stared at her as though she was simple. 'Because Felix has obviously stood before the Mirror of Truth—'

'You mean he's dead?'

'My dear child, how else would the gods know who to avenge?'

That was the trouble when one leads a zealot's existence, she thought. Tarchis' vision was as narrow as these corridors hewn out of the rock and Claudia wondered whether Gaius had genuinely taken to the priest as a friend or simply exploited his standing in the local community.

'Your husband told you nothing about Felix's trial?'

Claudia was his trophy, not his soul mate. 'Why would he?' They rarely met, much less conversed.

Tarchis leaned forward and folded his hands on the desk. 'Because, my dear, there were six men, not five, who bore witness against Felix.' He held her gaze for what seemed like eternity. 'The sixth witness was Gaius.'

Veive looked down the long shaft of his arrow, then tested the feathered flight with the tip of his finger.

Beside him, the winged avenger smiled.

Fifteen

Midnight, and rain lashed the hillsides of Tuscany, swelling the rivers and nourishing the roots of the vines and the olives. There was no lightning, no thunder, thus the Augurs of Tins had no need to be summoned from their beds and continued to snore soundly, oblivious to the drumming volley. For the Priests of the Auspices, however, there was no such luxury. As the clouds discharged their watery cargo, they interpreted the secret language of the sky, musing how the shapes of the puddles related to the Order of the Cosmos and whether the swirls of the rain would maintain Divine Harmony. Around them, drenched acolytes made the sign of the cross for the four sacred quadrants, chanting, *'This is my front, my back, my left and my right'*, while sodden altar boys laid bowls of bulls' blood on beds of laurel and poplar to propitiate Aplu the Weather God.

In her humble cottage on the Mount of Mercury, surrounded by relatives yet never more alone, Vorda's mother shed a torrent of her own. Life was predestined, she understood that, but to cut Vorda's thread before she'd danced was an act of unspeakable cruelty. The Priest of Uni insisted the rain was the tears of the Queen of the Cosmos falling in sympathy. The Priest of Fuflus told her the rain was swelling the grapes, ensuring little Vorda would live on in the vintage. The priests of the river gods consoled her by reminding her that Fraon the demon had been denied Vorda's soul, and that her daughter would walk the Everlasting Meadows with a heart as pure as her body. For the first time in her life, Vorda's mother found no comfort in the priests' words. Her baby, her baby, her beautiful baby was dead. Lying cold on the rough wooden table that served as her bier, Vorda's laughter would echo no more round this cottage. There'd be no more scolding her for not cleaning her teeth, no more decking the door with gorse together on the spring equinox, no more hugs before bed. Clutching her daughter's cold hand to her breast, Vorda's mother howled like a wounded beast.

In her room at the hot springs, the rain drummed down on the terracotta roof tiles as Candace studied her perfect, unlined reflection in the mirror. Kushites, she was assured, were the handsomest race in the world. They were tall, graceful and naturally slender, they lived to six score years without a day's illness and their bows were so strong that no non-Kushite could pull them. She had also been assured that the grasslands of Kush were populated by spotted beasts with necks so long that they could browse the tops of the trees, that there was a lake where not even a petal would float but sank to the bottom like stone, and that gold oozed out of the rocks along the Nile. These things Candace had been assured for the simple reason that the only personal recollections she had of her homeland were memories that left her with nightmares more than two decades on. But, as everyone knows, hearsay is unreliable. One needs hard facts, not rumour, truth rather than fiction, and she dismissed the tittle-tattle with a shake of her closely cropped head. There were far more important issues to concern a sorceress, and if she was to walk the winds that blew over the Elysian Fields and open gateways to the next world, then this summoner of spirits has to live up to her reputation of belonging to the handsomest race in the world. Carefully Candace tweaked her eyebrows into an arch.

Four doors along, Orbilio listened to the rain swirling down the gutter spouts and splashing into the butts below. He hadn't bothered undressing, for how could he sleep after he'd caught Claudia in his arms beneath the cascade and felt electricity surge through his whole being? He'd thought of nothing else since. His interview with Hadrian he'd had to write down; he kept forgetting what had been said. That report on

124

a local girl's suicide he must have read a dozen times, yet the details still failed to register. Claudia. It was all he could think of – Claudia, Claudia, Claudia – and he was as powerless to harness his emotions any more than he could harness the wind – or harness her, for that matter. She was untamed and untameable, unprincipled and unpredictable, a forest fire out of control. She could not, would not, trust anyone as a result of her past, and he would not, could not, risk harming her further. What she needed was time – lots of time – and if she married him as a matter of expediency to prevent Darius taking control of her business, he'd give her as much time as she needed. As for sex . . . as much as he yearned for her, any move there would have to come from her, and the reason he was happy to wait was because after yesterday he realized at long last why she persisted on keeping him at arm's length. Not because she wasn't interested. Hell, no. He saw – oh gods, how he saw – how her eyes darkened to pools when he gripped her. Felt the tremble that ran through her body. Claudia, he realized, was scared. Not scared of what happens when two bodies unite. *But what happens when two souls fuse together.* For the second night in succession, Orbilio sat at his desk, poring over his case files, and tried not to think about being turned down.

One floor below, Rex patted the concubine on her bare rump and tipped her an extra sesterce. Always felt better when he came to this spa place. Must be the air or something, but he never felt liverish here, and he was glad now he'd brought his son along. Do him good to get out and about. Bloody shock to see Marcus when they drove in, mind, but that was his own bloody fault, he supposed. Shouldn't have told Eunice he was bringing the boy; woman never keeps a damn thing to herself. Can't blame her, of course. Have to feel sorry for a respectable widow being taken advantage of by a lounge lizard like Lars. Scandalous. Absolute bloody disgrace. Rogue's only after her money, any fool can see that, though as it turned out, there was no harm done by her blabbing. Hadrian didn't tell Marcus anything he hadn't told him before, though god knows what the lad's father would say, may he rest in peace, having his son poking his nose in business he's no right to be poking in. Hardly a chip off the old block, young Marcus. Still. That's a millstone we all have to bear, what. Rex snapped his fingers and called the whore back. Perhaps she could do that last thing again? Pretty sure he was up to it this time.

Across the hallway, Hadrian sobbed into his pillow and the same word echoed round in his head. *No, no, no, no.* If only he could undo the things he had done. Unsay the things he had said. But he couldn't, he couldn't, and because of him Lichas was dead, and there was nothing he could do to bring him back. Not one bloody, damn thing. Hadrian turned his pillow over and proceeded to flood the underside.

Down in the cramped cubby-holes that passed for the slave quarters, a girl with dark olive skin and a nose like a hawk's and a man with the same olive skin and the same sharp nose went through their paces in silence. Their stretches were graceful, feline, lithe and athletic, Judith's movements in perfect harmony with Ezekiel's. The only odd thing about it was that the couple were two floors apart.

In her small stone hut in a grove of sweet chestnuts, old Etha stared at the bowl of soup on the table. She had to eat. Aye, she must keep her strength up, for already Deathmist hovered outside the door, waiting for her to bid him enter. She would not. So long as hope for Tages burned in her breast, Etha would not let him in. A spoonful at a time she sipped the broth. He was a smart boy, her Tages. Too smart to have got himself killed, and if he'd slipped in the storm they'd have found his body. Aye. They'd have found his body by now. Wouldn't they? In the pen, his sheep bleated pitifully. She'd milked those ewes that didn't have lambs the best she could, but her joints were stiff and her heart was aching, and one of them needed a thorn pulling out and two of the lambs had ticks. Etha was waiting for Tages to come home and fix that. It needed nimbler fingers than hers, and he'd come home. Sure he'd come home. He was a good boy. A smart boy . . .

126

Old Etha pushed the bowl away, laid down the spoon and rocked herself in the chair. Outside the door, Deathmist inched a little bit closer.

Alone in the workshop where her brother carved toys, Rosenna sharpened a small stabbing dagger. She had no qualms. She'd played it through many times in her mind, and besides, the omens were good. Blood was red. Her hair was red. She would strike on the night of the red-headed moon. Three reds, for three was an auspicious number. It was the number of gods in the triumvirate: Uni, Tins and Menvra. It was the number of favourable auguries in the sky: north, south and east. And, when the Brides of Fufluns danced in the firelight and all eyes were upon them, three was the number of lives Rosenna would take in retribution: Hadrian, Rex and the patrician. With deadpan indifference, she kept the edge to the grindstone.

'*Mrrrow?*'

Drusilla wove herself in a figure of eight between Claudia's ankles, but for once no stroke was forthcoming. In one liquid leap, she was up on the table, head-butting her mistress's chin.

'*Mrrrrow!*'

'Damn right, poppet.' Claudia ruffled the cat's ears with her free hand as she traced Tarchis' gridlines with her finger. 'It's extremely irritating, but no, I haven't found the connection between Lichas and the six witnesses at Felix's trial.'

Nor, for that matter, any connection to Tages and Vorda.

'But I will.'

Just give me time, and I'll have Felix connected to them so tight he won't be able to move, but in the meantime let's consolidate what we already have. Five decent, honest, hard-working freemen, who were ridiculously easy prey in this superstitious religious climate.

'Whereas Gaius was the odd one out.'

As a producer and merchant of fine wines, not to mention a pragmatic Roman of equestrian status, Gaius Seferius was no soft target for Felix's revenge. You couldn't ruin his livelihood by simply poisoning a well! On an estate of this magnitude and with this number of slaves, you couldn't set fire to his vineyards or sabotage his vintage and hope to get away with it, either.

'And friend Felix certainly intends to get away with it!'

If he didn't, he wouldn't be so bloody subtle. Revenge would be reward in itself and he wouldn't give a toss what happened to him.

'*Prrrrrr.*' Drusilla clambered up on to Claudia's shoulders and wrapped herself round like a fur collar.

'Yes, poppet, I do realize that nothing horrible has actually befallen Gaius's nearest and dearest. Yet,' she added softly.

Because it was highly unlikely that, simply because Gaius was dead, Felix had decided to abandon his campaign against the sixth witness. Not when Candace turned up out of the blue, casting spells to avert an epidemic of bad luck. Not when Darius appeared on the scene, wanting to marry a woman old enough to be his mother.

'There's only one conclusion, I'm afraid.' Claudia stared into Drusilla's crossed blue eyes. 'Felix and Darius are one and the same.'

In assuming the identity of a bona fide horse-breeder (and had anyone actually checked on the *real* Darius's whereabouts?), Felix installed Candace to frighten Larentia and make the poor old trout dependent on him.

'*Brrrp?*'

'You mean those remarks of his at the market?'

'*Candace is the main reason I'm pushing Ren to fix a date for the wedding. More and more, your mother-in-law is becoming dependent on that woman's visions and spells, and I'm not convinced that's a healthy development.*'

'Weasel words, poppet.'

Trying to make out he was against Candace, when in reality it was the opposite.

'*Can't find out one damn thing about her. Other than the fact that she's Kushite by birth, our lovely sorceress remains a mystery, and mysteries, my dear Claudia, trouble me greatly.*'

The hell they did. By shedding suspicion on Candace, he's effectively clearing himself, adding to his own credibility by intimating that there's no point in anyone else checking her out, because if a wealthy horse-breeder can't uncover her past, then who can? And all the while the pressure increases on Larentia to marry him quickly.

'We have Gaius cheering his mother on from the Underworld. Her late husband giving the wedding his seal of approval. Even Darius's cough is supposed to make her feel guilty about keeping him away from his good southern health!'

Claudia's instincts had been right from the outset. The bastard *was* after taking control, but not purely from the financial angle. Yes, running Gaius's business would be the ultimate in revenge. But once he assumes control, it is total – and imagine the satisfaction of being in a position to marry off his enemy's widow to a three-legged dwarf if it pleased him, or contract Gaius's unworldly daughter to an elderly lecher. As he'd calmly destroyed the brick-maker, the paper merchant, the tavern-keeper's families, so he can sit back and ruin Gaius's impoverished sister and her weak and vacillating husband, pulling his strings on the puppets they were and watching them dance to his tune. With the most lavish portion reserved especially for his enemy's mother.

'You callous bastard,' she whispered into the night.

Leading a vulnerable old widow on, purely to set her up for rejection and humiliation. A man might divorce his wife for infidelity and cruelty, but thanks to Rome's entrenched chauvinism, it was virtually impossible the other way round. Having married Larentia, he could treat her like a dog and she'd have no choice but to endure, and suddenly Claudia recalled the locked gazes between Darius and Candace the night the spirits were summoned. Hard and assessing on both sides.

'Unless I miss my guess,' she told Drusilla, 'this puts the happy pair in partnership.'

How cruel does a heart need to be in order to plan installing the mistress before he's even married the wife? *How evil?* His voice hadn't just trod the path to Hell, she reflected. The bastard had dragged Hell back up with him.

'*Mrp.*' Drusilla disengaged herself from Claudia's neck and settled down on the desk with her front paws folded in front of her.

'Make the most of it,' Claudia warned. 'It's only a matter of time before Felix-stroke-Darius tosses you down the nearest well, too.'

'*Hrrrrrowl.*'

'Oh, don't worry.' She flattened the cat's rising hackles and kissed her firmly between the ears. 'It won't come to that.'

There were many places where hemlock grew wild around here, though Claudia sincerely hoped it would not come to that.

Colchicum was much more painful.

In the dank, dark subterranean caverns where no daylight penetrated and the sighs of the hopeless twittered like moths, Veive fitted three more gold tips on his arrowheads.

Beside him, the winged avenger dipped them in poison.

Sixteen

When Eunice said Terrence threw the most lavish bashes anyone could ever hope to attend, she wasn't kidding. To celebrate the Festival of the Lambs, he'd not only invited the entire town, but he'd filled fountains with wine for their benefit, created wine lakes connected by wine channels in which miniature warships bobbed merrily, and since one ox wasn't enough for this number of guests, he'd slaughtered at least half the world's ox population to turn on the spits. In addition, he'd built a miniature house out of nuts and sweetmeats for the children, and created a magnificent edible Trojan horse in which a snail had been stuffed inside a dormouse, which in turn had been stuffed inside a quail, which had also been stuffed inside something larger, until finally a horse comprising different layers of meats stood proud with a mane of . . . wait for it . . . sorrel.

The witticisms didn't end there. He'd hired musicians, clowns, acrobats, fire-eaters, jugglers and mimes to entertain the masses. Gladiators fought in a makeshift arena, wrestlers and boxers competed for honours, buffoons dressed in motleys ran riot – and the most amazing part of it all was that the events didn't just run simultaneously, they ran continuously too.

'I thought the Lamb Festival went rather well, didn't you?' Thalia asked, wringing skeletal white hands that didn't look as though they could kill two birds with one stone, much less a seasoned banker. But then Eunice never suggested Thalia had strangled her husband. His heart gave out at the hot springs, she'd said. Old age, Claudia wondered? Overexertion? A combination of both? And yet even the weakest of hands can drip poison into a glass. It was time to delve deeper into Thalia's mind – a journey, she suspected, that wouldn't take long. There weren't exactly great depths to plumb.

'I thought it went exceptionally well,' she replied, linking her arm with her new best friend's.

'The children looked adorable wrapped in their tiny fleeces,' Thalia said wistfully. 'Though I do believe Lars needed to snarl a bit more in his wolfskin when he chased them, and Terrence perhaps a *teeny* bit less. Not that there was anything wrong with what he did,' she added quickly. 'No, no, it was only that one little boy who burst into tears. And a couple of the toddlers. Of course, though I expect they were overtired by then . . . Sorry.' She shot Claudia a tight smile. 'I do ramble on, don't I, and Terrence gets so cross with me—'

'You're doing fine, Thalia.'

'You think so?' The smile that flashed across her face lit up her enormous green eyes. 'Oh, good, because I wanted to say that I thought Marcus got the balance just right, chasing the babies, and my word, Claudia, isn't he hand-some!'

'That's the word they use to describe the Emperor, and he's bow-legged.'

Thalia giggled. 'You are wicked, but I don't think he's bow-legged. Marcus, I mean.' The smile dropped from her face and her expression became haunted again. 'Do you see him? The man talking to Terrence right now?'

Claudia couldn't see anyone for Terrence's sandy mop, but said yes anyway. Agreeing is what best friends do.

'Terrence invited him here as a prospective husband for me, but I'm not going to marry this one, and I don't care what he says. Terrence, I mean. Not the bridegroom. Well, yes, I don't care what he says, either . . . Oh, there I go again. Sorry. Verbal diarrhoea, Terrence calls it, which I think is terribly vulgar, and I keep meaning to ask him to refrain from phrases like that, but then he gives me these little brown pills and then I can't think straight . . . Am I boring you?'

'Quite the reverse.'

Claudia patted Thalia's arm in the way best friends always

pat and led her away from children raucously racing toy chariots and playing tag to the rose arbour, where it was quiet. Several early varieties were already in bud, she noticed, and beneath them pinks and cerastium ran riot.

'You were telling me about Terrence and the pills?'

'Was I? I get so confused, you know, but that's why he says I should take them. After my husband died . . .' Thalia glanced round over both shoulders to make sure no one could hear. 'Claudia, I've done a terrible thing. To my husband, I mean. Well, when I say *did*, I didn't do it myself, but I killed him all the same.'

Thank Jupiter! Claudia held one of the fragrant pinks to her nose while her best friend unburdened herself.

'Terrence says it's nonsense. He says I couldn't possibly have murdered him just by willing him dead, but it's true. I wished my husband dead and – *pft!* – he died the next day, and Tarchis says that if one invokes the Dark Gods, they always answer the call . . . Oh, Claudia, do you hate me very much? For what I did to my husband, I mean, not the blathering. Although you probably hate me for that, as well . . . Ooh, look, look! Do you see the magistrate's wife?' Thalia peered through the twining branches. 'She's wearing a grey robe, and I *swear* it's the same colour as the one Terrence forbade me from wearing because he said it clashed with my hair and made me look pasty.'

'Sadly, Thalia, I think your brother was right.'

'But who *cares* whether something's suitable or not? Why can't I do something I *want* for a change, without constantly having to worry about what other people might think? I *like* grey.'

'So do I, but getting back to your husband . . .'

'Exactly. *He* wouldn't let me wear that shade, either, and I'm going to tell Terrence that the magistrate's wife is wearing it and . . . and . . . well, I don't know what else I'm going to tell him, but I think he ought to know!'

And off she swept, leaving Claudia wishing that Terrence would give her a handful of sedatives. God knows five minutes with Thalia was enough to drive anyone crazy. No wonder the banker was grouchy.

As the sun sank, torches and cressets blazed to turn night into day round the villa. This was the cue for the water-wrestling to begin, in which naked, oiled athletes were required to hold their opponents under for a mere count of twelve, which was proving harder than it sounded, since they were constantly slipping out of each other's grasp. On the far side of the terrace, a man clad in a bearskin danced with a live bear, another paraded monkeys dressed in military tunics, while masked actors performed a satire on marriage and a girl wearing a horned helmet twirled a bull-roarer with both hands that drowned out the musician entertaining a crowd with his pan-pipes.

Too much, too much. With all that had gone on since talking to Tarchis yesterday, Claudia's mind hadn't stopped whirling. She needed somewhere to think. Somewhere quiet. And Terrence's maze offered the perfect retreat.

Especially since every dead end resulted in a forfeit of wine!

She collected four goblets, then took them to one of the marble benches that had been placed at regular intervals for weary exit-hunters and thought that that was the trouble with the aristocracy. When you're born in the slums, a sense of direction becomes second nature, every bit as keen as touch, hearing and smell. Terrence's soft-living guests would need every seat he'd laid out!

The throb-throb-throb of a drumbeat pulsed out across the immaculately clipped topiary, and she could almost picture the dancers swirling and twirling to their hypnotic rhythm. Downing the first goblet, she wondered how Flavia was getting on. Timi, the instructress at the Temple of Fufluns, could not have been a day under seventy, yet she was as supple as she was graceful – but best of all, she was strict.

'The girls run through their routines with me until I'm satisfied they're step-perfect,' she'd explained crisply, showing Claudia the rehearsal room. 'Only then do I allow them to enter the god's chamber –' She'd pointed to a low, narrow door cut into the rock face '– to work on their self-expression in front of Fufluns. But I warn you: if your step-daughter thinks it's an hour to skive off, she's in for a shock.

When her time's up, she will be required to dance for me the way she danced for Fufluns, and I can spot instantly if her movements aren't polished through the additional practice.' She snapped her fingers. 'If they're no different, back she goes until they jolly well are!'

A thought occurred to Claudia. 'That's the same for all the Brides?'

'It is,' Timi said, bending backwards to touch her heels.

'So when Vorda finished the night she died, was she step-perfect? You didn't make her go back and practise again?'

The dance teacher straightened up with a scowl. 'Young woman, if you're implying I was responsible for Vorda's state of mind that night, think again! I have no idea what improvements she'd made to her routine, because once the measuring candle burned down, I knocked to tell her and, dear me, she didn't even look at me when she came out. Pushed straight past, which was not like her at all. She was singing like a lark when she went in—'

'No indications at the start of the evening that she intended taking her own life?'

'Between you and me, my lady, I rather hoped in Vorda I was training my successor. She was a natural, that girl. Far better than me at that age, and she loved showing me the various nuances she'd added, and with the red-headed moon approaching, she was as excited as ever. Singing, laughing, eyes bright when she went in, but like Tarchis says, what can you expect when the Herald of Death has summoned you to His hall?'

Inevitability and predestination had its merits, Claudia supposed. People became saddened by death, but not devastated, since all things were the will of the gods . . . which was fine when you were distanced from it in terms of family and friendship. Rosenna, though, had taken her brother's murder very badly and Claudia couldn't help wondering how Vorda's mother was coping with her daughter's sudden death, either.

'May I?' She indicated the narrow door.

Timi smiled proudly. 'Fufluns will be very pleased to welcome you, my lady.'

With a well-practised gesture of obeisance, she opened the door to reveal a chamber hewn out of rock, whose walls were covered with sensual rather than erotic paintings and in which fragrant oils burned from a handful of strategically placed lamps. Hyssop for purity, oregano for peace, sage for sanctification. The idol inside was life-sized, carved out of wood and realistically painted, right down to the leering expression, and though Lars had warned Claudia that Fufluns had horns, he forgot to mention how many. Or where!

'He certainly seems pleased to see us,' Claudia murmured.

'The Brides' purpose is to arouse their bridegroom, my lady. We cannot have them thinking their husband is disinterested.'

Oh, that effigy was definitely not disinterested!

'Thirteen virgins representing the full maturity of their respective moons marry the earth god on the night of the red-headed moon,' Timi explained. 'Then they dance to arouse His divine passion, that His seed will fructify the precious vines and the cycle of life will continue.'

Claudia walked slowly round the chamber, feeling the rock face as she passed. 'There's only the one entrance?'

'Like Horta, whose soil we turn with our ploughs, Fufluns makes His home in the earth. Even one door is an intrusion into the world of the gods, which is why the opening is kept small and remains locked when not in use.'

Yet the Herald of Death got to Vorda somehow, and he couldn't have been hiding in here. Not for the day or so between rehearsals. Claudia absently sniffed the contents of a bronze chafing pan. Ugh. Catnip leaves. Definitely not Roman! And for heaven's sake, look at that. Something else seemed to have shrivelled and died in that horrid bowl. She moved closer to one of the oil burners and let their sweet fragrance smother the pong.

'Did anyone come in while Vorda was dancing?'

'Lady Claudia!' Timi's face was a picture of outrage. 'Lady Claudia, this is a *bridal* chamber. The girls dance before their bridegroom in absolute privacy. I stand guard outside myself and no one – I repeat, no one – may intrude upon this sacred space while the girls rouse Fufluns' passion!'

Claudia tried to picture Flavia arousing anyone's passion,

much less a veteran godly seducer, but contented herself that whatever rabbits Timi managed to pull out of the hat, at least Flavia would learn discipline in the process, and god knows she needed it. Her foster parents had overindulged her and their authority had grown lax, enabling Flavia to give them the slip and meet Orson on the quiet.

Orson!

Bugger.

Between arranging for Flavia to dance on the full moon and sorting out the Darius affair, Claudia had completely forgotten about Orson! In the quiet of the maze now, she prayed to Justice and Fortune that the ugly lug had got that preposterous notion of helping Rosenna out of his head, because forget what Orbilio said – evil had already tapped two seventeen-year-old boys on the shoulder. And two was more than enough . . .

Reaching for the second goblet, she wondered just how much evil there was around here. Lichas was dead. Tages was in danger. Vorda had taken her own life. Moreover, five men had been brought to the brink of ruin through hardship or emotional distress, sometimes both, their families dragged through hell with them. Now the descendants and dependants of the sixth witness were about to be put through the same mill, and what could Claudia do?

She couldn't alert the authorities. Without proof, they'd laugh her out of the barracks – and, dammit, if the five men who were responsible for Felix's conviction don't recognize him, how on earth was she going to prove they were the same man? The fact that Darius doesn't look anything like Felix is immaterial, but the authorities wouldn't see it that way. They would agree with her that any man who intended coming back to Mercurium to wreak vengeance on those who had wronged him was hardly likely to announce himself – but they'd be expecting Felix to adopt a disguise by growing a beard or something else obvious, something that could be denounced immediately. Darius was far more subtle.

Indigo says Darius is clever.

Through the mouths of babes, Claudia thought. Through the mouths of babes!

What was it Amanda asked, peering closely at the razor in his room? *Why does Darius shave his head?*

At the time, Claudia dismissed it as a childish mistake, but now she realized it was no error. No doubt ten years down the silver mines hones revenge to the sharpest of points, but who'd have thought that by shaving his head and combing the rest of his hair over it, Caesar-style, it could pass as a disguise? Darius wasn't balding at all. He just pretended to be – and what were the odds that Felix had had a thick head of hair? Curly hair, too, because Darius kept his closely cropped. She could not use his cough as proof of working the silver mines any more than she could show he took balm of Gilead buds as a painkiller against the bad back that ten years' hard labour had undoubtedly bequeathed. Since the leaves were a well-known remedy for unproductive coughs, who's to say an apothecary hadn't muddled the physician's prescription? Dammit, everything about Felix was different.

Ten years of swallowing dust had left him with an unrecognizable gravel voice.

Ten years of wielding a pickaxe had bestowed on him an athlete's body.

Ten years of shifting rocks had changed the way he walked, his gestures, even his nature.

But take this to the authorities and they'd see nothing more than the bleatings of a self-seeking widow whose stepfather was about to wrest control of a business which, as a woman, she shouldn't be running anyway – and besides! She's already had her two years of state-allocated mourning. Doesn't the law decree she should re-marry?

That was one jar of worms Claudia had no intention of opening up – and, dammit, she couldn't confide her suspicions to Larentia, either. Not without concrete evidence to prove Darius was a monster who had nothing but hardship and humiliation lined up for his bride! The fact that he'd packed no cameo of his late wife surely showed admirable tact and discretion for a man about to be married. A lack of personal mementoes reveals a simplistic nature, a trait the parsimonious Larentia would admire. And how can you say

138

he's spent all this money on the villa to feather his own future nest, when there's no proof he's not the real Darius? No, no, the minute Claudia started to discredit her suitor, Larentia would view it as mischief-making and go running to Darius.

Can't have that. If Darius thinks the game's up, his most likely course of action is to run. Five out of six ain't bad, he could argue, and he'd disappear into the mist before you could say 'retribution and justice'.

'You're not going to get away with this, you bastard.'

Not when so many people have suffered so horribly for his petty grudge, and right now he's proud of his achievements. Devastation has rippled round their families like an earthquake, leaving death and destruction in its wake, while not so much as one finger of suspicion points back at him. What better time to attack than when he's sure of himself?

But to attack, Claudia needed weapons – weapons she didn't have, because the best way to attack this man was through facts and either Larentia was unaware of Gaius's involvement at Felix's trial (women not being privy to men's business) or she'd forgotten it, because she certainly hadn't connected the epidemic of bad luck to the other witnesses. Why should she? In all her years at the villa, she'd mixed with the same people, led the same narrow life, and even though she'd started out as the wife of a common road builder, she'd risen far enough through society not to mix with the likes of millers and tavern-keepers. And if the paper merchant and the brick-maker viewed their calamities as nothing more than misfortune, all the more reason to place her faith in Candace. Were Claudia to broach the subject of Felix's trial with Larentia, it was more than likely the old bat would ask Candace to contact him the next time she walked with the spirits. Sod that.

Realizing the second goblet was empty, Claudia reached for a third.

Undoubtedly, the best source of information had a rich baritone voice and carried a faint hint of sandalwood around with him, but she couldn't go to Orbilio, either. As much as the newly installed head of the Aquitanian Security Police would love the credit for solving a case involving treason, even he couldn't take too long an extended furlough. He was close to cracking this business of Lichas's murder, which meant he'd be heading back to Gaul in the middle of his investigations into Felix, thereby dumping the case back on to the local authorities – and, excuse me, haven't we been through this already?

Shit. Claudia drained the glass and hurled it into the laurels, where it smashed into a thousand satisfactory smithereens. Overhead, stars twinkled brightly, with no hint of the clouds that had left such a deluge overnight. She watched them tramp slowly round the heavens and thought, fine. All these are things I can't do about Darius.

Let's work on the things that I can.

The God of Revenge simply laughed.

Seventeen

'There you are, you poor thing.' A sandy mop tutted sympathetically over the top of the topiary. 'Lars said he'd spotted you entering the maze by yourself, but that was simply ages ago. Come, my dear.' Terrence offered his arm. 'I'll show you a sneaky way out.'

Claudia was about to point out that she wasn't actually lost, when he reached down and suddenly one of the neatly clipped laurels turned a ninety-degree right-angle to reveal a gap in the hedge for them to pass through.

'This particular tree stands in a tub that I've buried,' he laughed, 'but *sssh!* Let's keep this between you and me, because I would hate word getting round that I cheat.'

'I rather got the impression you cheat on a lot of things. Loopholes in the law, I believe you called it.'

Tuscany's favourite playboy twizzled the pot back into position and brushed the dirt from his hands with a carefree gesture. 'The State decrees each citizen must pay their taxes, Claudia. They don't stipulate that they have to be fleeced in the process. A clever accountant finds ways and means, just as you and I circumvent the law when it comes to maintaining our freedom. Or am I being too blunt?'

'Not at all.' Claudia was comfortable with straight-talking men. Especially thirty-eight-year-old bachelors who owned half of Italy and knew how to throw a good party.

'Do you . . . er . . . fancy a game of featherball?' he asked, his large green eyes narrowing in shrewdness.

She followed his glance to where teams were being picked and saw that, innocuous though the game was, it was scheduled to take place between the piggy-back jousting and a boxing contest, both of which were high-profile crowd pullers.

'Perhaps you could set aside a little time to talk privately?' he'd suggested, when they bumped into each other at the market. *'There's a little business matter I would like to discuss.'* With a gentle clink, the coin dropped, and if Claudia could have purred like a cat, then she would have.

'Opposite sides?' she said.

'But of course.'

'Then you might as well congratulate me now, Terrence. I've never lost at featherball yet.'

A lie, but a psychological advantage never hurt, and when asked which team she wanted to join, red or blue, there was no contest. She'd take the fit townsfolk any day over round-shouldered lawyers, but even then her team was still short.

'Two more,' Terrence yelled. 'Any volunteers?'

'Oi'll join.'

Orson lumbered over from where he'd been watching the boxing and Claudia breathed a sigh of relief. Thank Jupiter he'd found better things to do with his hands than carve toys in Lichas's workshop!

'What about you, Rosenna?' he called. 'You in?'

Was Claudia going deaf? 'Did you say *Rosenna*?'

'Aye. It weren't easy, marm, getting her to come here tonight,' Orson admitted, limbering up for the game. 'But there's a time to grieve, Oi told her, and a time to mourn, and melancholy dishonours the dead. Come along, Rosie.' Grabbing the wrist of a po-faced redhead, he dragged her into the middle. 'Let's show them Blue Bloods what stuffing us poor folks is made of.'

Something changed in Rosenna's eyes as she weighed up the opposing team. A sharpness took over, banishing the indifference. 'Them and us,' she murmured to no one in particular, kilting up her fringed skirt to the knee. 'Och, we'll bloody show them, Orson. We'll show them bastards right enough.'

'You were right,' Terrence wheezed half an hour later. 'Claudia Seferius, I do indeed congratulate you. Blue were well and truly trounced by the finish.'

'We had a secret weapon,' she puffed back, watching Rosenna merge back into the crowd, wiping the sweat from her face.

'Yes, who *was* that redhead?' he asked. 'I've never seen such passion in a ball game, especially from a woman! She went for every damned shot whether she had a hope of reaching it or not . . . I say, wine?'

'I doubt I could whimper,' Claudia quipped back, refreshing herself with a glass of cool dry white whilst wondering how that spangled Arab over there managed to swallow a whole sword and not give himself indigestion. As her eyes ranged over the dark hills all around, she remembered just how much land Terrence owned. 'You do a lot for the locals, don't you?'

'Philanthropy is all part of the aristocratic process,' he said, fanning air down his sweat-sodden tunic. 'When one inherits land, one inherits obligations, and it strikes me that change is moving across the Empire at such a pace that it's in danger of overstretching itself. Like most other cultures, the Etruscans embrace change, but evolution needs its own tempo, Claudia. As long as Rome and Tuscany have opportunities to mingle at functions like this, the ties of friendship remain strong.'

'And Fufluns?'

'Same thing. Providing people see that they haven't had to give up *everything*, they're happy to adapt to those things they're required to.'

'Lars thinks they'll be calling their wine god Bacchus before long.'

'Not while I'm in charge,' Terrence said firmly. 'People talk about the temple being on my land, but more accurately it's the *access* to the temple that's mine. And if I continue to allow them to use the road, what they do inside is their own business, not Rome's. Lars and I work very closely on joint Etruscan issues. It's something we both feel strongly about and . . . Ah, Claudia, I'd very much like you to meet—'

'Sorry, old chap, can't stop.' A small round man with a small round face kept on jogging. 'I'm in the Cheese Merchants' Relay.' He wagged a jaunty baton to prove it. 'Catch you later!'

'That is – or rather *was*,' Terrence corrected with a chuckle, 'the fellow I've earmarked as Thalia's husband. Decent fellow. Doesn't womanize, doesn't gamble, doesn't take drugs, what more can a girl ask?'

'Choice in the matter?'

His chuckle deepened to laughter. 'Not every woman is like you, Claudia. Believe me, my sister couldn't choose between two identical buns, and I know you think I bully her, and I do, but Thalia needs a steady hand on the tiller.'

'Her seas do seem a little choppy.'

'Choppy? The silly bitch is even convinced she murdered her husband, which is absolute bollocks; he suffered a massive apoplexy at the hot springs and it served him bloody well right. Doctors told him to lose weight, drink less and exercise more, but he didn't take a blind bit of notice.'

The hot springs, the hot springs, always the hot springs.

'So why is Thalia so certain that she killed him?'

'Because they were always arguing, those two, and I know you must find it hard to believe when she appears scatter-brained and simpering now, but my little sister's extremely highly strung.'

'Is that why you give her pills?'

'There's a poppy that grows wild in Sumeria. I'm told you extract the latex from the unripe capsules and it calms the nerves.'

'Whilst turning her into a gibbering idiot.'

'Better an irritating fool than a self-confessed murderess,' Terrence snapped. 'I've worked hard to establish a rapport with the people of this town.' His voice softened to a chuckle. 'I told you once that I have enough glory to last me a lifetime, but no man can be too popular, Claudia. All joking apart, though, Thalia's claims are bullshit, but they're the very sort of wild declarations that attract scandal, and shit sticks. I will not have my sister undermine the trust I've established with these people. Like Caesar's wife, she too must be above reproach. Now, unless I miss my guess, that's the three-legged race about to kick off.' He shot Claudia a warm grin. 'How about you and I tying our legs together and cementing our business arrangement?'

'My left to your right good enough?'

'Perfect,' he said with a wink.

* * *

144

As dawn broke through the bright new leaves of the chest-nuts and the grove filled with the song of the birds, Etha knelt on the bare soil behind her stone hut staring into the east. Through the trees, on the far side of the valley, rheumy eyes could just about make out the first of Cautha's fiery rays lighting Master Terrence's enormous white villa. All through the night, she had watched with empty eyes the flicker of torchlights burning around it and, as she'd sat staring out into the blackness of the valley, she'd pictured the folk of Mercurium laughing and drinking, dicing and feasting. Aye, he laid on a good spread, did Master Terrence. But the townspeople's happiness was like a vice round her chest, crushing hope from her heart until every last drop drained away.

She had spent the past week praying to the gods of the sunrise, but the gods of the sunrise were powerful gods. They'd be too busy answering the prayers of rich men and priests to bother with an old woman like her. So she'd turned to the deities of good fortune to the north, for fortune is noto-riously capricious and rash, and who knows what games the gods might be playing this time on mortals? But as the old woman waited, she'd received no signs from the north wind. What little breeze there was blew warm from the south, and Etha took that as an omen. With tears dribbling down her wrinkled cheeks, she lifted shaking hands to the sky.

'O wolf-headed Aita, who makes thy home at the edge of the Universe and presideth over the Dead, I offer this wreath of myrtle.' Myrtle was the death tree. Aita would understand. 'But before I open my heart and let Deathmist enter, I beg thee to speak to the gods of the south, that they might be persuaded to give up my grandson.'

If he's dead, let the earth no longer conceal his body. Let Horta, Fufluns and the rest of the gods who dwell therein surrender his corpse that Etha might send Tages to the Afterlife with the proper rites, and though it weren't in the Order of the Cosmos for the old to bury the young, it weren't right, neither, that his soul be denied entry to the Hall of Purification. Despite the pain in her arthritic bones, Etha bent low to the damp soil and kissed it.

'If my boy's dead, as I accept he must be, at least grant him a resting place where the Guardians of the Graves can watch over his immortal soul,' she begged the earth. 'I ask this for Tages, thou understands. Not myself. But I beseech thee, with all my heart I beseech thee, don't deny the poor lad.'

The earth gods were good gods. Even as she was reaching for her stout laurel stick to straighten up, she heard footsteps on the path. The footsteps were heavy. Etha turned and saw Philo, her neighbour, and though his face told his story, it was not at his face that Etha was staring. It was at the blanket-covered bundle he held in his arms.

The heavy rains of the night before had washed away the earth from the boy's shallow grave.

The Guardians had a place to stand watch, after all.

Eighteen

If there was one thing Orbilio had noticed about Mercurium, it was that news travelled fast around here. Locals joked that this was the reason the town had been named after the messenger of the gods. Gossip travelled on the same invisible winged sandals. Marcus could well believe it. Even before Etha's neighbour had taken Tages home, news of the discovery had reached the townsfolk – and since most of them were wholeheartedly maintaining the ancient tradition of celebrating right through the night, it was at Terrence's villa that the news broke.

As it happened, Orbilio was among the first to hear it. This was pure chance, since he had participated very little in the festivities. Not because he hadn't wanted to. He'd thoroughly enjoyed climbing into a wolfskin and scattering little lambs hither and thither. Their delighted squeals lifted his heart, reminding him how he longed to father a tribe of his own, hoisting one on to the crow's nest of his shoulders whilst another whirled from his waist as – I don't know, another two, maybe three – danced around him like a maypole until finally they all collapsed in one dizzy, idiotic heap. Oh, and did he mention dogs? Wolfhounds, poodles, hunting dogs, mongrels, he didn't care what breed they were, or how many, so long as they loped beside him and his kids as they gathered baskets of mushrooms from the forest floor or stretched out on the river bank, tickling trout.

He had no doubt such pleasures lay in store, but meanwhile, given the choice, who wouldn't have preferred joining in the footraces Terrence had organized, or putting his name down for the tug-of-war, to bypassing the festivities in favour of a backlog of files? However, when he accepted the post as Head of the Aquitanian Security Police, he'd accepted responsibility, loyalty and commitment to Gaul. On previous trips back to Rome, he'd been accompanied by a chest full of case notes and Milo, his scribe. The difference was, on this trip it was Milo who had done all the hard work! Thus Orbilio contented himself with admiring the skills of the rope-walkers from a distance while he annotated his scribe's meticulously prepared reports and added to the ever-growing list of actions for his return. His return . . .

After only a week with Claudia Seferius, Santonum seemed a lifetime away.

An expert at compartmentalization, Marcus stuffed that particular demon back in its box and snapped the lid shut. One thing at a time, he reflected, and, as Terrence's guest, he'd felt duty bound to put in regular appearances throughout the night, introducing himself to all and sundry and generally making the right noises. Surprised at seeing Rosenna, he would very much have liked to have taken the girl aside and talked privately for a while, but each time he approached, she ducked away and he had to respect that. Her brother had only been dead a week, and attending Terrence's party was Rosenna's first step at overcoming her grief. This was not the time for him to rake over her sorrow.

But Claudia, he couldn't help noticing, had managed to cast aside her worries about Darius. Every time Orbilio made a tour of the revels, there she was, in the thick of it, playing featherball, competing in the three-legged race, clapping at the mimes, gasping at the fire-eater, laughing at the antics of the clowns. Terrence seemed to be clinging like a shadow, that same fixed oily smile plastered all over his face, but Orbilio wasn't going to lose sleep over that. Claudia had seen at first hand how he bullied his sister, undermining what little confidence Thalia had, until the poor cow was so frightened of saying something stupid that she always ended up saying something even more stupid. But it felt right, somehow. Looking up and seeing Claudia there. As though that's how it was meant to be . . .

Another lid snapped shut on another compartment. One thing at a time, old son, remember?

'Ah, Rex!'

'Marcus, m'boy.' The general's eyes were puffy from lack of sleep, his jowls hanging heavier than usual. 'What can I do for you?'

That old patrician trait, he reflected. No matter how tired or weary one was, be polite, be interested – be what one was expected to be, and never show what you really feel. Orbilio pasted on a suitably gracious expression of his own.

'News has just filtered in about Tages. The shepherd boy who went missing the night of the storm.'

'Found him, have they?'

It was because Rex was tired, he supposed. But the general didn't say, 'turned up, has he?' He asked if the boy had been *found* . . .

'His body was discovered late yesterday afternoon,' he explained. 'From the state of him, it looks like Tages had been dead for a week.'

In fact, decomposition had wedged him so firmly between the rocks that it took the rescue team several hours to retrieve him, but it was important to the Etruscans that their dead be despatched to the afterlife in as perfect a condition as possible. They'd have beavered away for days if needs be.

'Glad for the old woman,' Rex sniffed. 'Terrible thing, not knowing what's happened to your loved ones, but now she knows he slipped in the storm, it gives her closure, what. Listen.' He patted Orbilio's shoulder. 'Would ask you to join me for my customary constitutional, but don't mind admitting I'm done in. Not bothering with breakfast. Going straight home for a kip.'

From the corner of his eye, Orbilio noticed slaves with blue headbands clearing up the debris while a squad with red headbands laid breakfast out on the trestle tables. Hot bread, pancakes, cheeses and fruit were being heaped up, plus there were still great piles of leftovers from last night's feast for people to help themselves from. The townsfolk were not averse to a free meal, he observed dryly. Hardly any had filtered off home, and he truly admired those die-hards who were still at it, playing bounce-ball or clipper, jogging round the lake, taking a dip, while those sober enough to aim true

149

(or inebriated enough not to care) were engaged in darts, discus or the javelin as children trundled hoops and spun tops.

'The thing is,' he said evenly, 'Tages didn't slip. The area had been canvassed several times in the past week, and the reason the search team missed it was because the body had been banked over with earth. Earth, which the recent down-pour uncovered.'

Rex dismissed buried shepherd boys with a snort. 'Storm most likely the culprit. Same way the rain washed it out, it probably covered his corpse in the first place. Just hope the lad wasn't alive at the time, eh?'

'Oh, Tages was dead, Rex.' Orbilio looped his thumbs in his belt. 'The rescue team say his throat had been cut.'

'Wolves. Bloody things are a menace. Take my lambs, they would, if I didn't fence my bloody pastures. Even then, I have to mount a guard.'

'Some of the big cats have been known to hide their kill from the competition, but I've never heard a wolf pack do that.' Marcus puffed out his cheeks. 'And by a strange co-incidence, wouldn't you just know it? The place where Tages was dumped was a mere fifty paces from the yew tree where Lichas was killed, and do you know what's *really* bugging Hadrian, Rex?'

The tiredness dropped like a stone. 'If you're accusing my son—'

'I'm not.'

As he'd told Claudia, he'd had Hadrian pegged for the toy-maker's murder until he'd wangled that session beside his prime suspect at the hot springs. Softly, softly had been his attitude. In rekindling their childhood friendship (if that was the word), he hoped to win Hadrian's trust and that, combined with the soothing warm mud and a relaxing massage, he'd wring out the boy's confession. The technique was successful. Having swapped do-you-remembers and some rather bland childhood experiences, the warm mud started soothing, the massage began relaxing and in no time the lot came tumbling out.

He loved Lichas, Hadrian said. Lichas was a good person,

a kind person, and maybe the oils were too fragrant and the steam too calming, because this outburst immediately prompted an extensive list of the toy-maker's worthy deeds which, if Orbilio remembered correctly, included a contraption to help a crippled boy regain the strength in his legs and a doll's house for a poverty-stricken orphan called Jemma.

Right. Boy meets boy, but not round Mercurium, because both Hadrian and Lichas had to come to the hot springs to meet like-minded souls. And Hadrian had admitted sneaking out after dark, because he was shit-scared of his father's reaction should Rex get wind that his son's homosexuality wasn't the passing phase he had hoped. So far, so good – but at this point Orbilio's softly-softly technique threw up a response as startling as it was unexpected.

'I was prepared to leave everything to be with him,' Hadrian blubbed. 'I loved him, I'd have done anything for him, but Lichas said it was madness, throwing my life away.' Tears made runnels in the mud plastered to his pallid face. 'He said he loved me too much to let me waste my future on someone like him. He said I didn't know what he had done. I said I didn't care. He said I should, and when it got out my father would disown me, so I told him again I didn't care. Lichas said, *"that's what you say now, but what about when we're broke, when we're the scandal of the town and no one will talk to us, and when the luxury you've been used to and the family who raised you are both cut off irrevocably?"* That's what we rowed about, Marcus. That's why my big honey-babe took his own life.'

Orbilio ran his hand over his jaw and heard the scrape of his own stubble. (*Honey-babe?*) 'Were you aware that your son genuinely believes Lichas committed suicide?'

Rex looked startled. 'Bollocks.'

'Hadrian is convinced Lichas fell on his own dagger after their row, and that somehow Lichas either crawled to the river to throw himself in and finish the job quickly, or he tried to ease the pain with the water and fell in, or else he got disoriented stumbling around in the dark and somehow missed his footing.'

The general ran his tongue under his lower lip. 'Pity my

151

son didn't tell me that at the outset, but can't be helped, I suppose. If it was suicide, it was suicide. End of story.'

Orbilio tugged at his earlobe, because they both knew full well that the knife was too deeply embedded for Lichas to have yanked it out himself. Not when he was in that kind of agony. 'What about Tages?'

'Isn't it obvious? That snide little queer killed him, then covered his tracks best that he could.'

'His motive being?'

'Equally blatant, I would have thought. Couldn't bugger my son, so he tried his luck with the nearest available male, only Tages spurns his advances, so Lichas kills him.'

'And then commits suicide?'

'Absolutely. Filled with remorse. Realizes what a monster he's become. Does the decent thing.' Rex threw back his shoulder blades and tossed his chin in the air. 'Case solved, d'you hear me? Case – let me make myself absolutely clear, Marcus – closed.'

Orbilio sank down on the low stone wall that encircled the fishpond and buried his head in his hands. He didn't believe it. More to the point, he didn't want to believe it. A hero of *how* many campaigns? All the values he'd been raised to appreciate, all the qualities he'd come to admire in one of Rome's finest living generals, shattered like glass at his feet. Where was the honour in saving one's own skin? Where was the integrity in conspiring to cover up murder? He thought back to watching with pride as a child as the Emperor laid crowns of laurels and oak on the head of the man his own father had been proud to call a friend. *Which crown for cowardice, Rex?* He spiked his hands through his hair. God knows, his father would be turning somersaults in his grave, knowing his son had forsaken the family profession in favour of lowly investigative work, but what would the old man make of his friend's betrayal of patrician principles, he wondered? *What would the two say when they finally met?*

'When a chap sits there with a face like a walnut, there's only one possible conclusion,' a voice breezed in his ear. 'That just when you think things can't get worse, life proves you wide of the mark.'

Orbilio felt his bad mood lifted from his shoulders like a weight. 'Do you want to know the truth of it?'

'Good heavens, Marcus, surely you know me better than that!' She sat down beside him and he inhaled the richness of her spicy, Judaean perfume. 'So what happened to leave you looking like you've sat on a wasps' nest? Did you come home and find your girlfriend in bed with another man?'

'I'd have given him a bloody good hiding, too, if it hadn't been her damned husband.'

Claudia's laughter was like a drug to him and he drank deeply. He repeated his conversation with Rex.

'What are you going to do?' she asked, producing a linen cloth bursting with warm, sticky pancakes.

'Not going to let it drop, that's for sure.' Orbilio hadn't realized he was hungry until he reached for a second one. 'But Rex isn't only a local hero, he's a national icon – and he wields a hell of a lot of power around here.'

'Well, you know my motto. If at first you don't succeed, quit.'

He licked the honey off his fingers. 'Oh, so if all else fails, lower your standards?'

'There's no sense in being obstinate, Marcus. You can't win 'em all.'

'Agreed.' This time, he selected a pancake bursting with raisins and figs. 'But I'm buggered if I'm going to let Rex get away with two murders.'

Was it stubbornness on his part? A refusal to back down, even though he risked his career? Or was it because Rex had been a close friend of his father's, and he was worried he'd be tainted with the same brush of corruption? Both, probably, but at the root it was knowing he could not in all conscience turn his back on justice. Justice was blind out of impartiality, not bias.

'Then come to my house tonight,' Claudia said, dabbling her fingers in the fishpond. 'Having eaten all the pancakes, you'll probably be too stuffed to want dinner, but Candace is walking the winds again, or so Larentia tells me.'

'*All* the pancakes?'

'Every last one.'

Oh, well. No point in leaving that last plump little raisin, then. 'And what exactly do you expect me to gain from summoning the dead?'

'While the gateway's open, you might ask to speak to Lichas.'

He tipped back his head and roared. 'Now that *will* set the cats among the pigeons!' He sobered instantly and the pancakes turned to butterflies in his stomach. 'But how about you? Time's running out if Larentia decides to set a date to wed Darius, which I presume is the object of tonight's exercise.'

Another time he would have expected her to quip, *'Did you say exorcise?'* Instead, Claudia pursed her lips and stared into the distance.

'Darius,' she said slowly, 'is proving a much bigger problem than I'd imagined.'

'Are you having second thoughts about him?' he asked, the butterflies fluttering uncontrollably now.

'Good heavens, no. Once a girl has second thoughts, she finds there's a third, then a fourth, and before you know it, she's thinking for ever, and you know how dangerous it is when we women think.'

His smile was as tight as hers, though, he noticed. Was she as nervous as him? He coughed. Shuffled. Stuffed his hands under his armpits. This wasn't how he'd planned it. Unshaven, dishevelled, it was hardly the time or the place to ask a girl to marry him . . .

'Have you thought about my proposal?' he blurted.

'What?' The faraway look disappeared as she spun round to face him. 'The marriage thing?'

'Yes.' There were so many butterflies now, he was scared that if he opened his mouth they'd fly out. 'The marriage thing.'

'Well, Marcus, if you must know, I think it's an absolutely brilliant idea.'

Her dark eyes gleamed with something that might have been satisfaction, might have been pride, but which he hoped was something entirely different. Even though he had no right to hope it.

'Look.' She held out her hand. 'I even have a betrothal ring. Do you like it?'

He laughed. Relief. Excitement. Elation. Fear. 'Actually, I'd rather hoped that was something we could have chosen together, but . . .'

What did he care? What the hell did he care who chose the bloody thing, or whether it was rubies or sapphires? She'd said yes, hadn't she? That was the main thing. *Claudia Seferius had agreed to be his wife.*

'Oh, you Security Police,' she tutted comically. 'Always so thorough, but you don't have to worry about my – what did you call them the other night? My lying, cheating, stealing, fiddling taxes, making fraudulent deals, forging documents, signatures and seals? From now on, Marcus, I promise, cross my heart, I'll be a good girl and you can claim all the credit you like for solving the cases. Plus I won't even gamble, which is also against the law as you very kindly pointed out, and hell I'll probably even be there, waving to you as you climb the steps of the Senate.'

Butterflies began to turn into thumping great elephants. Had he missed something? 'Claudia, I realize it's only a marriage of convenience—'

'Convenience? Orbilio, who on earth contracts themselves to someone for something as mercenary as expediency? Not when there's this much money at stake.'

There was a joke there, he realized, but he couldn't riposte. The pancakes were threatening to come up. Every last bloody one.

'Money?' he muttered stupidly. 'How much money?'

'You'd have to ask Croesus and Midas that question, then double their combined income for what Terrence is worth.'

'*Terrence?*'

'You will come to the wedding, won't you? We've booked the Ides of June. Always propitious! I do so hope you won't miss it.'

Nineteen

You had to hand it to these patricians, Claudia thought as she made her way up the steep, cobbled alleyway. They take their obligations seriously.

On the one hand, you could argue that six sweet pancakes would test anyone's digestive system and it served him bloody well right, being sick in the fishpond. She turned left into Saturn Street then right at the fountain, where a bored-looking mule slurped noisily while its rider adjusted its pack. Unfortunately, there had been a pain in Orbilio's eyes that suggested throwing up hadn't been payback for greed, and there was only one explanation. Marcus Conscientious Orbilio had been so shaken by Rex's betrayal of his class that it had made him physically ill.

At the public ovens she paused to admire the gorgon's head that had been painted on the doors, with a curse underneath on any nosey parkers who felt like peering inside and ruining the rising process.

In fact, Orbilio had looked so utterly wretched that she'd been tempted to console him by reminding him that it was his idea to thwart Darius with remarriage, and hoping that by congratulating him on his cracking idea it would cheer Old Green Features up. However, it's not easy making polite conversation to a chap who's feeding six sweet pancakes to the carp, so she took another look at her betrothal ring (Terrence was no slouch on the gem front), gave it a rub for good luck and came straight up here to Mercurium. And oh, ho, ho, who's this, then, gawping at the goldsmith's intricate skill?

'You really shouldn't wear so much jewellery at any one time,' Claudia murmured in Candace's ear. 'One of these days, you're going to get robbed, and for that amount of gold the thieves'll mean business.'

'No one is going to murder me for my money,' she replied in her rich, velvety, dead-communing voice.

'You can see that in your crystal?'

'Any would-be thief is aware of my powers.' In the sunlight, her oiled skin shone like the ebony wood of her native Kush, her beauty enhanced by wine lees rubbed into her lips and cheeks, turning them tawny, while a blackcurrant pigment on her eyelids added to the stunning effect. 'They know that if they touch me, their skin will blister and their eyeballs will burn, they will die in torment as their bowels corrode and their livers explode, and my curse will follow them beyond the grave, where they will be consumed for eternity in hell fire.'

'But I'll bet it hurts, lugging so much metal around every day.'

'No more than a warrior going into battle.'

'Except warriors don't fight every day.'

Glittering eyes bored into her. 'Gold oozes out of the rocks of the Nile. Gold is my birthright, the symbol of Kush, and cursed is he who attacks my country.' Candace turned into the shop. 'I will walk the winds in pursuit of the blasphemer,' she hissed over her shoulder, 'and see his wickedness punished.'

Good for you, girl, good for you. You keep up the charade, but you're not fooling me.

Claudia checked her directions. First on the left past the shield-maker's shop and you can't miss it, the apothecary had said. It's the only inn on Juniper Square with vermilion lintels. At the time she'd thanked him for such clear directions, but what the apothecary had failed to mention was that every Etruscan tavern decked their lintels with greenery. She had to walk round the entire square, stretching her neck like a giraffe to determine paint colour until finally, under a welter of pine (for healthy lungs) she spotted a hint of vermilion.

'Milady?'

If the landlord was surprised to find a young unchaperoned wine merchant's widow strolling round his premises admiring walls decorated in bold, earthy colours depicting scenes of Fuflunic delights, he hid it well. But then, for a man whose cart's axle had broken, costing him not only its replacement but thirty gallons of wine after three amphorae had smashed – as well as his stocks turning to vinegar overnight – she suspected very little interested the poor man beyond financial survival. Which, looking around, seemed decidedly doubtful. Claudia was the only customer in the place and the flowers planted in pots outside the door only acted as a magnet for dogs.

'A large jug of your best vintage wine, and a hot pie if you have one.'

Ordinarily he was a big man, a jolly man, the life and soul of the place, she suspected. Today his eyes sat in black hollows and the skin hung slack round his jaw.

'Reckon I can do you the pie, ma'am. Wine went off again in the night.'

'All of it?'

He shook his head sadly. 'Fufluns has cursed me, that he has, milady. Don't rightly know why, but I sure do know how, and though I've hung prayer ribbons outside begging him to pass me over – '

And here was her, thinking they were there to add gaiety!

' – and made every offering you can think of to appease Fufluns' wrath, his curse descended upon me while I made revel last night, and Tarchis says if the gods decide vengeance, vengeance cannot be avoided.'

Good old Tarchis. Nothing like a dyed-in-the-wool zealot to lift flagging spirits.

'Then I'll have a jug of your best vintage water, landlord. And don't forget that hot pie!'

'You sure?' The tavern-keeper looked at her as though he'd been covered in spots and she'd catch a bout if she stayed another five seconds.

'Absolutely.'

Claudia pulled out a small, round stool from under one of the tables and sat down. Many of the wall paintings seemed so achingly familiar – satyrs chasing maenads, maenads chasing satyrs, all amid much cymbal clashing and upending of goblets – that she wondered whether Bacchus mightn't be another Etruscan trophy that had been off to Rome in triumph.

'I was going through my husband's old papers when I

came across notes of a trial that took place several years ago, and . . . well, Gaius wrote about you in such glowing terms that I simply had to come and meet you myself.'

'Me?' For a big man, he turned ever so coy. 'Gaius Seferius wrote about *me*?'

As he rattled off to stoke the wood-fired oven in his kitchen, he was beaming from ear to ear and she knew then it was just a matter of time.

'Look what I found!' He returned with a flagon painted with garish purple grapes that he'd filled to the point of overflowing. 'It's white wine, milady, but I suddenly remembered squirrelling it away in the corner, even though there's not much call for white round these parts. But I've just broke the seal and tested the quality.' He winked. 'Reckon it's only red wine old Fufluns has a beef with.'

Divine providence? Or a saboteur also failing to notice that particular amphora tucked away in the dark reaches of the cellar?

'Pie'll be along shortly, and I've got herbed chicken legs fried in olive oil . . . well.' He grinned as his natural bonhomie bubbled back to the surface. 'Not me personal, like! My legs is more hairy!'

He pushed out a plate of relishes to go with the wine. Claudia pushed out a stool for him to join her.

'Gaius spoke very highly of your cheerfulness and wit.' Idly she wondered whether acting was in the blood. 'As he did about your honesty and integrity at Felix's trial.'

'Felix?' The landlord rolled his eyes. 'Now *there's* a name I never expected to hear again this side of the Styx.'

Claudia poured wine into her glass and filled one for him. 'Treason, the notes said.'

'Aye, though you'd never think it to look at him, ma'am. You'd have taken him for honest as the day was long, but there he was, embezzling funds from the Imperial Treasury, and between you and me, milady, he was lucky to get off with ten years.'

Hear that, Darius? Lucky to get off with ten years.

'Gaius was rather more specific,' she said. '"Guilty as hell" were his words.'

159

'No question of it, milady.' The landlord leaned his elbow on the table, rested his head on his hand and stretched out his legs to make himself comfortable as he related the story.

Felix, he explained, wasn't from around here. He came from Cosa, which Claudia happened to know well, being the Etruscan port where Seferius wine was still shipped from. The Gaius connection started to fall into place. According to the tavern-keeper, Felix didn't inherit his wealth. He came from a poor but freeborn family and started life as a daytime donkey (which she assumed to mean porter) on the quay down at Cosa, working his way up to become an oysterman, and eventually farming them for a living. Only two other men had ever tried farming oysters, he added, and though Felix's initial efforts off the coast here were none too successful, he discovered that the Bay of Naples was infinitely more conducive to the cultivation of his little molluscs.

Naples. Another cog clicked into place. Naples was the port where Darius shipped out his famous racehorses. No wonder he was so familiar with the south.

'Why would a man who was so successful want to embezzle funds from the Treasury?'

'Search me.' His big shoulders shrugged. 'Guess when you're born with no money, you can't never have enough.'

How *very* true. 'What I don't understand, though, is why a man born in Cosa and farming oysters in Naples would be tried for treason in Mercurium.'

'Oh, that'd be his marriage, milady.'

The tavern-keeper switched elbows and launched into a reminiscence of Felix's marital history. How he'd married the blacksmith's daughter when he was very young, for the simple reason she told him she was pregnant and he wanted to do the honourable thing by her.

'But she wasn't, I assume?'

No wonder Darius wasn't amused when Claudia cracked that joke about Larentia on market day. Too close to home for comfort, that one!

'False alarm, *she* said, but people who knew Felix back in them days said he knew straight off he'd been conned. Set out to trap him right from the start, she did, but them marriages never work out. It was a sham from the beginning; he never loved her, and that's why folk believe he worked such long hours. To take his mind off his loveless marriage, because there was never any question of his wife going to live with him in Naples.'

But then, the landlord said, after fifteen years, Felix visited Mercurium on business and here he met Mariana.

'Love at first sight for both of 'em. Soul mates, milady, no other word, and the very first thing Felix did was ride over to Cosa and divorce . . . cor, what was her name? Ophelia? Emilia? *Aurelia!* It's all coming back now. Felix divorced Aurelia before you could blink, bought a house here and hardly set foot in Naples again. No one said it was fair on the first wife, but I knew Mariana, milady. Lovely girl. Absolute angel. And a man can't help how he feels, can he? You only get the one life.'

Not if you're a Gaul. They were firm believers in scourging themselves to make it better for their incarnation. Live tough and live miserably, that was their motto. Because when you die you can do it again.

'How did Aurelia take to being usurped?'

'Not a peep out of her, and let's face it, she couldn't have been any happier in her heart than Felix, and you have to remember they was both young still. Pretty girl in her prime with a hefty divorce settlement? Probably the best thing that happened to her in the long run.'

While he broke off to fetch the pie, the hot crispy chicken legs and to refill the wine jug, Claudia wondered what had happened to turn Felix into a monster. Had he still been trapped in a disillusioned marriage, she could have understood bitterness gnawing away down the silver mines. But here he was, the archetypal working-boy-made-good, starting over with a girl who adored him. It didn't make sense. Felix was rich. Felix was happy. Felix was in love. Why risk everything by stealing from His Imperial Majesty's coffers? Burrow into a bank vault, steal your neighbour's money chest, break into a merchant's house and rob him of his valuables, by all means! You get caught, you make restitution, you compensate the victim for any distress, blah-blah-blah, then you spend two years on somewhere like Capri or in Athens in what is supposed to be exile. After which, you come back with a tan, a few new experiences, some good tales to tell, then – hey presto – it's business as usual.

So what inspired Felix to dip his fingers in Imperial funds? Of all people, he would have known that, if he was caught, the State always made an example of the thief – no exceptions – by seizing his assets and sentencing him to the very minimum of ten years' hard labour?

Which was all very interesting and certainly aroused Claudia's curiosity. But went absolutely nowhere towards proving Felix and Darius were one and the same!

'How did you come to be involved at the trial?' she asked, biting into a herb-encrusted drumstick and tasting garlic, parsley, oregano and thyme.

'Me?' The landlord wiped his hands on his canvas apron and rejoined her at the table. 'Saw him taking the money from the Treasury clerk and packing it in his saddlebag. Right under that silver birch there, matter of fact. With the lights from the tavern, they was lit up like a sunrise, them two, but then if you're open about your dealings, people tend not to take any notice. Didn't then, to be honest with you, ma'am. It was only later, when the soldiers came asking questions that I remembered seeing them there.'

The crime tumbled out. There was so much gold missing from the Treasury that it was noticed at once. The clerk was arrested before he'd even joined the main road to Rome, and instantly betrayed Felix as the mastermind. Indeed, the horse on which he made his escape was proven to come from Felix's stables and the bulk of the gold was still in Felix's saddlebags when the authorities conducted their search. The clerk also admitted to handing it over outside the tavern, believing, like the inn-keeper, Felix's attestation that the more open one is, the less one is noticed. Except in the end six citizens of unimpeachable character happened to be in the square at the time.

The inn-keeper saw them through his tavern window, no doubt the paper merchant had been returning home after a long day, the brick-maker out buying his wife a birthday present from the goldsmith's for instance, and so on, and so on, and so on . . .

Claudia cut into the rich partridge pie. 'I can't remember what Gaius wrote about how he recognized Felix. His lantern jaw, was it? His dimpled chin?'

Some other feature that was highly conspicuous to mark him out as separate from Darius?

'Felix? Bless you, ma'am, there wasn't nothing that stood out about him, though there was nothing weak about his face, either.'

Good.

'But he always rode the same sorrel mare, did our Felix, and I suppose, if I was honest, I'd have to say he was a bit of a dandy. Wore quality clothes in the manner of a man used to wearing 'em – '

Like Darius.

' – but wore a gold headband to keep his curls out of his eyes – '

Knew it!

' – and, of course, what did set him out from the crowd was that, unlike most freemen, Felix didn't favour white tunics. Bright blue was his colour. Wanted folk to see he'd risen up through the ranks, and though he'd been promoted to equestrian status like your late husband, Felix only tended to wear his purple-striped tunic on state occasions.'

So a man with a neat Caesar crop, wearing a crisp white linen tunic, dazzling white woollen toga and wearing high patrician boots wouldn't be lumped in the same social class as the johnny-come-lately dandified Felix. Especially if he adopted different mannerisms and gait.

Claudia polished off the partridge pie along with the relishes. Sabotaging the wine would have been easy for anyone committed enough to want to bother. Five earthenware *dolia* were set in the tavern's stone counters like gigantic toilet seats. Simple matter of dropping the contents of a phial into those during the night, then nipping into the cellar, removing the spigots from the casks, souring that wine, then re-plugging them without leaving a trace. But to plan this, Darius would have had to have been inside this tavern, and twelve years ago was too far back to rely on mere memory . . .

163

'In Rome, artisans tend to drink at their various guild houses,' she said. 'Is it the same here?'

'Oh, aye.' The landlord explained that his clientele fell into two types. Shopkeepers and residents of the apartments above them who ate here on a regular basis, and barflies who never left, at least when there was wine to be had! 'Not wishing to sound snobby, ma'am, but that type tend to comprise the lower orders, if you get my drift, or else those fallen from grace, who just drink themselves stupid.'

Damn.

He ambled off to the kitchens and returned with a steaming hot pumpkin tart that he set down with a bang on the table. 'Course, we do get gentry like yourself occasionally.' He sliced it with the same knife that had cut the partridge pie. 'Not often, but it happens.'

'Yes, now you mention it, I do believe Darius said he'd been in here a while back.'

Pine. It was the pine over the lintel that gave him away.

'Do believe you're right, milady.' The landlord nodded sagely. 'Not often, but like I says, it happens. Here, you sure you don't want a piece of this tart? The missus bakes 'em herself.'

'No.' Claudia was too excited to eat. 'No, I don't, but I'll tell you a secret,' she said. 'It's not something I share with everyone, but I've just had a vision.'

'A vision, ma'am?' His face twisted in the manner of a man worried that the partridge was off.

'A vision,' she said. 'And in my vision, I saw Fufluns, and do you know what? He was lifting his curse from your tavern.'

There'll be no more sour wine in this place, my friend. Felix has just met his match.

The first thing that struck Rosenna, returning from shopping, was the smell of freshly carved wood. She hooked her basket over her arm and thought, daft. This was a toy shop! She was used to the prickly sensation at the top of her nose. Well used to the dry, dusty air. All the same though . . . She swapped the basket to the other arm. The vividness of it caught her right off guard, reminding her of when Lichas sat hunched over his chisels, and she realized with a start that it had been eight days since she'd last inhaled that timbery smell. Three days during which she'd been out of her mind with worry. Five days during which she'd gone out of her mind with grief . . .

She ducked under the counter and thought, no. No, it wasn't like when Lichas was working. Her brother'd sit in the corner, rasping away, his tongue clenched between his teeth in concentration. Orson moved his stool right up to the street, often stopping to show the kiddies what he was working on, explaining how he was going to turn this offcut of cypress into a soldier, why fig was the best wood for making a hoop, and why grain oak was good for the crossbars of lyres. And when he wasn't surrounded by curious kids, he'd be humming away to himself. 'Whistle while you whittle, Rosie,' he'd laugh. And that was another thing: no one had ever called her Rosie before.

'Oi'd have thought it were the first thing that sprung to mind,' Orson said when she told him. 'What with name, your rosy round cheeks and hair that's the colour of rosehips in autumn.'

'Not my rosy nature, then?'

'Oh, that'll come back,' he'd assured her, fixing the hinges to Jemma's doll's house. 'Like a tide coming in on a steep-shelving beach, you don't see it creep up, but it do. Pass them tacks over, would you?'

'I don't have a rosy nature to creep back,' she told him, steadying the miniature cottage as he tapped the nails home.

'No?' Broad hands satisfied themselves that the structure was rigid. 'Then who's responsible for painting them jugs in the kitchen? Who stencilled those floral swags on the walls?'

Jugs? Swags? Did he honestly think such things mattered? Rosenna returned his wave with a jauntiness she didn't feel and thought, justice is what counts. Not flowers. Not sodding paint. A life for a life, and with Tages' body being found late yesterday afternoon, it wasn't one murder she'd be avenging when the Brides of Fufluns danced for their god. She'd be doing old Etha a favour as well. Climbing the stairs with a heavy tread, she laid the contents of her shopping out over the table. Leeks, peas, beans, onions. A clutch of freshly laid eggs. And, thanks to those kiddie-sized flutes he carved out of that old leftover pine yesterday and got her to paint Pan faces on, she could throw a coney on the table as well, for they'd sold like hot cakes, them flutes. It weren't fair to punish Orson for the sins of the Romans. Oh, he were a Roman, she knew that, but he weren't the double-crossing, skin-saving kind of Roman – and hell, he deserved a decent meal at the end of the day for helping little orphaned Jemma and the crippled boy.

'No, no, you keep that, Rosie,' he'd said when she'd offered him a half share of the takings. 'Reckon they thinks Oi'm a goose that needs fattening for Saturnalia, Oi'm that well fed up at that villa.'

'Fancy titbits, aye. But do they feed you rabbit stew with lentils and leeks?'

A look of longing crossed his freckled face. 'Thick gravy?'

'So thick, you'll need a knife,' she promised, and Rosenna had never broken a promise in her life.

She proceeded to strip the skin off the coney and joint it. By the time she'd finished chopping the vegetables, the herbs and the spices, the blade she'd been using was blunt, and she resolved to sharpen it on the grindstone, but not until Orson packed up for the night. She didn't want anyone to overhear the spell she cast while she honed it. The spell that would carry it straight to the heart of three bastard patricians: Hadrian, Rex and the other one. Marcus.

She hefted the cauldron on to the stove. Aye, Marcus, they called him. Not one of your soft types like the coward who betrayed her brother, nor the bullying kind, like the father, which only left the other kind. The kind who tried to bribe you to keep your mouth shut. Oh, don't think she hadn't seen the way he followed her around last night! Trying to catch her attention, so he could stuff gold in her pockets – as though *that* would bring Lichas back! But she was glad now that she'd gone with Orson to the festivities. She hadn't wanted to go, but he insisted that, rather than dignifying the dead, too much mourning dishonoured them, and if Lichas was half the man she had claimed, he must've been a chap who'd taken life by the horns and she could do worse than follow her brother's example. Part shamed, part inspired, what had tipped the balance was that Orson had no one else to go with. Flavia was stuck at the temple, he said.

'Reckon it would give us both a treat, Rosie, for you and me to horse around for a couple of hours.'

And show those bastard patricians how to play featherball, she thought triumphantly. That'll teach 'em – and while she was up at Terrence's mansion, she'd got the chance to look all three of her enemies in the eye, too. Nits and lice, just like she'd said, and no one thinks twice about exterminating *them*.

'Dinner smells good,' Orson called up.

'Looks good, too,' she called down, giving the pot a hearty stir with the paddle and adjusting the seasonings.

That was one heck of a big stew, but he'd probably scoff the lot, would our Orson. Strapping fella with a wise head on broad shoulders, and a heart of gold on the inside. Why, look at the amount of time he'd spent on that contraption Lichas had been designing to help the crippled lad walk.

'Still ain't right though, is it?' he'd said in the end, but he weren't giving up. 'Leave it with me, Rosie, and Oi'll see what Oi can do. Reckon it needs three wheels, see. One at the back here, to steady the frame and stop it from tipping forward.'

As the light began to drain from the sky, Rosenna lit the oil lamps and resolved that, before the red-headed moon waxed to its full, she would will this workshop to Orson. She'd have to get a document that was drawn up all legal, like, to prove she'd given it to him *before* she'd killed them patricians. Because afterwards the State would crucify her for what she had done, but them Romans weren't getting their hands on this shop. No way.

But Orson now. Orson liked wood. It didn't matter a jot what happened to her, but this way Lichas's memory would live on through his wood. Orson would see to that.

'Supper's ready,' she called down the stairs. 'And don't forget that knife for your gravy!'

Twenty

Candace stared into the shining crystal on the centre of the table, while Larentia explained to her dinner guests how she was able to see the future through the visions it produced. Vaguely, she was aware of Eunice's heartfelt hope that Candace couldn't see her future wrinkles; she had more than enough at the moment, thanks, and if that crystal even *mentioned* the word 'fat', she'd smash the thing with her shoe.

Candace continued to stare, knowing that it would be interpreted by the assembly as the first stage of her trance, since silence and stillness were as integral a part of her wind-walking ritual as the persona she had developed of wearing rich, bold fabrics, a plethora of gold and honing her naturally deep voice to this melodious drawl. Yet it was not for professional reasons that Candace stared into its glistening facets, and it was not for its visions that she carried the prism around.

Her mind travelled back on a journey that took her down a long, dark, distant tunnel. And though she had never given up hoping to see lush lowlands at the end of the tunnel, where giant grey beasts with a fifth leg coming out of their forehead trumpeted loudly, where long-necked, long-legged creatures grazed the treetops and where striped horses ran wild in herds, no such visions had ever formed. It was always only more darkness she saw. A terrible blackness in which people were screaming, making terrible gurgling noises from deep in their throats, a blackness where fathers pleaded and mothers sobbed, and terrified children screamed . . .

Staring into the crystal, the memories solidified like the rock itself and shimmered every bit as brightly.

Kush was a land of plenty, she'd been told. Apart from

the gold that oozed out of the rocks, there was brisk trade to be had in supplying Rome with exotic creatures and huge profits to be made from the enterprise. Candace had never been to Rome, so it was only through hearsay that she'd learned about huge spotted cats that spent all their lives up trees, and snakes thicker than a man's thigh that could swallow a billy goat whole. Indeed, it was through such tales that she'd heard about the grey five-legged monsters whose footsteps shook the ground and from whom giant logs of ivory came. Candace needed no telling that the Kings of Kush had grown rich from this ivory – very rich. Or that rich men grow powerful – very powerful. To the point that, when one of them dies, no one questions whether it is right or wrong that three hundred and twenty-eight men, women and children be buried along with the king. Or that he'd stipulated they should still be alive.

How old would Candace have been? Four? Maybe not even that, for she had no memories of life before that fateful day. All she recalled was being dragged in chains into that pit and seeing people strangled one after the other. Some were strangers, some were from her own village, many came from her own family. As her mother's turn came, she remembered the ribbon being wound round her neck as she sobbed and pleaded and begged for her baby's life. Candace recalled the startling warmth of the ribbon as it was wrapped round her own throat. Remembered the constriction, the pain, her vision blurring as the haze turned to red, but then, as she fell forward on to the corpse of her mother, a hand clamped round her mouth and a voice hissed in her ear,

Make a sound and I'll finish what I started.

Candace made no sound. Not a whimper. She lay there, face down and frozen with terror as her mother's corpse slowly cooled, and she listened to the gurgles and screams until finally, mercifully, only silence filled the air. As darkness cast its cloak over the burial pit, she felt a rough hand pulling her out, but this, she discovered, was no humanitarian rescue. She'd been snatched for pure profit, sold on as a plaything for a rich Roman family. A black toy for white children to tease and torment.

'As I was telling Terrence this afternoon, I got a letter from Cousin Julius to say old Auntie Antonia has lost her mind completely,' Thalia was twittering.

'Hardly a disaster,' Eunice retorted. 'It was a closed one, anyway; no one'll miss it.'

'Especially Antonia,' Terrence added dryly.

Candace didn't smile. Her features remained wooden, her eyes distant and, trapped in her memories, her mind travelled forwards. To the time when she was too old to continue as a source of childish amusement and was sold on again, this time as a slave. Do this, do that. I'll pinch you again if you don't do it quicker. Ah, yes, but slaves earn money . . . Some more than others, admittedly, it didn't matter. In addition to her upkeep, she was entitled to a small sum of pocket money to spend as she liked, and the crystal was her very first purchase. A lump of native rock on sale in the market at a price she'd had to pay for in six monthly instalments, but once she had it – once she clutched it to her breast – that shining glass would surely bring back her homeland. It would bring back her mother, her father, her brothers, her sisters. All the memories the old King had killed along with their persons.

But as the past stubbornly failed to materialize, so Candace could see the future . . .

Not through visions in the rock. She saw how she might use its reputation, for if others had tried to see the future and failed, surely it was because they weren't Kushite? The same instincts that had guided her as a child to keep her mouth shut during The Terror guided her then. She hadn't gone straight to her mistress. She began to convince other slaves that she could see their future, bland predictions that were nonetheless straws to clutch in a world where you owned nothing, not even your own soul. Word rippled up through the ranks until one day she was summoned. Basically, through rhetoric she had practised and gestures she'd rehearsed, it boiled down to nothing more than the Mistress encountering troubles and tribulation, but rising above them like migrating cranes. As the stupid bitch lapped it up, so Candace became a pampered pet with her own quarters, her own slaves, and

170

slowly perfected her act. For a start, she made it clear that she couldn't 'see' every day. It was the crystal that imparted the sight; she was merely the instrument of prophecy. Picking and choosing these times gave her control, and by studying the ancient oracles, Candace mastered the art of juggling ambiguity, guesswork and gossip with the well-heeled's insatiable insecurity. As her reputation grew, so did her money chest . . . and her contempt for them and their class.

Once she'd saved enough to buy her own freedom, she adopted more sophisticated techniques to separate them from their money. *The forces of the supernatural are all around us, my child. I am merely their instrument.* So why hang on to this empty block of glistening glass? Why keep this crystal which shows neither future nor past?

Like the prism itself, Candace had no answer. Instead, she brought her mind back to the present, demanded silence, for lights to be extinguished, for incense to be lit to propitiate the dead.

'I remind you. The shades of our ancestors inhabit a world of darkness and quiet. If they are to walk again, even for one night, an atmosphere must be created in which they feel comfortable, even though for the rest of us, it will feel cold.'

She bade the assembly link hands, cautioning them to ignore the chill and concentrate on the rhythm of the harp. Let the music fill their minds, she intoned, for the harp was the gateway to the Afterlife.

'Through the circle you form,' she picked up a blade and shook back her sleeve, 'and the blood that I sacrifice,' she broke off while it splashed into the little bronze bowl, 'we create a dark demi-world in which the dead live and the living are dead, and now I cover the sacred Crystal of Kush that time may be as frozen as the air that sweeps over us from the distant Isles of the West.'

In the dark, the gold thread of her veil shimmered like sunlight on water as she threw it over the table.

'O Vanth, Demon of Death, who has eyes on her wings and sees everything, I summon you to walk among us tonight.'

Three loud raps reverberated round the dining hall, echoed by gasps from Eunice and Larentia.

171

'O Leinth, who waits at the Gates of the Underworld and drinks of human tears, I call upon you to turn your faceless face to the stone and approach.'

Three more knocks.

Candace drew a long breath and deepened the pitch of her voice.

'By the Falcon of the Sun, by the Vultures of the Moon, I bid ye spirits enter.'

Twenty-One

'*By the Falcon of the Sun, by the Vultures of the Moon,*' Candace had said, '*I bid ye spirits enter.*'

And enter they bloody well had. In their droves.

From a marble bench by the gate in the courtyard, Claudia watched the moon rise over the roof of the stable block and thought, no sooner had Candace summoned the dead than the dining hall had filled with a thousand moaning, groaning, whispering echoes. Smoke seemed to come from all four corners of the room, swirling, choking, bringing with it the foul smell of Hades.

'Stop them, Candace,' Thalia had quavered. 'M-make them go b-back where they came from.'

'She can't,' Larentia said, and her voice was no steadier. 'She's fainted.'

'Then for gods' sake don't anyone break the bloody circle,' Rex growled, 'or the bastards might never go back.'

'Rex?' The voice was gentle and cooing. 'Rex, my darling, is that you?'

'Honoria?'

But as soon as he called out his wife's name, she was gone, and then swishing sounds filled the air, a flute trilled close to Claudia's ear and she'd felt the soft brush of a hand against her shoulder. When the gold shawl that Candace had thrown over the table lifted clean into the air, Thalia screamed and tried to pull free. Claudia tightened her grip on the girl's wrist, and felt a squeeze of reassurance in her other hand. How sweet of Darius to care . . .

And that was it, wasn't it? Everything in the end came back to Darius. Evil was proving as slippery as he was shrewd.

'Pale moon doth rain, red moon doth blow.'

And dear me, not only had the sorceress summoned the dead; she had also conjured the devil.

'White moon bringeth neither deluge nor snow.'

He sat down on the bench beside her, and she smelled a combination of cough drops and balm of Gilead above the floral scents that dominated the courtyard. So help me, if you're any kind of healer, she told Apollo, your divine powers will ensure both have gone off.

'I suppose that's why you wait to prune the vines,' Darius rumbled. 'So warm breezes can blow the frost away.'

That's it, Felix. Keep on pretending you're not from these parts.

'Frankly, I neither know nor care,' she retorted. 'I'm a city girl, which means that where I come from, gazing up at the moon is reserved for drunks in the gutter.'

'Are you saying you don't like Tuscany?'

'How can one like nothing? Because Jupiter knows, there's enough of the bloody stuff around here. Hills, trees, rivers, fields – good grief, the nothingness never ends, and if you think Rome's noisy, Darius, it's small fry compared to the commotion that starts here at dawn.'

'I think you're lying,' he said gently. 'I think you like this place very much.'

'And suppose I say I don't care what you think.'

'Then,' he laughed, 'I'll *know* you're lying.'

It was tempting – oh, god it was tempting – to stuff Terrence's ring under his nose and wipe the smile off his face. But if Claudia was to savour the moment, truly savour it, she had to ensure the timing was right. *'It wouldn't be fair to steal Larentia's thunder,'* she'd told Terrence with her prettiest pout. *'We should wait until she and Darius have announced their betrothal before announcing ours.'* That was the time to watch the smile freeze on his smug, vengeful features! To flash her sapphire triumph into his face. When he's standing in front of a crowd of compatriots, secure in the knowledge that he's finally taken control of his enemy's business, his enemy's mother, his widow, his sister, even his enemy's naïve teenage daughter. Oh, yes, Felix Musa. That's the moment for you to realize you're standing on quicksand.

'Tonight there were no conversations,' he said. 'Gaius didn't come through for either you or Larentia. No one did. It was pure mayhem that Candace unleashed in that room.'

Claudia tried not to think about the shawl wafting about of its own accord, the crystal hurling itself on to the floor, the sniggerings from everywhere and nowhere.

'Rex's wife called him,' she said.

'And was quickly suppressed, if you remember. Claudia . . .' Darius moved his lean, hard body close to hers. 'Claudia, I have to get Ren away from this. It's bloody dangerous.'

You're telling me! 'What do you have in mind?'

'I don't know, that's the problem. I thought maybe if I talk it over with you, we might come up with a solution between us.'

Like Indigo said. Clever.

'If I suggest whisking her off to my stud farm, she'll only want to bring Candace with her, and holy heralds, what can I say? Should I refuse, I come over as some domineering, chauvinist pig, and if I agree, the problem persists.'

'Damned if you do, damned if you don't?'

'Precisely.'

Bless him, he'd never said a truer word! Evidence was mounting that would eventually unmask the monster beneath, and already – thanks to the tavern-keeper and Darius himself – Claudia could track his campaign back to its start.

Passing himself off as the suave, horse-breeding patrician, Felix begins by reconnoitring the area, touring Mercurium and its environs to re-familiarize himself with the geography, the culture, the people in order to tailor his vengeance. It had been no lucky guess on her part, suggesting Darius might have called in at the tavern. The pine over the vermilion lintel gave it away. Oh yes, pine, my suave clever friend. That greenery obliterating the door planted an idea in your head, reminding you of the old wives' tale that pinewoods filter germs and keep the lungs healthy. Why not take it a step further, you thought, and have them filter bad luck?

Also, as part of the 'Establishing Darius' process, Felix would unquestionably have spent time at the hot springs, if only for the gossip he was bound to pick up. Gossip about Eunice and Lars, for example, which set another train of ideas in motion. Whether he'd known Gaius personally was moot, but one self-made man quickly identifies with another – and he'd know Gaius's mother was nobody's fool. Wandering around Lavernium, ideas would have bubbled like the hot springs themselves, and in a town where charlatans abound, Candace's reputation would have preceded her . . .

Having tracked down his sorceress, Felix's campaign was free to shift from theory to practice. While sabotaging the livelihoods of five of his victims and destroying their families, their finances and their peace of mind, 'Darius' befriends Larentia – and *friend* is the operative word. Nothing overt. No flowers, no gifts, no poetry, no moonlight. Keep it light, keep it friendly, but for gods' sake keep it going. Once that friendship has been established, though, he contrives for a message to be delivered, calling him back to the stud farm on business, but (kind heart that he is) he arranges for Larentia to be pampered at the hot springs in his absence where, surprise, surprise, she meets Candace.

Larentia does not suspect any overlap – why should she? – and astute though she is, she's still a working girl at heart, filled with working-class superstitions. All it takes is a few crystal gazes, a few walks on the winds, and she's swallowing that guff about the town being cursed like a man in the desert gulps water. Candace becomes her ally. She can help her. She can cast spells to counter the misfortune, but for these to be effective, Larentia must purify herself up in the hills and filter out the bad humours. Naturally, while she's filtering away, a letter arrives from dear, darling Darius saying that, as a special treat, he's renovating the villa while she's gone. Allowing him to not only make whatever changes he wants to his future home, it enables him to install those all-too-important folding doors. Yet here he is now, cool as

176

a cucumber, trying to convince Claudia that he wants rid of the woman he installed in her house in the first place!

'If you could have a think about how we can put paid to this dangerous nonsense, I'd be grateful,' he said, then rubbed his hands together briskly to change the subject. 'Tarchis tells me Flavia's progressing famously.'

'Does he really?'

'Ah.' He scrunched his jaw sideways in the manner of someone who's just realized he's put his foot in it. 'I'm sure our Red Priest will get round to telling you, only he and Terrence are like this – ' he crossed his fingers '– and given Terrence's reputation for hospitality, the old boy becomes somewhat garrulous after a few glasses. Indeed.' He grinned. 'He and Thalia seem well matched when it comes to the exchange of gossip.'

And naturally Felix would want to cultivate someone with his finger on the local pulse! Through Terrence, he had access to as perfect a pair of fishwives as one could hope to meet in society, and small wonder Tarchis made the connection between the victims so fast. He'd been talking about them often enough!

'That's how I came to hear about the Bridal Dance . . .' Darius was saying.

Liar. You knew about it because you married Mariana.

'And why I thought it might help Flavia.'

Felix's message, dammit, was clear. Cast aspersions on the paragon of virtue that I've created, and no one in this town will believe you. He was right, too. All the evidence she had amassed – the disguise, the persona, the pine – was circumstantial and wouldn't stand up to close scrutiny. Even if Candace confessed and Claudia could prove every point, it amounted to nothing more than malicious reprisals on the men who had sent him to jail. Hardly the sort of crime to jolt the authorities into action. Naturally, they would demand restitution for the victims, but if Felix should happen to go on the run, the State was unlikely to hound him down. Far quicker to close the case by compensating the victims, no harm done, good public relations and all that. Unfortunately, for justice to be served, Claudia needed to place the knife that killed Lichas and Tages in Darius's hand, and for this she needed someone who knew Felix from the old days. Someone who could see beyond the Caesar-cut and altered mannerisms to expose him for the impostor he was.

In short, she needed Mariana!

'How's Orson coping with his sweetheart's absence?' Darius asked.

Claudia looked at the moon, no different in colour from any other moon as far as she could see, and sighed deeply. 'With his customary practical sense, I'm afraid. Bored with a life of luxury, our young carpenter has taken his skills into town, where Rosenna provides him with board and lodging.'

'Rosenna? You mean the toy-maker's sister?'

Something congealed in her stomach. Dammit, she'd forgotten how dangerous Felix was. Drop your guard, even for an instant, and the tiger gets you to lead him to another tethered goat . . .

'It's only temporary,' she said swiftly. 'Until the Brides dance for Fufluns.' But the damage was done.

Now it was no longer a question of needing hard evidence against him. She needed to find it before another boy died.

Twenty-Two

The only thing different at the Temple of Fufluns was that, instead of rain clouds gathering overhead, the sun streamed down, turning the sacred pool to shimmering glass and inciting the temple kittens to even greater levels of skittishness. Lyres and flutes produced the same haunting music that penetrated every nook. Herbal garlands still wound up every pink column, bronze chimes pealed softly, the same lamps burned in their thousands. Lars had laughed when Claudia mentioned last night how the soothing atmosphere was in contrast to the energetic scenes depicted in the frescoes.

'To appreciate all that fine wining and dining and bedding you see on the walls, we Etruscans need to step back. Relax. Unwind. Cast aside our day-to-day worries. Then, once our souls are refreshed, our offerings laid and our prayers asked, we lift our eyes. Remind ourselves what Fufluns stands for – and *then* we binge, gorge and bonk ourselves stupid.'

Stupid? The Etruscans were anything but stupid. Her footsteps resonated down the vaulted stone corridors, and once again she was struck by the dedication it had taken to excavate this subterranean maze. Darius must have visited here. What thoughts as he drew deeper inside this tunnel of rock? Was he jittery, fearful of another stripe on his back? Or was it the other way round? That, seeing this sacred place where sanctity was mined, rather than ore, would it have hardened Felix's resolve?

'Ah, Tarchis! Just the chap!'

She needed to know exactly how much this red-hatted blabbermouth had been tattling about the Felix connection – and to whom.

'On that subject, Lady Claudia, my lips have been sealed,' Tarchis assured her, once he'd got his come-forth-and-welcome speech out of the way. 'The winged avenger has already been unleashed on the wicked. No useful purpose can be served alerting those whom Thufltha has targeted, much less broadcasting His retribution across the whole town.'

'You fear panic will spread?'

'The commandments of the gods are unequivocal, my child. When vengeance is Their will, Their will must run its course and warning the wicked can only compromise divine justice.' The old man leaned forward on his desk and laced his fingers together. 'Suppose, for example, I were to tell the miller that he is the target of Veive's vengeful arrows and the miller, realizing how his iniquity has brought his family low, then commits suicide?'

'Aren't priests the gods' messengers?'

'Holy Horta, my dear!' From his expression, you'd think Claudia had propositioned him. 'The augurs scour the skies, the signs of nature and the organs of sacrificial animals in a bid to interpret Their holy wishes,' he said. 'It is my task to impart them, then counsel my flock if they fall by the wayside.'

'Not to prevent them from falling?'

'That,' Tarchis said with a benevolent smile, 'is for the gods to determine, not for me.'

Don't stop them sinning. Just tell them afterwards how wicked they were. 'Suppose someone asks you for help?'

'Again, it is to Fufluns, not me, that supplication must be directed, for I am a vessel, passive and humble. Priests, Lady Claudia, cannot change fate.'

Really? What about Thalia's guilt over wishing her husband dead? Did Tarchis console her? Did he hell. Invoke the Dark Gods and they answer the call, he had told her. By sitting on his skinny backside in this underground cavern, he changed fate by doing nothing. And was that why a thirteen-year-old girl took her own life? Because the poor little cow had no one to talk to? *Or had Vorda come to him and been rebuffed?*

Claudia smiled radiantly. 'You haven't talked to Terrence about Thufltha?'

Terrence and Tarchis were finger-crossing close, Darius had said, and through Terrence, Darius would have picked up most of his information.

180

'As usual, Terrence and I discussed the forthcoming Bridal Dance and how, between us, we can keep local interest high.'

'Is it waning?'

'When so many traditions are being swallowed up by your culture – and I admit our proximity to Rome doesn't help – there's a very fine line between the old ways and the new.' The priest took off his mitre, rubbed his forehead where the band had dug in, then replaced it with care. 'I do not understand how you Romans can trivialize your gods. With us, every single aspect of life is spiritual. The gods move among us, speaking to us through the language of nature, and we supplicate ourselves before them, whereas you,' his voice harshened, 'you Romans treat them with appalling disrespect. "Make the noses of my hunting hounds keen and I'll give you this ring",' he mimicked. '"Give me a bumper crop of beans this year and this onyx flask will be yours." That is not worship, Lady Claudia. That's horse-trading!'

'Which is no more or less successful than your way.'

He looked down his thin nose at this uppity creature who clearly didn't know that her place was in the kitchen. 'Maybe,' he grunted in a manner that conveyed the opposite, 'but without Terrence backing Fufluns, the paintings on these walls would be plastered over. This shrine would close in favour of a glistening marble edifice to someone called Bacchus.' He almost spat the name out. 'Then there'll be no more dancing, no more brides – and I warn you, young woman, Fufluns will curse you for turning your back on Him. Without His seed to fructify the earth, your vines will shrivel and your hillsides turn barren.'

'Then we must take care not to reject Him,' she said sweetly, distracting his tirade by pretending to have an itch on her calf and giving him a flash of her shapely ankle. 'Going back to Felix, you said he was stripped of his assets . . .' Word association helps, too.

'Every penny,' the priest said, delighted that her itch was persistent. 'Even the house he'd built for his parents in Mercurium. The State confiscated the lot. Turned the old couple on to the street in full view of the populace, and the very next morning Felix's father fell on his sword with the shame of it.' His wrinkled face creased up in recollection.

181

'His mother drank poison, I think. Or maybe she drowned herself. It's such a long time ago; I don't recall all the details. The point is, they were a decent freeborn family who could not live with the dishonour their son visited upon them.'

'What about Mariana, his wife?'

Tarchis shook his red-painted head. 'Sad. Very sad,' he said. 'She was a lovely girl and no one had an ill word to say about her, yet the instant sentence was pronounced, her family disowned her. Treason does this, of course. It taints those it touches, and the stain is ineradicable. One thus understands their desire to disassociate themselves from imperial wrath, as one empathizes with the pain it undoubtedly caused them in renouncing her.'

'Maybe Felix should have thought about that before he dipped his sticky fingers in the Treasury.'

'Surely you are missing the point, Lady Claudia?' The priest leaned back in his chair and studied her with dark, glittering eyes. 'For Thufltha to be invoked and justice served, there has to be a guilty party to punish. If Felix Musa has called on the gods and his plea has been heard, he has stood in front of the Mirror of Truth and been judged by the purity in his heart.'

You can't have it both ways, you sanctimonious bastard. Felix is either dead and innocent. Or he's alive and guilty as hell!

'Mariana was pregnant,' Tarchis said wistfully, 'and such is the suddenness of fate. One day, she is radiant at carrying their first child, the next she's tossed in the gutter like a broken cook pot with little more than the clothes she stood up in. Somebody took the girl in, of course. Once again, I cannot recall who, but Mariana was much loved in Mercurium.'

Claudia began to understand why Felix had embarked on his campaign of vengeance. It might be misguided, but the passion was real enough. Felix Musa wanted the families of those who had wronged him to suffer the way his own loved ones had suffered . . .

'Where can I find Mariana, Tarchis? I realize twelve years have passed, but I really need to talk to Felix's wife.'

'Finding her is easy, Lady Claudia. Talking to her, less so.' A sad smile settled over the old man's face. 'Mariana died giving birth to Felix's stillborn child.'

Twenty-Three

Even as Orbilio approached the temple precinct, its serenity and stillness radiated out. From each salmon-pink column to the mighty oak doors, from the black bowls of divination to the fat sacred cats, Fufluns, god of wine, god of happiness, god of earthly pleasures, was determined to separate his devotees from their daily anxieties. And as these worries dripped off them with every step they took up to the temple, their spirits would be lifted by painted acrobats, dancers, musicians and banqueters brought to life by flaming torches set high on the walls and by thousands of oil lamps flickering like stars in the night sky.

Happiness and pleasure was their birthright. It was Fufluns' job to see to that, so over here the horned god dressed in his customary goatskin toasted newcomers with his brimming goblet. Over there, maidens in bangles and bracelets that encircled ankles and arms, and wearing great silver disks in their ears, danced in welcome, while overhead, instead of the celestial paintings Orbilio was accustomed to seeing, painted roots entwined with Etruscan iris, a reminder that Fufluns made his home deep in the earth, and that this was his world devotees were entering, and that they had left theirs behind.

'I know you!' a little voice chirruped at Orbilio's knee. 'You come to the villa and hold hands with the old witch.'

'I do?'

'Yes, but I don't think Claudia's *really* a witch, because she hasn't changed anyone into a frog, and besides, she's not very old, either. I'm Amanda,' the chirrup continued, 'and this is my bestest friend, Indigo.'

He looked down, but saw only the one bright-eyed child with freckles on her face almost as large as herself.

183

'Ladies.' He performed as deep and gracious a bow as he had ever made. 'Your servant, Marcus.'

Amanda burst into giggles. 'You live in Rome, don't you, servant Marcus?'

'On the Esquiline Hill,' he replied solemnly, before realizing that actually, no, he did not live there. Not any more. His home was now far away. In south-west Gaul . . .

'I wonder if *you're* my father?'

Mother of Tarquin, he hoped not. He wanted children, sure. But not illegitimate ones thrust at him several years after some casual coupling.

'Am I your father? Hm, let me see.' He pretended to consider the matter. 'Do I have your lovely blonde hair?'

'No.'

'Do I have your lovely blue eyes?'

'No.'

He swooped down and pinched her nose between his index and forefinger. 'But I do have your lovely snub nose!'

'Give it back, give it back,' she squealed delightedly, jumping up for the thumb she thought was her nose.

'Only if you're a very good girl.'

'Oh, I'm never good,' Amanda sighed. 'Me and Indigo are *always* in trouble, and if Mummy catches me here at this temple, I'm dead meat for sure.'

'Mummy?'

'You know the things, Orbilio,' a female voice muttered from the corner of her mouth. 'Come from Egypt. Old, wrinkled and completely brainless.'

'That sounds like my mummy, not hers,' he murmured as he replaced Amanda's nose amid another bout of giggles.

It was no coincidence, bumping into Claudia. Ever since he'd requested the report on Vorda's suicide, he'd been wanting to question Timi, and when he returned to the villa this morning and was told Claudia had left to check on Flavia's progress (like hell!), it seemed the perfect opportunity to sound out her dance teacher.

'So then.' Claudia plucked a sprig of oregano from one of the herbal garlands that snaked round the pillars. 'What brings you to the temple this fine, sunny morning?'

'Don't tell me you've forgotten!' Amanda assumed the question had been addressed to her. 'It's the Trumpet Parade, silly! Mummy said I could go into town and watch the procession, only Indigo said we should come here instead, because Mummy says we're not allowed near the temple and that *really* bad things happen to little girls who come here, but I like it, don't you?' Blue eyes widened as they travelled up the pillar to what must have seemed like the sky at the top, it was so far away. 'Promise not to tell, either of you, but I'm coming back tomorrow to play with the kittens. They're *cute*.'

'I tell you what, Amanda.' Marcus knelt down. 'You go down and play with the kittens now, then I'll give you a ride into town on my horse and that way you can still watch the Parade of the Trumpets.'

'You mean I get it *all*?'

'You're a woman,' he said, ruffling her hair. 'Of course you get it all.'

'Out-of-bounds temple, kittens, trumpets, the lot?'

He winked. 'I'll even buy you a bun when we get to Mercurium.'

'Oh, servant Marcus, I love you, I love you, because I'm *ever* so hungry. Did you know I haven't eaten since breakfast?' She tried to wink back at him and failed.

'All of two hours, eh? Then we'd better make it two buns, one for each hour.'

'Excuse me, but it'll be *three* buns by the time we get there,' she sniffed, skipping down the steps.

'Oh, lord, what have I got myself into?' he groaned.

'Serves you right for ignoring your own army training. Never volunteer, remember?'

'I will next time!'

Claudia took a bench facing a fresco of sated nymphs and satyrs sleeping contentedly in Fufluns' sacred hazel grove, their empty goblets sprawled beside them. 'I don't suppose this visit is because you're planning to convert to the red religion?'

'It's the celibacy that worries me,' he replied, taking the opposite seat. 'I don't fancy giving it up.'

185

He liked it when she smiled. The way it started off at one corner of her mouth, as though struggling out against her will, then spreading so that her cheeks bunched up until it finally danced out of her eyes.

'Vorda's death bothers me,' he said, leaning back against the wall. It was a shame he'd missed out on the fun and games with the spirits last night, but he'd needed to speak to the girl's mother. 'Suicide seems right out of character, yet she drowned in the river, Lichas drowned in the river—'

'And Felix's mother might have drowned in the river, as well.'

He sat up. 'Who's Felix?'

Something fluttered over her face and closed down her expression. 'No one. Local legend. Fairytale. What were you saying about Vorda?'

She was lying. Claudia Seferius was doing it again. Dammit, why would she never tell him the truth? When was she *ever* going to trust him?

'Do you think Vorda's death was murder made to look like suicide?' she said in the hurried manner of someone desperate to change the subject.

'No.' He stretched out his legs and crossed them at the ankle. 'Talking to the rivermen – heroes, if you listen to Vorda's mother, who risked eternal damnation diving into that pool – they're quite clear her belongings were neatly arranged on a rock. Shawl folded. Amulets on top.' Of course, it wouldn't be the first time a killer had staged such a scene. However . . . 'It was a still, warm night when she went in, and Kol the goatherd was sleeping not far away.'

Wolves choffed down newborn kids every bit as eagerly as they choffed down newborn lambs.

'He'd seen Vorda earlier, bathing in the river. Dirty little devil crept up to watch, because she was naked, but the problem was, she was crying.'

The impression Kol gave was that if she hadn't been, he'd have stayed a bloody sight longer, but at eleven years old the boy still had a conscience. Feeling that he was prying, he went back to his goats.

'Kol insists he would have heard any struggle, never mind

screams, and he's equally sure no one else came down that path.'

'It's a pity you hadn't been able to inspect Vorda's body,' Claudia said, and when she pushed her hair back from her face, the gesture highlighted the curve of her breasts. 'If she'd fought for her life, there would be abrasions to betray her attacker.'

Orbilio cleared his throat and his impure thoughts. 'I questioned the rivermen about bruising. They insisted there was none.'

'And Vorda's mother would certainly have mentioned it,' Claudia added.

Indeed. No matter how conscientious the believer, the will of the gods only stretches so far.

'There was one odd thing,' he said slowly. 'The divers say her folded shawl was wet when they picked it up, and that struck me as strange. I mentioned it to her mother, who confirmed it was still damp when they handed it over, and I took a good, hard look at that wrap. It smelled of sorrel and the smell was strongest over a series of red stains that were not, I hasten to add, blood, but cochineal dye.'

'Perfectly understandable, Orbilio. Sorrel's a bleach and, though the Etruscans paint their skin, they tend to steer clear of their clothes. For a girl with few possessions, Vorda would be unlikely to want her best shawl stained.'

'I realize teenage girls are over-emotional, but they don't throw themselves to eternal damnation because the dye won't come out of their wrap! Dammit, Claudia, Vorda's death is connected to Lichas and Tages somehow.'

Like the hunch that told him right from the start that Hadrian had not killed his lover, he could feel it. All right, he'd strayed from his theory, but he'd paid the price of listening to his head, not his gut. Somehow Vorda was connected . . .

'Maybe she saw something?' Claudia asked.

'First thing I asked her mother, but Vorda was home the night of the storm, and as far as I can determine, she'd never spoken to Rex.'

They weren't simply miles apart in terms of location. They

were miles apart in class distinction and Rex, as he knew, kept the distance as great as he could.

'I feel like I'm swimming in a thick fog,' he said, 'and what's more, I'm swimming out to sea, not towards the shore.'

'And I thought you said you didn't crawl to your superiors!'

'It beats the breast stroke,' he quipped back.

For several minutes they sat opposite each other, lit by the flickering oil lamps and surrounded by enduringly happy people. Finally, Orbilio scratched at his neck.

'Will you join Amanda, Indigo and me for processions and pies?'

'Typical patrician. Two women are never enough.'

'I shall only worry about that when I start actually seeing Indigo,' he laughed. He stood up. 'No trumpets?'

'I blow mine quite often enough, but Marcus . . .' She stood up and lifted her eyes to his, and now there was no laughter in them. 'If *you* were a seasoned soldier, a general for instance, how would *you* kill somebody on a dark, stormy night?'

The question surprised him. What was she saying? That it wasn't Rex after all? Bullshit. Who else had a motive? Hell, who else knew Lichas was meeting his lover?

'If you mean method—'

'Well, well, what a small world!' Eunice's trill echoed through the lamp-lit cavern. 'Are you two planning on taking up the red religion?'

On her arm was Lars, as was to be expected and indeed welcomed. What was neither expected nor welcome was that they were accompanied by Thalia and her playboy brother.

'When I said it was important to keep the numbers up,' Terrence laughed, 'I was rather thinking of locals.'

Orbilio steadfastly refused to look at the betrothal ring on Terrence's finger as he gripped his wrist in greeting. Even though the bloody thing outshone the lights in the temple.

'Well, you know my motto,' Claudia breezed. 'Think like a local, drink like a local, and Fufluns is the fellow for that!'

As Terrence leaned forward, a look passed between him and Claudia that might have been affection but then again might have been something else. Orbilio couldn't tell because he was focussing on a kiss that landed a hair's breadth from her lips. He hadn't realized he'd been biting his cheek until he tasted blood on his tongue.

'Since *this* lovely man is the temple's chief sponsor,' Eunice said, squeezing Terrence's arm, 'and this lovely man is its keenest publicist,' she wrinkled her nose affectionately at Lars, 'I saw absolutely no reason why these two handsome devils shouldn't show Thalia and me around. After all, it's so terribly primitive and tribal, this dance of the thirteen virgins tomorrow. I mean, can you imagine it in Rome? They'd never even *find* thirteen virgins, much less get the girls to go public!'

'Eunice, you get worse,' Terrence chided with a laugh.

'Don't say that, man,' Lars retorted. 'The woman takes it as flattery.'

'Exactly how it's meant.' When he kissed Eunice's hand, he completely blocked Thalia from view. 'How's Flavia progressing, my sweet?'

'Timi's doing her best,' his sweet replied, and Orbilio thought, yes, Timi had also confided to him that she'd get better results with a three-legged donkey in clogs.

'I'll have a word with Tarchis,' Terrence said. 'See if he can't arrange for extra tuition after the festival. Right, you girls seen enough? Because we need to take our places for the trumpet parade. Claudia?' He held out his arm.

'Thirty seconds,' she promised.

'I thought you said no trumpets?' Orbilio said when the quartet had wandered off.

'I didn't say no,' she said. For gods' sake, his *sweet*? 'I just said no to your offer of a lift. I already had mine arranged.'

'With your fiancé?' He stressed the last word.

'With my fiancé.' So did she.

'I'm sure you two will be very happy,' he said levelly.

'Oh, we are, Marcus, we are.' But there was a glint in her eye that he didn't trust. 'Though there is one other thing before I go. Have I ever asked you for a favour before?'

'Dozens of times.'

'Apart from those?'

He couldn't help the soft snort of laughter that escaped through his nose. 'What do you want?'

'I'd like you to arrest Orson, please. Only my jewel chest is missing, and I think you'll find it in his room in the toyshop, but do hurry, Orbilio. Before that dirty thief pawns my best gems.'

When the Five-Headed Serpent rose from the Darkness and coiled herself round the Chaos, she created Order by dividing the sky into four holy quadrants.

From then on, Order was controlled by the sign of the cross, which signified not only the four different points of the compass, but stood for in front, behind, the left and the right, as well as the future, the past and the here and the now. Then there were the three sacred dimensions, typified by the holy trinity of Uni, Tins and Menvra. Three and four. These were the divine numbers through which Order was kept separate from Chaos and to which all gods contributed equally. Some – like Tins, who wielded the all-powerful sceptre of justice – might enjoy higher status, but the same tireless effort was required by all. Vesta must constantly watch over the fire and protect those hearths that she guarded, just as Vitumnus was obliged to breathe life into the foetus and Thalna obliged to deliver that child into the world.

But with life comes death. It is as much a part of Order as Zirna sustaining her silvery cycle and Horta giving strength to the crops. The gods of the west worked no less industriously.

The Nymphs of Prophesy conferred in hushed undertones with the Seraphs who measured the span of human life with sand that trickled through a holed jug, while the Demons of Death directed the Guardians of the Graves to the tombs where they must stand watch for eternity. Beside wolf-headed Aita, who judged the hearts of the dead before the Mirror of Truth, spells were cast, magic made, contingencies conjured, and there was no rest. Often Charun was required to make two trips in his boat to ferry souls to the west, such was the queue. The fountains from which the pure drank the Waters of Innocence required endless replenishment.

But while Envy and Greed stirred their sulphurous cauldrons and wraiths were guided to walk with their ancestors in the Isles of the Blessed or be chopped into pieces and burnt in the fire to annihilate their souls and their sins, a young man strode through the shadows with confidence. Like Terror and Ignorance, Rumour and Fear, the God of Revenge never slept, and all that was required to engage his services was an oath.

I have perpetrated no falsehood against man.
I have done no wrong in the Place of Truth.

Veive had heard Felix's pledge and was duty bound to obey. It was not his task to question whether the oath was a lie. That was for wolf-headed Aita, who sat on the Throne of Reckoning.

But behind the throne, silver-haired Time sharpened his sickle and the Seraphs measured carefully the thread of one more human life.

Twenty-Four

The day of the Bridal Dance dawned murky and grey, but for the folk of Mercurium this was unimportant. The redheaded moon was the red-headed moon whether she shone brightly or not, and given that so many of their practices had been absorbed by Rome, it was no surprise that this had developed into the single most important date in the Etruscan calendar. It was a day in which to reinforce their national identity. To confirm their proud ancient heritage.

Wandering round the streets, Claudia saw that Romans, too, had become caught up in the excitement. Shops were shuttered, schools had closed, and even the commercial area around the basilica, which was entirely Roman in construction, had been given over to men, women, children, even babies, promenading with red-painted pride. Shoe points were compared, to see whose was the longest and whose curled up most at the tips. Hair fillets were scrutinized for intricacy and innovation, braiding admired round hems, the efficiency of various amulets exchanged in competitive clamour.

'Doesn't it make your blood run that wee bit hotter, seeing our primitive ways at such intimate quarters?' a familiar brogue chuckled.

Under the Etruscan corona, the tunic, the traditional wrap, the only thing to distinguish Lars from the masses was his perpetually smiling face. There was a woman with him, also in national costume, and Claudia remembered that he'd spoken once in passing of a sister. She wondered why he didn't introduce her.

'Seeing isn't necessarily believing,' she retorted. 'I can't understand a word anyone's saying.'

With Latin the principal language these days, her only experience of Etruscan was the written language, which, since it looked like Greek, she'd assumed it would sound like Greek. When Lars's old school friend came through the night Candace first walked the winds, they'd jabbered away in Etruscan, but the conversation had been brief, interrupted by Eunice's rather persistent cousin, and of course the boy was only eleven years old when he'd died. Given the shock of that night, Claudia felt she might be forgiven for not taking much notice, plus you'd expect some distortion in sound quality when the poor kid had trekked all the way up from Tartarus!

'I'll tell you something else,' Lars said. 'We write back to front, as well.'

'That goes some way to explaining the gibberish,' she laughed back.

As he linked her arm with his and led her round the square, translating some of the ancient songs that were being sung, re-enactments of Etruscan history, she was conscious of his musky scent and firm muscle tone. With his over-long nose and stocky build, you could never accuse Lars of being handsome. Yet sex appeal oozed from every pore. The nickname Red Gigolo should be embraced as a compliment, she thought. Not an insult.

'Over here, you see Tyrrhenos leading his people to this land from the east, to escape famine. Those soldiers in armour are retaking Rome, so don't look, don't look!' He pretended to cover her eyes. 'Watch the priests from the College, instead. They're re-enacting the son of Genius rising out of the soil to give his divine pronouncements for Cosmic Order.'

'What happened to Fufluns? I thought this was supposed to be his festival?'

'When we only have the one day, we cram everything in that we can,' Lars said dryly. 'Fufluns takes centre stage when the sun sinks, though. Then the fires are lit, the idol is brought out, the Brides take their oaths and then they dance through the night.'

'Lucky Fufluns. Thirteen times in one night.'

'Like I said, when you only have the one day, you make the most of it,' he chuckled, and turned to the woman on his other arm. 'Isn't that right, pumpkin?'

Eunice?

193

'Don't look so shocked, darling. Tonight I'll be the Roman merchant's widow again. Respectable matron attending the festivities as an honoured guest, and I'll be in robe and slippers, tiara and fan, flanked by a zillion dutiful slaves.'

'With a deliberate smudge of red paint on your cheek,' Claudia said.

'You do, you know me too well!' Eunice laughed. 'But why not? I'm married to an Etruscan who is fiercely proud of his ancestry, and the Empire might look down its nose on what I'm doing today, but I don't regret a single moment.'

Lars took his wife's hand in both of his. 'I never asked this of you, Eunice, and I never expected it either,' he said huskily. 'I'm proud of my heritage, mighty proud, but I'm prouder today than any man has the right to be and I thank you from the bottom of my heart for the way you've honoured me this morning. And that's true? You've no regrets?'

'All right, one.' She leaned towards Claudia. 'Not only does it take an age to paint this wretched stuff on,' she scratched at her forearm, 'but the dye is one stage down from indelible. By the time I've finished scrubbing, my skin will be just the same colour as when I started, I'll be that bloody sore.'

Lars rolled his eyes. 'And to think we're hanging on to this tradition!' He turned to Claudia. 'You'll be at the Dance?'

'Wild horses wouldn't drag me away,' she assured him. 'This is the moon that's going to launch a thousand pruning shears across my vineyards.'

Their laughter was still ringing in her ears as they moved arm in arm on through the crowd, and she watched long after Eunice had turned and shot her a broad, conspiratorial wink over her shoulder.

Is any man better placed to dose his wife with extra minerals every day?

Claudia thought of Eunice screwing her face up as he forced her to sip the vile brew.

It's no great science. You pulverize herbs, turnips, lettuce and broccoli until you're left with the juice. Oh, don't twist your face, woman. With a pinch of mustard, it's practically palatable.

Would he still be cracking jokes as his rich wife tried to

lift her arm and discovered it would not move? That she could no longer swallow? Or speak? Or breathe? Would he still take her hand in both of his as Eunice slowly suffocated to death, her heart and her brain still healthy and fighting and keenly aware of what was happening to her? Would Lars kiss his wife's paralysed eyes and tell her how proud he was then?

As the sun began to push through the clouds, Claudia left the main square and wandered through the twisting narrow streets, where herbs and flowers had been strung between storeys in gaily coloured ropes and pennants flapped in the breeze. On every street corner, musicians thumped drums or clashed cymbals and Claudia thought she would either go deaf or return to the main square, but as she turned the corner by the basilica, well, well, well, guess who?

'That's why they play those percussion instruments,' Larentia said, and once again Claudia was struck by the skilfully dyed hair, the fine golden fillets that had been woven through her exquisitely pinned curls, the pleated and flattering gown. 'To drive away evil spirits.' Larentia sniffed down her long nose. 'Obviously the system is effective.'

'Ren!' Darius chided through a throat full of gravel. 'It's too early in the day to be catty.'

'No, no, that's quite all right,' Claudia breezed. 'Talk to any snake charmer and they'll tell you that they need to squeeze the venom out before they can get any charm.'

Larentia's neck shot forward like a tortoise's out of its shell. 'Did you just call me a . . .?'

'Asp me no questions and I'll tell you no lies, Larentia. Oh, and before you say something you might regret, don't forget you're in company.'

Claudia smiled radiantly at the rest of their party. The debonair playboy, looking particularly smart in his toga for this prestigious occasion. A well-turned-out Thalia in a green robe that complemented her eyes. And the little round man with the little round face that Claudia had met at the Festival of the Lambs. The future husband, she remembered. The one in the Cheese Merchants' Relay.

'Did you win?' she asked him.

'Second,' he said ruefully. 'Rex's team won by a considerable margin, even though he's a producer, not a merchant, and fielded a squad of army-trained runners. Still, it's those tactics that won us an Empire, so I'm not complaining.'

A decent, jolly little man, who didn't deserve to have Thalia foisted on him. Especially an edited version! Claudia studied her, empty-eyed and as quiet as she was yesterday in the Temple of Fufluns, and realized that Terrence must have upped his daily dosage. In the eyes of the cheese merchant, Thalia was a docile, maybe even heartbroken widow. In reality, her brother had drugged his sister into compliance . . .

And this was the man Claudia was supposed to announce her engagement to?

She glanced at the ring on her betrothal finger – sapphires, Mercury's stone – and her mind travelled back to a tall, dark-haired patrician being violently sick in the fishpond. She'd wanted to cheer him up by reminding him it was his idea to thwart Darius's takeover with a marriage of convenience, but pulled back in the nick of time. Girls with criminal backgrounds don't go blabbing to the Security Police that they've worked it so that their bridegroom jilts them at the altar! Dear me, no, but as Terrence said, there were sufficient loopholes in the law, providing one knows where to look – and he hadn't reached the ripe old age of thirty-eight and stayed single without looping himself dizzy. In the eyes of the State, though, betrothal was equal to marriage and once a sweet, innocent party has been jilted, it's back to square one in the eyes of authority. Game, set and match, she'd thought at the time, and honestly, had any woman looked more sincere when she'd promised the long arm of the law that she'd forsaken her criminal habits for ever?

But that was then.

I like grey. Yes, indeed. Why couldn't a thirty-year-old woman do something she wanted without constantly having to worry about other people's opinions? Yet Thalia wasn't even allowed to choose her own frocks, much less her own husband, and to ensure her obedience Terrence plied his sister with opiates. No wonder the poor cow rebelled when-ever she got the chance! When Claudia married Gaius it had been a pact. A mutual agreement which (regardless of

196

Larentia's poison) both parties had entered with their eyes open. Having already palmed his sister off on an old man for reasons of political/financial/class alliance, which took absolutely no account of Thalia's feelings, Terrence was set to do the same thing again, and who knows how an honest cheese merchant might react once he realizes he's been duped by a self-centred neurotic shrew?

'It was an absolutely ghastly marriage.' Eunice's words echoed back. *'Hubby was a banker, much older than her, and they were constantly at each other's throats, with Thalia never able to remember what the quarrel was about, while he could never forget.'*

At the time, the notion of Thalia arguing with anybody struck Claudia as odd. Now she realized that they'd quarrelled because argument was the only way Thalia could express herself. That was why she couldn't remember what it was about. Nothing to do with forgetfulness or stupidity. She couldn't remember for the simple reason that it wasn't important. Fighting back was all that had mattered – the desperate need to exert some independence, prove she had some form of identity – until finally, between her husband, her brother and no doubt his father before him, the last flame of spunk was doused when the banker died at the hot springs. She hadn't killed him. His own ego had seen to that, drinking too much, eating too much, exercising too little. Yet Thalia had been so conditioned by bullies that she actually believed she killed him, simply by wishing him dead. How much had Terrence paid Tarchis, she wondered?

'Won't you join us, my sweet?'

When he planted a kiss on her cheek, Claudia felt her gorge rise. 'As much as I'd love to, darling, a problem's arisen with the shipping of last year's vintage.'

'Can't it wait till tomorrow?'

''Fraid not.' Fortune, there are times when I could kiss you! 'Here's my ride now.'

The hired gig clip-clopping over the cobbles wasn't hers, but Terrence wasn't to know, and as she ran off to hail a very confused driver, she saw Larentia knocked aside by three boisterous youths waving an upended wine jug. As her

197

mother-in-law went flying, Darius rushed forward and lifted her to her feet, and while the others fussed over the shocked Larentia, brushing the splattered dregs from her robe and checking for bruises and grazing, Claudia noticed that Darius had taken off after the drunken trio. She watched him grab one by the scruff of the neck. Yanked him back. Forced him to apologize to Larentia.

'Cosa,' she told the driver.

No longer the confident, spiteful old battle-axe, was she? Just old. A frail old woman whose hands were shaking, whose hair had fallen loose and whose rouge stood out on her cheeks like ink spots.

'Sorry, missie.' The driver shrugged in apology. 'I'm booked to drive the magistrate's brother to his villa out in the country.'

Claudia slipped off a silver bangle set with mother-of-pearl. 'Is that a fact?'

'No, miss, don't reckon it is.' The bangle disappeared with a grin that showed every one of the driver's three teeth. 'Reckon the real fact is that my poor mule went lame and I couldn't make the appointment.'

As the mule cut a swathe through the actors and dancers, she glanced back. Above the bob of Etruscan caps and priestly mitres, Terrence's sandy mop towered over Darius's close Caesar-crop, Larentia's squiffy gold ribbons and his sister's immaculate coiffure. A day for theatricals in every sense, she reflected, as Larentia leaned on her fiancé's arm. But wait!

Suppose Felix was *innocent?*

Suppose, for a moment, Tarchis was right and Felix ended up serving ten years down the silver mines for a crime he didn't commit? How bitter would that make him?

The driver chatted amiably as the gig passed through the city gates amid hordes of clamouring beggars, but for once his gossip fell on deaf ears.

Claudia began to draw up a picture of a man who started out labouring – daytime donkeying, the tavern-keeper called it – and rose to riches through farming oysters in the Bay of Naples. A man who didn't give up. When his first efforts off Cosa didn't succeed, he moved south, to where presumably the climate, the tides, the rocks were more suitable, and he'd stuck with his disastrous first marriage for fifteen whole years. Years, moreover, that weren't simply loveless but childless, and for a self-made man the desire to perpetuate his name must have been strong indeed.

As the gig trotted past the Temple of Fufluns, its bronze tripods gleaming in the sun that had now banished all clouds, she fleshed out her portrait of Felix. Coloured in the parts where loneliness and despair turned into joy with Mariana. How he moved his parents to Mercurium, one big happy family, even to divorcing Aurelia without acrimony. Hardworking, kind, caring, honourable. The picture grew – but there was a gap. A gap between the exhilarating moment, a mere few months after his divorce, when his new wife announces she's pregnant and when his world collapses at the trial.

Same old question: why would a man who had never been happier and was eagerly awaiting his first child dip his fingers into the Imperial treasury? The assets that the State seized after his sentence proved he hadn't needed the money. So what then? Not enough thrills in his life, he needed more? Well, he got them. Ten years' hard labour, during which his father commits suicide, his mother ditto, while his in-laws disown his shamed pregnant wife, who has to lodge with a neighbour before she dies giving birth to their stillborn child. If Felix was guilty, he'd got all the thrills any man would need in a lifetime. But if he was innocent . . .

If he was innocent, he'd have plenty of time to ask himself who set him up. And if six stalwarts of the community had independently testified in open court that they'd seen him taking money that he hadn't taken, surely, he'd argue, it must be to cover their own tracks? Felix wouldn't know why and by the time his ten years were up, he'd care even less. In fact, after ten years breaking rocks it's doubtful he'd care about anything. He'd be released devoid of feelings, of all emotions, save one: revenge. Revenge, which he plots like a draughtsman as he sets out to destroy those who destroyed him.

Nice hypothesis, she thought as they approached the hot springs, only there was a problem. Darius has money. Lots of money, in fact, and this wasn't the first time she'd questioned his wealth. One of her earliest actions had been to check on the artisans who'd carried out the renovation work and confirm that the bills hadn't been charged to her. But no. The men had been paid cash for their efforts. (An opportunity Felix would surely not have overlooked, had the poor man but known he could have bankrupted what was left of Gaius's estate!)

Fine. If Darius is who he claims to be, his hands might well be as tough as those of a man who'd spent the last decade mining ore, and his skin might well be naturally tanned, rather than quickly brought up to colour quickly after being bleached from living underground like a mole. But if Felix was masquerading as Darius, how did he get his hands on so much cash? Felix's assets had been stripped from him, every last copper quadran. It's why his parents were thrown out of their home. Why Mariana couldn't afford a place of her own, or pay for a physician to guide her through childbirth. It was money, or rather lack of it, which cost her life and probably that of her child.

And there lay the root of the problem. The Felix who stood trial twelve years ago could not *possibly* afford to install Candace in Larentia's life, much less fund major renovations at the villa. Plus changing names, appearance, indeed planning every last detail entailed an awful lot of hard work and effort for a man who was guilty! So could Claudia be wrong about Darius? Could Felix be innocent after all?

Yes, of course.

And the sun would shine right through the night, and the moon would drop out of the sky!

Claudia leaned back in the gig and stretched her feet out on the buckboard. This ought to work out quite nicely. Swap Felix for a clean sheet and I'm home and dry on the Security Police front! Not that she'd wanted to spring Felix on him as a total surprise. Humiliation is never an asset in one's quest for a deal. But she was proud of the way she'd laid the foundations.

If you were a seasoned soldier, a general for instance, how would you kill somebody on a dark, stormy night?

By raising the question, it would occur to Marcus Cornelius sooner or later that, had Rex wanted to kill Lichas, he would have killed him. No messing, the boy would have been dead. None of this stab 'em and dump 'em stuff. Rex would claim self-defence and who wouldn't have believed his story? Even Rosenna couldn't be certain her brother hadn't picked a fight with the wrong man. Same with Tages. *He jumped me, I killed him.* Quite right. National heroes do not hide murder. Rex would have left the bodies in the open as proof.

'Stop,' she ordered the driver. 'Pull over to the side for a minute.'

Through the willows and poplars she'd noticed a soft, swirling ribbon of mist as the steam rose from the river and the air had filled with the sound of water rushing over the rocks, and the faint smell of sulphur. Everything hinges on these wretched hot springs; they were central to every move in the game – and every player. Eunice and Lars. Hadrian and Lichas. Darius and Candace. Thalia and her husband. Terrence, who owned the land, while even Rex feared Candace would be accessing the Gateway to the Underworld here. What was the old war horse worried about, Claudia wondered? Was it genuine altruistic concern, in his capacity as influential patrician, about a possible resurgence in local superstition that would put a barrier between Etruscan and Roman? Or something deeper, and far more personal?

Through the archway that led to the square of Lavernium, she watched acrobats tumble and jugglers tossing cups, while actors in cork masks performed humorous mimes and dancers swirled and gyrated in rainbow tunics shot with silver and gold.

'Judith and Ezekiel,' she murmured softly. 'Judith and bloody Ezekiel!'

'What was that, miss?'

'Nothing.' She indicated for the driver to move on. 'I thought I recognized some friends of mine, that's all.'

It wasn't the Hebrew twins in person, of course. They were firmly ensconced back at the villa, going through their creepy paces as usual. But the performers in the square made the connection in her mind – all the performers, as it happened – and a slow smile settled over Claudia's face as another piece of the puzzle dropped into place.

High in the sky, the moon prepared to comb her lovely red hair.

Twenty-Five

*B*oom, *boom, boom-a-doom-a-dum-dum.*
   The pounding of the drums, soft and insistent, cut through the night like a heartbeat.
   Boom, boom, boom-a-doom-a-dum-dum.
   There was no blare of trumpets, no clashing of cymbals to signal that the transition from the day spent rejoicing in Etruscan heritage had become the night when Fufluns was worshipped. Just the lazy brush of stick against stretched animal skin.
   Boom, boom, boom-a-doom-a-dum-dum.
   Over and over again.
   A hush descended on the sanctuary. A thousand people fell silent. The flames on the torches were dimmed. Sacred incense wafted over the precinct, a heady blend of frankincense, cedar, cinnamon and juniper, and in the Pool of Plenty, where moths fluttered round the floral garlands that wreathed the marble satyrs and nymphs, the moon reflected silver and proud. As the drumbeats continued to pound, a procession emerged from the darkness. Priests in mitres descended the steps, followed by acolytes in soft caps, and now chanting filled the air from the choir, soft, wordless, like a gentle exhalation of musical breath. A whisper. A blessing. A boon. His long robes swishing the ground, Tarchis stepped forward, raised his hands to the heavens and made the sign of the cross.
   'Today the powers of Zirna have proved greater than Her brother Aplu's,' he pronounced, 'for the Moon Goddess has sent His clouds scurrying and captured the stars for Her own.'
   These were good portents, he added solemnly, not just for the Bridal Dance, but for the fruit of the vineyards and the fruitfulness of the earth.
   'Through Silver Zirna, the sky gods have given the

Marriage of Fufluns Their blessing. Let the ceremony begin.'

In a finger-snap, reverence gave way to revelry as the musicians upped tempo, the choir lifted their voices and the whole crowd began to clap, cheer and stamp their feet. Sulphur was sprinkled on to the torches and, as the flames flared, a gilded litter appeared at the entrance to the temple. On the litter sat the famous red idol of Fufluns, so heavy it required a score of muscular bearers to manoeuvre it down the steep steps.

'By the Falcon of the Sun, by the Vultures of the Moon,' Claudia whispered, 'I know how you do it.'

'What do you know, my child?'

There it was. That deep, rich smile that never quite made the journey to her eyes. Was it the smile of a cold, scheming bitch, milking the gullible for all they were worth? A smile tempered by caution, lest human emotions betray the facade? Or was Candace hiding something? Even – possibly – scared? Claudia thought back to that first night she'd summoned the spirits and the feline look she'd held with Darius. She remembered the hot springs and the long, evaluating glance she'd given him from the corner of her eye, and to his granite gaze as she swept into the bath house, flanked by her silent servants. Claudia was wrong. Candace wasn't his mistress . . .

'I know you extinguish the lights, burn a tree full of incense resin and employ a harpist to enter the gateway to the afterlife,' she said.

'I create an atmosphere where the dead can feel comfortable, yes.' Candace nodded. 'The perfume and the music honour them.'

'Actually, they mask any foreign smells brought into the room by your accomplices and drown any sounds they might make.'

The sorceress swivelled her head to look down on her. 'Whether you are a believer or not, the forces of the supernatural surround us all. I am—'

'Merely their instrument.' Claudia shot her a radiant smile. 'Just like your harp. Just like Judith and Ezekiel are your instruments, too.'

Thirteen virgins skipped down the steps in time to the boisterous music. Each bride wore a different costume but

each had her skin stained with the same cochineal . . .
Correction. *Twelve* virgins came skipping down. The third
from the back lumbered like an arthritic carthorse. Good old
Flavia. Always stands out from the crowd. Claudia cheered
her stepdaughter on as the brides formed a semi-circle round
their carved, leering groom, but when Tarchis stepped in to
the ring, the mood switched back to one of solemnity.

Boom, boom, boom-a-doom-a-dum-dum.

'I know about the folding doors,' she told Candace.

And while the priest blessed each moon in turn that she
would fulfil her promise of richness and plenty for the forthcoming year, Claudia spelled it out. How Darius had hired
her. Arranged for her to meet Larentia at the hot springs.
How Candace had persuaded the poor woman to take herself
into the hills to filter the epidemic of bad luck that was going
around. She ran through how, during Larentia's absence,
Darius set about his renovation work, which, after consulting
with Candace, included the installation of pipes leading up
from the villa's boiler room. Because there was only one
place where a surge of smoke could escape in puffs on
command: the dining hall, which sat directly over the furnace.
And since such pipes required considerable demolition work,
Darius had no choice but to go the whole hog and knock
out a wall. With the miracle of folding doors, who would
notice the additional plasterwork all round the sides?

Boom, boom, boom-a-doom-a-dum-dum.

'That's how the smoke got into the room, the sulphur, the
voices – and there was no cold air.'

Only an illusion created by constantly referring to the chill
that descended and rubbing her arms. And the loved ones?
Only someone close to the bereaved would be able to draw
out pet names and that's why the conversations were brief.
Keep it going too long, and whichever dupe Candace had
targeted would quickly pick up on the odd speech and mannerisms of their dear departed. Oddities that she couldn't guar-
antee would be smoothed over by constantly passing them
off as Stygian errors!

'Then there's the touchy-feely business,' Claudia said before
the sorceress had time to interrupt. 'It bothered me that not

only was smoke and sulphur infiltrating our lovely linens, or even that our loved ones were chatting to us as though they were in the next room, but that they could *see* us.'

Which, of course, they could. Not in the dark, but that's why Candace gathered the group in to such a tight circle. So her accomplices could run round the room, having practised beforehand and in the sure and certain knowledge that every piece of furniture was where Candace promised it would be. She'd taken care to make any adjustments – straightening chairs, moving tables – while lighting the incense burners, so that, dressed in black and with their skins blackened with soot, Judith and Ezekiel were invisible as they crept up from the furnace room through a trapdoor beside the folding doors. They trained so regularly that every movement was synchronized, each knowing what the other was thinking, so while one imitated Rex's late wife or, say, Larentia's dead son down in the boiler room, the other moved around the dining hall, brushing a shoulder, an arm, a hand as they passed to reinforce the presence of the spirits.

Boom, boom, boom-a-doom-a-dum-dum.

Once they were together in the dining hall, they were no longer able to project their voices, using sighs, sobs, whispers, sniggers to make it seem the spirits were everywhere and nowhere, and now of course they were free to hurl vases, overturn figurines, pick up Candace's gold-thread shawl and shake it, co-ordinating their well-rehearsed routines with precision.

'If this is true,' Candace said stiffly, 'then I am as much a victim as anybody else. Remember, I was in a dead faint every time.'

'*Victim?*' The crowd hissed for her to shush when Claudia laughed. 'The only victim here was the plant you ripped up to prepare your potion, and I'm guessing it was black hellebore.'

They grew in abundance up in the Apennines, inducing the deepest of sleeps which could be regulated by the dose.

'Your cynicism falls off me like rain from a palm leaf,' Candace drawled, though Claudia noticed there was a tighter set to her jaw than when their conversation started. 'I know my powers.' In the artificial light, the skin on her unscarred forearm gleamed as she held it out, clenching her fist in defiance.

'That?' Claudia snorted. 'You doused the lamps before rolling your sleeve up, and all you cut through, Candace, was a piece of black vellum containing a small bladder of pig's blood.'

'Then where was it?' The velvet contempt still carried conviction. 'If Judith and her brother daren't risk entering the circle, who cleared away this mysterious patch?'

'Oh, Candace, give it up!' Claudia was getting cross now. 'Darius took it, who else? For gods' sake, can't you see that it's *over?* It's not just what I know, it's why. Why Felix impersonated Darius.' That shook the bitch. 'Why he hired you, why he's destroying the lives of so many people. Hell, I even know why you crop your bloody hair!'

To control it. Just as the hot springs were central to the actors in this sordid charade, so was control. It was why Candace kept her springy fuzz short and why she smelled of the incense she burned. Not because she used so much, but to control a different smell. A balm of Gilead smell. One whose painkilling properties would not only help a miner's bad back, but would ease other problems, emotional problems, because control was everything here.

'And drugs. Mustn't forget them.'

Drugs were also a form of control, though god knows everyone used them in one form or another. In homes and in temples, lavender oil was used to calm, mint to stimulate, lemon balm and chamomile to refresh, but the effect was no different. They were intended to alter another person's mood, generating that transition without that person's knowledge or consent, though for the most part the change was as benign as it was well-intentioned and welcome.

'Have you noticed how everyone uses them?' Claudia clapped as the holy sacrament of marriage between moon and earth was blessed with wine. 'Terrence on Thalia, Darius on himself, you on Larentia to keep her happy.'

One finely plucked brow rose in disdain. 'I cast spells to protect your mother-in-law. I am not responsible for her state of mind.'

'Wrong again. Without you slipping her happy pills – and this time my guess is lime flowers dried, crushed and added to her wine – Darius would have come unseated at the very first bend of the racetrack.'

Candace tossed her head dismissively. 'Your mother-in-law laughs because her spirits are high. She jokes because she is at ease.'

'Would she be at ease if she knew her suitor was Felix?'

Candace swallowed. 'Felix has done some bad things, but he is not a bad man.'

'Then you're even more callous than I took you for, you miserable bitch, or doesn't murder count as a "bad thing" in Kush?'

Feline eyes narrowed. 'Don't talk to a Kushite about murder! I could tell you tales that would freeze your blood and turn your hair white, and what if Felix *is* tortured by memories? What if he *is* tormented by the fate that befell his wife and his family? This has only come about through the injustice of a conspiracy involving your own husband, and don't pretend to me Gaius Seferius was an angel.'

'If you must know, Candace, he was a bastard.'

Ruthless and brutal in his business dealings, while socializing meant touring the child brothels in search of small boys. Claudia hadn't shed tears for her husband. But in many ways Gaius was an honourable cove, and the idea of him raiding the Imperial treasury seemed anomalous to the point of incredulity. Also, if he and the other five had been co-conspirators, his mother would have made the connection . . . and so would they.

Darius, Claudia realized, wasn't as smart as he thought . . .

'But at least Gaius was an uncomplicated bastard,' she told Candace, 'while you, my little wind-walking fraud, have been used. Played like the harp you use in your charades – and I suppose he conned you into funding his exploits?'

Candace laughed. 'See? You know nothing! What I earn is mine. Mine!' She held out her arms to reveal the welter of gold, and yes, always gold. Maybe that's why she took balm of Gilead? To counter the pain of carrying so much weight. 'I told you on Market Day, no one can take this away from me, not Felix, not a thief, not even your State, so there will never be any question of *my* breaking the law.'

With a crash of cymbals the marriage ceremony was brought to an end, thousands of tiny candles were lit round the idol and the tempo changed again. With wild music and free-flowing wine, the Bridal Dance was about to begin. In the reflection of the sacred pool, the moon rippled silver and full.

'This is about more than money,' Claudia said. 'More than just control.' There was something Candace still wasn't telling.

'I have lived through things I should not have lived through, endured what no living person should have endured,' the sorceress hissed. 'Gold paves the road to freedom like no other. Never more shall I be enslaved!'

The passion exploded like a ripe melon, and suddenly Claudia saw the reason for Candace's mask. How do you preserve your own identity when you have none? You create it. By surrounding herself with mystery and magic, then portraying herself as an instrument of the supernatural, slave becomes master at last.

'Except somewhere along the line, morals become blurred, ethics fade and compassion dies like a thirteen-year-old girl with a rock tied round her waist.'

As the crowd surged forward, eager for a better view of the virgin moons, a child was sent flying and began to cry.

'How dare you!' Candace pressed her nose to Claudia's and the light in her eyes was pure fire. 'This gold is not for the pursuit of avarice. This gold assures our future . . .'

'Whose future? Lichas'? Tages'? Vorda's?' The child's crying was closer now, and more harrowing for its insistence. 'Whose freedom are you buying with the blood of their innocence?'

But the answer was not the one Claudia expected, nor did it come from Candace's mouth.

'Mummy, Mummy, Indigo's hurt! Someone trod on her and she's bleeding,' a tiny voice sobbed, stuffing a grazed elbow under Candace's nose. 'Kiss it better, Mummy! Kiss it better!'

Twenty-Six

Many things change but the land never does, and regardless of who conquers whom, the soil is enduring and the cycles of the moon never waver. She begins as a crescent, young, fresh and pure. The virgin who waits her turn. Then she matures into womanhood, ripe, round and fecund, adored by all who gaze up at her. Finally, though, her time comes. She grows old, shrinking away until she fades into nothingness, then a brand new moon is born and the sequence starts over again.

No moon is ever the same. What has passed once can never be repeated, not in the same manner, Aplu's weather staff will see to that. Each moon is revered for her own self, and there was a saying among the Etruscans: no moon, no man – meaning that any child born between the moons was cursed by the gods – and thus, of all the traditions dear to their heart, it was this the people held closest. Fufluns and his brides stood at the very soul of the fatherland. Life versus death; harvest versus crop failure; happiness versus sorrow. The cycle of three, like the cycle of the moon. Sacred. Respected. Sacrosanct.

Each moon had her role to play in the farming year, and no role was more valuable than her sister's. Without the planting moon there could be no harvest moon. The ploughing moon was as crucial to farmers as the hunter's moon, the lambing moon and the midsummer moon.

Claudia watched the first little bride take her place inside the candle-lit circle, but her mind was not on the dance. She saw only a small girl with fair hair and freckles whose face was creased up in pain, yet who still turned to her best friend first. The invisible Indigo.

'I found her in the mountains when she was a baby,'

Candace mouthed over Amanda's head as she ferociously cradled her daughter. 'She'd been abandoned, exposed and left to die, and believe me, I know how that feels. I gave her a home and I gave her love, and that's why I keep earning,' she added. 'That's why I need gold so badly.'

Claudia sighed. If only money was what children needed! It helps. God knows it helps. But what Amanda needed more was her mother's time, not her money – and the girl needed stability, too.

'Darius told Mummy that Indigo was bad for me and Mummy should stop moving round and that would get rid of her, but I told Indigo not to worry, no one's going to get rid of her, because why should Mummy listen to what Darius tells her? She'll be moving on soon, we always do, but this time it won't matter, because Indigo and me are running away to live with my father in Rome, only you promise not to tell Mummy, won't you?'

Dammit, the bastard was right. It wasn't fair on the girl to keep uprooting and moving on. She needed real children to be friends with.

Taking a deep breath, Claudia had clenched her fists and broken her oath to Amanda.

But it was better Candace heard from an impartial source that her daughter was so unhappy that she planned to run away, and it shocked her rigid to learn that Amanda preferred to start a new life with an imaginary father and an imaginary friend, rather than continue with the life she already had. Feeling like an intruder, Claudia had left mother and daughter mingling their tears of pain, hugging each other tight. Will anyone ever understand love, she wondered? Has anyone ever actually got it right?

Absently, she watched the little moons dance in the flickering, fairy-lit circle. The first was dressed in diaphanous silver, another in a headdress of crescent horns, the third clad in a costume of clinging ivy. And *now* Claudia's attention was focussed.

For a split second, she swore she could smell the stale sweat of the sailors, hear their coarse jeers ringing once again in her ear. She was their age when she began, too. The difference was, it had been every night, not just once a year, but orphaned, penniless and alone in the slums, dancing was her only escape. Like a dam bursting its barricade, memories flooded back with every sensual sway. The rhythm. The pulse. The arched back and the come-on look in the eye. As the fifth moon swept into the ring, chin held high, skirts billowing, Claudia recalled her own half-parted lips, the pretence to each leering sailor that this dance was for him and that she couldn't get enough of his pawing as she stretched, coiled and gasped her way through her routine. *Except the performance here tonight was authentic.* As the fire moon stroked her budding breasts with teasing sensuality, arousing the earth god with the thrust of her hips, Claudia realized the girl wasn't acting. Of course, it wasn't the same for all the performers. Three had danced stiffly and had been acutely self-conscious. But when a virgin bride peels off her clothes and gyrates with erotic abandon . . .

'I see you have to scrape around to find a virgin these days,' she quipped to Timi, standing at the edge of the circle.

So far, three out of five needed no husband to initiate them into the art of the bedchamber. These were practised seducers who knew exactly what they were doing.

'Lady Claudia!' Timi bridled with indignation. 'It is the girls' very innocence that arouses Fufluns to the state of excitement where He can no longer contain His seed and in spilling it, makes the earth fertile. I *personally* verify my pupils' virginity!'

'If they're not pure, they don't dance?'

'Virginity is the gift they bring to the earth god,' she snapped. 'Without it, they dishonour Him.'

'But there are no half measures here,' Claudia pointed out. 'The girls are either completely inhibited or . . . um . . . they're not.'

Timi flattened her hackles. 'That is the god's own will,' she stated. 'I must admit, I have been extremely surprised by some of my brides. Their movements are more . . . how can I say . . . *suggestive* than any choreography I've taught them.'

She let Claudia into a secret. That it was her quest to enlighten her pupils that, although they lived in a male-dominated society, there was no reason for men to have it all their own way. There was fun to be had for women too in the bedchamber, and, although she didn't tell Tarchis, she emphasized the pleasures of receiving, rather than giving.

'But they're not,' Claudia said. 'What those girls are enacting out there – in fact, *exactly* what your little fire moon is doing with that tinder stick at the moment – is pleasing her man.'

'My point precisely,' Timi said, smiling. 'We can impart our personal viewpoints till the cows come home, but when the time comes to dance, it is the god's will inside the pupil's, not a mortal's. It is Fufluns who shows His virgins the way.'

Maybe so, Claudia thought. But it wasn't Fufluns who showed Vorda how to tie a rock round her waist. And it wasn't Fufluns who stuck a knife into Lichas!

I can see you working out how Candace did it, what Darius's game is, what's behind the run of bad luck and why Lars married Eunice before the moon combs her lovely red hair.

Perhaps it was seeing Supersnoop over there, leaning nonchalantly against a pillar with his arms folded over his chest, that made Orbilio's words echo in Claudia's head. But either way, she had done it. She'd worked out how Candace summoned the spirits, what Darius's game was, how he was behind the run of bad luck, why Lars married Eunice, and now here was the moon combing her lovely red hair.

Except Claudia hadn't been able to connect Felix to Lichas . . . or Tages . . . or Vorda – and without hard evidence the bastard would walk.

Frankly, she had a better chance of solving that political crisis in Mauritania.

The flames of the torches flickered on the temple walls, and the candles round the idol shimmered like sun on the ocean. As the wine flowed freely and the music grew wilder, the harvest moon skipped into the circle and as Flavia offered herself to the earth god, no one noticed a young woman with flaming red hair pass through the crowd.

Or the knife in her hand.

The patrician she sought was leaning with his back against one of the salmon-pink pillars. He had his arms folded over his chest and was concentrating hard on the dance. Rosenna waited until he raised his hands to applaud.

Then aimed her blade straight for his heart.

Twenty-Seven

The day dawned warm, soft and golden, bathing the landscape in the same glow that had suffused it for centuries. Subtle and gentle, tranquil and pure, the sun promised springtime and growth and renewal. For the people of this land, the people who had, for the same centuries, farmed its fields, fished its rivers and hunted its woods, the dawn was a time of contentment. Exhausted from revelry, satiated from wine and secure in their time-honoured identity, they slipped away from the temple. Thousands dwindled into hundreds, hundreds became scores, scores filtered away into nothingness until only the smell of incense and stale wine remained in the precinct.

That, and a pool of dark blood.

Kneeling over it, Claudia stared at the sticky puddle. Shouldn't it be blue, she wondered dully? Shouldn't it at least have been blue? Rocking on her knees, she could not leave this place. The Etruscans believed in Guardians of the Graves who stood over the tombs and protected the soul for eternity. But what of blood? Who guarded the blood to stop blowflies from feasting? To stop rats licking it up? To prevent ghouls from stealing his lifeblood away?

Life.

She tried to say the word aloud, but nothing could get past the rock in her throat, and you'd think it would hurt, but it didn't. Everything was numb. Leaden. Completely without feeling, and for some reason she couldn't see properly, her mind wouldn't work, nor would her legs or her arms. And there was rain falling now. Rain from a clear blue sky, that bounced down to leave crown-shaped imprints in the blood. Oblivious to the tears that coursed down her cheeks, Claudia rocked herself back and forth. So much of it. Like her mother's, it was the quantity that always surprised her. How much blood one stupid body contains . . .

Marcus.

But she daren't speak his name aloud. If she did . . . if she did . . .

When she closed her eyes all she could hear was the wild, wild music, and all she could see were the dancers. Every one whirling, swirling, blurring into one by the lights of the flickering candles.

Flavia.

This time Claudia didn't even try to say the word aloud. She would never speak it again. She hated the name. Hated her. *Hated*, you hear? Because while she was waiting, watching that little bitch run through her dance, Rosenna was sticking her—

No, don't. Don't think about that. Forget Rosenna. Forget Flavia. Forget everything. Forget, forget . . .

Please Jupiter, let me forget.

Twenty-Eight

The mare galloped through the arched gateway and up the long drive to the villa, foam flecking its mouth from where it had been ridden so hard. In the courtyard, Claudia jumped down but there was no groom rushing forward to take care of the horse. Twenty-four hours of non-stop revelry had taken their toll, and whether bailiff's house or dormitory, stable yard or guest room, snoring emanated from each open window. Even the dogs were too tired to snuffle and lay slumped on their sides in the yard or draped over doorways, paws and noses twitching in sleep.

She flung open the atrium doors, but nothing moved in this ghost villa, save a butterfly searching for a way out and even those wings were silent. She paused at the fountain and sluiced cool water over her face. The reflection that peered back came straight from Hell. A gargoyle tormented by demons.

The temple physicians were good. They had to be, didn't they? Yes, of course they were. Competent. Professionals. They had all the skills, the equipment, the medicines, the technology. Life-savers weren't they, these doctors? Well, obviously. They wouldn't have bundled him into their infirmary so quickly if they didn't know what they were doing. *Or would they?* Who consulted the physics of Fufluns? Impotent men? Barren women? Drunks to be cured of the shakes? Beside the bust of Apollo, she reeled, grabbing the shrine to the household gods for support.

What support?

She tossed her head and squared her shoulders. What did the gods care? If they cared, they wouldn't have let that stupid temple acolyte throw a bucket of water over the flagstones and wash away Marcus's blood. Oh, she'd flown at the idiot, scratching his face, his arms, clawing his neck, but too late. Too late. The blood – so much blood – that ought to have been blue was already gone. All traces of him washed down the steps.

Now somebody . . . oh yes somebody . . . had to pay.

'Get up, you bastard!'

Darius pulled at the coverlet, but it was already in a heap on the floor.

'I said get up, you murdering coward.'

'Claudia?' Fresh from sleep, his voice held even more gravel. 'What's the matter?'

As he propped himself up on one elbow, she could see the stubble on his head where the hair needed shaving to keep up the pretence of baldness.

'What's the matter, he says, like he hasn't heard about Rosenna's settling of scores!' In a flash she was across the room, holding a knife to his throat. 'The girl's spitting nails, apparently, since one out of three is bad odds in her book.'

According to the temple guard who was first on the scene, Rosenna believed that by stabbing Orbilio, she'd improve her chances of killing Hadrian and then, while Rex was finally understanding how it felt to lose someone he loved, she would complete her mission and bring peace to her dead brother's soul. What happened to her didn't matter, she told the guard as he carried her away. But now, because she'd cocked up, the louse and its nit would go free. Remorse, it appeared, was not high on Rosenna's priorities.

'Do you know the penalty for stabbing the Security Police with a skinning knife?' Claudia pressed the point of her own into Darius's throat. 'Cruci-bloody-fixion.'

And Rosenna didn't damn well deserve it. She was as much a victim as Lichas, because, in killing her brother, Darius put that knife in her hand.

'I had nothing to do with that.' He wasn't frightened. Concerned, yes. But not scared. *He should be.* 'Ask Larentia. Ask Terrence. I was at the front with them when she struck.'

It took every ounce of restraint not to plunge that blade into the artery that throbbed in his throat.

'And where,' Claudia hissed, 'was Felix Musa?'

He blinked rapidly. 'Felix Who-sir?'

Still bluffing, eh? Even now, you're still trying to bullshit your way out?

'Felix,' she whispered, leaning so close that she felt the heat from his body, 'is the scumbag who sees the six upright citizens who witnessed him pocketing bags of Imperial gold as members of some kind of conspiracy, which they supposedly concealed by framing him.'

That got his attention.

'Felix,' she said, 'is the scumbag who spent ten years down the silver mines, making his heart as hard as the rocks he was breaking. And when his time was served, this scumbag visited the same suffering upon the witnesses as had been visited upon those he himself had loved, grinding them down by heartache and fear, making sure their assets were eroded as his had been taken, their lives ruined beyond salvation.'

'And what? You think I'm this Felix character?' His Adam's apple moved up and down, but his voice, though characteristically rusty, remained even. 'Claudia, I know you're upset about Marcus, but . . .'

'You want to take this argument public? Explain why you shave your head? Why your cough sounds like every other poor sod's who's served time down the mines, because their lungs have been scoured raw with the dust? Or will you just whip off the tunic that you cling so coyly to at the hot springs, to prove there are no lash marks scarring your back?'

'I keep my clothes on because I'm shy and . . . Look, I don't have to justify myself.' It's not easy to smile with a knife pressed to your throat, but he made a pretty good try. 'You're bound to fear the loss of control if I marry Larentia, it's natural, but you can keep the wine business, I don't want it, I don't need it . . .'

'Save your excuses for the Ferryman. I thought Candace must have been subsidising you, but now I realize you'd been skimming off some of the ore and salting it away while you worked. Perhaps you had a guard in on the scam, I don't know, but one thing's for sure: stealing from the State is a capital offence. There'll be no second chance for you this time.'

If she didn't know better, she'd almost believe she read relief in his amber-quartz eyes. 'You don't understand.'

'Wrong. I don't *care*, but you should know this, Felix Musa. So help me, I will see you in Hell if he dies.'

There. She had said it.

If. He. Dies.

But he must not. He cannot. She would not allow it. A pain welled up, the likes of which she'd never known. It happened so quickly, that was the thing. Laughing one minute, on the banks of the River Styx the next, and the worst part was, she hadn't even *known* until it was over. So busy watching some stupid dance . . .

She blinked back the tears and beneath the tip of the blade, Darius shuffled. 'They deserved what they got,' he rasped. 'The sour wine in the tavern, the fire at the parchment ware-house . . .'

'Don't sell yourself short, Felix! You didn't just torch it the once, you made sure the merchant could never trade from that building again, like the kilns you so persistently sabo-taged, the well that you poisoned, the donkey you killed, the old woman you led on, the axle you patiently sawed through—'

'Oh, for goodness' sake!'

As he jerked up in protest, the knife pricked his skin and a dribble of blood ran down his throat. He didn't seem to notice – or care.

'I admit I took advantage of certain incidents, helped them along a bit, but Larentia's right. Bad luck *does* breed bad luck. I set fire to the warehouse, I doused the kiln, but only the once, and when you're down on your luck, bad things follow as sure as sun follows the rain.'

He had a point. Pessimism does engender negativity, and in retrospect maybe she had attributed too many misfortunes to him. Accidents happen, calamities occur naturally. He couldn't have been responsible for everything on her list. *Only the ones that really mattered.*

'I'm not responsible for sloppy maintenance or clumsy practices,' he said and she'd forgotten how persuasive these conmen can be, 'and I sure as hell don't go round killing animals. All right, it *is* a nasty thing to do, leading Larentia on then dumping her at the altar, but Seferius was the only man smart enough of those six to organize the conspiracy, so it's only right his mother gets a taste of her son's medicine, and there's a difference between tossing sewage down a well and sawing through axles where somebody might have got hurt. You check. I'll bet that was rotted right through and quite honestly it served the penny-pinching bugger right. In fact, I don't care if they *all* go bloody bankrupt.'

How he must have punched the air seeing their despair lead to neglect.

'Except financial ruin wasn't enough for your greedy cold soul. You wanted emotional destruction, as well.'

'Wouldn't you? Claudia, those bastards set me up to cover up double dealings of their own.'

'And exactly what double dealings would those be?'

'How the hell should *I* know? I've been in prison!'

'You don't know? Suddenly, and with all those long, lonely years in which to think about it, you . . . Let me hear that again. You don't know. Let's fall down on our knees and give praise for paranoia.'

'I swear on my life those bastards set me up.'

'I can swear I'm the Queen of Sheba, but people still won't call me Your Highness. Because of you, Vorda risked condemning her soul to immortal obscurity—'

'Who's Vorda?'

'You cut short the life of a shepherd boy—'

'This is ridiculous. Now you're painting me as some kind of monster!'

'Am I? Sorry. But it's a mistake anybody could make when the person they're addressing has destroyed livelihoods, quality of life, peace of mind, and the pain has torn families apart . . . Oh, and did I mention the part where you inflicted such a protracted, painful, terrifying torment on a young man that his sister becomes maddened with grief and lashes out at the wrong people in her misguided quest for revenge? And guess what? This idea of the Furies pursuing the innocents on behalf of the guilty? It's bullshit. Drama for playwrights, Felix. Grist for the zealot's mill.'

The silence was deadly.

'You cannot prove I'm not Darius,' he said at length. 'By the time you send for the evidence I'll be gone, so if you're going to kill me, I suggest you do it now.'

Faster than she could blink, he'd caught her wrist like a manacle. She couldn't hold on. He twisted. The knife clattered harmlessly into the corner.

'It doesn't matter,' she told him. 'I never had any intention of killing you; I just wanted to get your attention.'

A slice through the jugular was too fast. She wanted lions and fear and a really slow build-up.

'Though, as it happens, I *can* prove you're not Darius. You see, after we had that cosy little chat in the plaza this morning, I took a ride to the coast. To Cosa, as it happens, and I brought back a souvenir.'

She called out and a pinched-faced woman looking a decade older than her forty-six years slipped into the room.

'Remember Aurelia, Felix?' Claudia paused. 'Remember your first wife? The one you were married to for fifteen years? Because if you don't, she sure as hell remembers you.'

Twenty-Nine

There was no way she could remain under the same roof as that bastard. The very thought of it made her sick.

Equally, though, she could not hang around while Fortune juggled her ball of chance over Orbilio. Had to do something. Anything. Fortune was fickle. Fortune had let so much blood spill in the precinct, far too much for one person, yet he was alive. Just. Clutching grimly to a thin thread of life, while the Fates stood poised to snip when given the order. Not yet, not yet! Claudia clenched her fists until the knuckles turned white. Let him grow old. Let his hair turn white and his skin crinkle before you cut that damn thread. Give him . . . Oh, pray to every Immortal up on Olympus, please grant Marcus his life. Her nails dug gouges in the palms of her hand. Too much tragedy already. Too many deaths. Too many lives ruined. Let it stop. Here. *Now*. She swung herself back on her horse. Isn't it enough that I've failed? Fine, I've exposed Felix for the monster he is, but the bastard's got away with it and that's not right. Please, I beg you, don't make it worse.

She turned the horse towards the gates.

All right, he was unlikely to harm anyone else, while Larentia had at least been spared public humiliation and the State would probably reimburse the five witnesses to keep a lid on the fact that they'd allowed a convicted criminal to return to Mercurium, wreak havoc and walk free. But she'd failed, because Felix escapes justice, and yes the money will help, but will it bring the blacksmith's children home from Rome? Already it was too late for the brick-maker, his business has been taken over and the paper merchant's storehouse is beyond repair. But, tragic though those stories were, they were nothing compared to the real victims. Lichas, Tages, Vorda and now . . . and now . . .

Don't think about it. Don't even consider it. He's alive. Hanging on by the skin of his teeth, but – praise be to Juno – *alive*.

Once out in the open, she kicked the horse into a gallop. The look of astonishment on Aurelia's face when confronted with the husband she hadn't seen for sixteen years had been priceless. Claudia lifted her own face to the wind. Since there was no question now of Felix denying his past, she supposed there was at least a crumb of satisfaction to be gained from that, and she couldn't in all conscience regret tracking Aurelia down, though heaven knows it hadn't been hard. She still lived in the same house that she'd shared with Felix in Cosa and which he'd gifted her as a divorce settlement. Neither had she remarried.

'I'm part of a new generation of women,' she'd explained, inviting Claudia to join her in grapes, cheese and wine. 'Women who cherish their independence.'

Reclining on a couch upholstered in clean but faded damask, Claudia studied her hostess. Her hazel eyes were small and unblinking, and seemed even smaller set in a thin, pointed face that had more lines than it should for middle-age. Her hair was streaked silver, dull and dry, a sign of too much time spent indoors, which also explained her pale complexion. A homebody, she thought, with no one to keep home for, and the independence Aurelia so desperately cherished had turned her into a recluse. Yet she seemed happy enough to talk about the past – though not curious – openly admitting that she wasn't wealthy, not by a long chalk, but that money meant nothing to her, since she hadn't known it before she met Felix, it wasn't what she married him for, and she'd had little use for it since.

Claudia hadn't confided the reason she'd wanted Aurelia to return to Mercurium with her, only that it was a matter concerning her ex-husband, and was surprised that Aurelia was happy to make the return journey with her there and then. But as her horse's hooves ate up the road, she realized her mistake was springing Aurelia on the cold, callous bastard who had divorced her. Claudia had acted on impulse because of Orbilio – doing something was better than nothing – only she'd blown it, through hot-headed recklessness, not thinking it through. She wondered what on earth had given her the idea that Darius would confess? *Oh no! There's my ex-wife, who'll testify I'm Felix! You'd better lead me straight to the lions!*

Stupid, stupid, stupid, the hooves echoed. Stupid, bloody stupid.

A look on a man's face once he'd been unmasked wasn't enough to convict him of murder. All Claudia had done was expose him, which meant she had failed. She'd failed Lichas and Tages, Vorda and Orbilio, and because she'd been too bloody arrogant to confide her suspicions about Darius, Rosenna had done her damnedest to kill the wrong man. A good man. A man who did not deserve to die . . .

Suddenly the air seemed too thin. She couldn't breathe. Panic uncoiled in her breast. Suppose she never saw that slanting smile again? Never heard that wicked chuckle? Suppose that thick, dark mop never fell carelessly over his forehead again, or his eyes never crinkled up at the corners?

There was no sign of activity at the temple. No acolytes filling oil lamps, no sweepers of floors, no purifiers of altars. Even the temple kittens were crashed out in a heap, a tangle of twitching pink paws and white whiskers. She approached the physicians' quarters with her stomach cramping. No one had been allowed in except temple staff. When she'd left at dawn, they'd been scurrying like rabbits. Now only one or two assistants were gliding silently back and forth, carrying bowls, bandages, pills, and avoiding her eye.

'Can I see him yet?' she asked the guard standing with his arms implacably folded outside the entrance to the medical quarters, and her palms were ridiculously damp.

'The Lord Tarchis says no visitors, milady. Will you wait?'

For ever, my darling. For ever.

'I'll wait.'

In the red, flickering labyrinth nothing stirred. The faces on the frescoes kept their same inane grins, the floral ropes round the pillars didn't slide or shed petals, the irises on the ceiling didn't wilt. Yet in continuity there was comfort, and the deeper she penetrated this underground cavern, the more comfort she gained. She looked back at the offerings – the plaques, the ribbons – and thought *I have nothing to give you, Fufluns*. Nothing to offer . . . Nothing except . . . Slipping off her sandals, she ran through the labyrinth to the god's private chamber. The only sounds that intruded were the occasional spit from a torch set high on the walls and the strange, ethereal music that emanated from the depths of the temple. Lyres, flutes and tambour.

'I have nothing to offer you, god of wine, god of pleasure,' she whispered, 'except this.'

Closing the little door quietly behind her, it was as though Fufluns had been expecting her. Oils burned, fragrant and calming, in braziers around the painted walls. Catnip smouldered in the chafing pans, along with something equally sour and unpleasant, but this was not about her. Claudia studied the god. Red, horned, proudly erect. Tarchis called it horse-trading but if trade makes the human world tick, why not the divine – and what else could she exchange for a life? No amount of riches would tip the balance, for if Orbilio, who had enough in the bank to make King Midas jealous, didn't have sufficient gems and precious metal to save himself, what chance did she have? Suggesting human life wasn't measured in riches . . .

'I give you my dance,' she told the idol. 'I give you my past for his future.'

Her glance fell on the silver platter on which a goblet of rich, dark wine sat, and a note.

Drink, sweet bride. Drink of my love while I drink of your beauty. Drink deeply, my love.

Claudia picked up the goblet and swirled it. The way it clung to the sides suggested the wine wasn't cheap, and in true Etruscan style it hadn't been watered, but the smell indicated that it had been poured out too long. Let a good wine breathe by all means, but like a fish out of water, it dies for lack of its appropriate element. But this was not the moment to start offending the earth god. Claudia tossed it back in three gulps.

224

As the music swelled, she took a deep breath, unpinned her hair, then began to dance the way she used to dance for the sailors. She had vowed never to do it again. Under no circumstances, she'd said. Yet slowly, erotically, she peeled off her clothes and with each layer that she discarded, she felt lighter. Not simply from the weight of the clothes, but her mind, her head, her thoughts all grew lighter until there was nothing but the dance. The heat increased inside the chamber and, swaying, twining, tossing her hair, she gyrated round the idol as she'd gyrated round the tavern a lifetime ago, exciting the earth god with the thrust of her breasts, the swing of her hips, the tongue pushed through half-parted lips. This was no virgin dancing for Fufluns, but this god embodied all earthly pleasures, and if trembling, shivering, arching and gasping had aroused half of Genoa, surely it would arouse him?

Round and round she swirled, caressing her skin with teasing sensuality, until the faces on the wall merged with the face of the idol, winged horses appeared, angels, blue-feathered demons, and now all the faces she had ever met crowded round her, applauding, cheering, egging her on. Her mother was there, her father, her husband. Orbilio, Felix, even his pinch-faced ex-wife. It was like a drug. The more she danced, the hotter she grew, and the hotter she grew, the lighter she became, until nothing mattered but the pulse of the rhythm . . .

Drugs.

She halted abruptly and the room kept on spinning. Drugs were at the centre of everything. Drugs were control, and control . . . Sweet Janus! *Faces!* She grabbed a chafing bowl with one hand while the other rammed two fingers down her own throat. Dear god, she had it all wrong. Yes, Felix was Darius, who'd tossed sewage down a well, set fire to the warehouse and led Larentia on with his courting. But Felix wasn't scared. Even with a knife pressed to his throat, he hadn't been scared – *because Felix had no reason to be.*

The drugged wine came up in a flood. Winged horses and demons galloped away. The faces receded into the mist. Barely pausing for breath, Claudia stuck her fingers down her throat a second time.

When a man's been sentenced to ten years' hard labour for a crime he didn't commit, then loses everything he loves in the process, you might think nothing can touch him. But Darius did care. He cared about Amanda's reliance on her imaginary friend. He cared about a stranger's creaking cart, and the strain on his oxen. He cared enough about Larentia to force the man who'd sent her flying to come back and apologize. So if that man still had feelings after all he'd been through, yet wasn't scared of a knife at his throat – and worse, didn't turn it on his attacker once he'd disarmed her – it was because that man had faced every terror he had ever needed to face.

Felix, goddammit, hadn't stolen the State gold at all.

Retching, sweating, Claudia spat out of the last dregs of the drugged wine and wiped her face with her discarded veil. Control. She'd known all along it was about control . . .

With her palms flat on the floor as she gulped for breath, she asked herself the obvious question. If the six men who testified at his trial believed they'd seen Felix taking heavy sacks from the clerk and the gold was found in his saddle-bags, who set him up? She already knew the answer. Those hazel eyes appeared smaller because of the jealousy and resentment that drove her. The same emotions that had pinched her face and made her old before her time – and the reason she was so happy to talk about the past was so she could relive her triumph. Suddenly Claudia understood the astonishment in Aurelia's eyes when she came face to face with her ex-husband. The bitch thought he was dead. She believed she had killed him by crushing his spirit in punishment for casting her off, but, as always, she had underestimated her man.

From the outset Aurelia was determined to make Felix hers, by feigning pregnancy to trap him in marriage. He'd grow to love her, she told herself, but instead it had the opposite effect. Once he realized he'd been tricked, he turned cold, throwing his passion and energy into oysters. Oysters! Not even another woman! Just some cold little molluscs down in the south, leaving Aurelia with nothing but her pride and a large empty house. No wonder money meant nothing to

226

her. Felix made her wealthy, but money did not buy his love. She consoled herself that at least she was still his wife.

And then, *wham!* Out of the blue he falls in love. Not a mistress. Not another business venture. It's the real deal this time and she knows it. Hell hath no fury like a woman scorned, and having spent fifteen years exhausting every possible means to hang on to her husband, Felix was taking the only thing she had. He was giving his name to some-body else.

He had to pay.

How clever to pretend she didn't mind! While the divorce went through, Aurelia smiled, and oh, how hard she must have smiled. Why not, she would have said. She was young, pretty, this was an opportunity for them both to start over. While all the time in her heart she was wishing him dead! When Mariana fell pregnant so quickly, that bitterness must have known no bounds. Claudia didn't know the details – how could she? – but she could imagine, and as she stag-gered to her feet inside the god's chamber, the tavern-keeper's words echoed back.

'Always rode the same sorrel mare, did our Felix . . . wore a gold headband to keep his curls out of his eyes . . . What did set him out from the crowd was that, unlike most free men, Felix didn't favour white tunics. Bright blue was his colour. Wanted folk to see he'd risen up through the ranks, and though he'd been promoted to equestrian status like your late husband, Felix only tended to wear his purple-striped tunic on state occasions.

It wasn't hard to picture the barren, rejected Aurelia hiring herself an actor. Dressing him up in blue tunic, headband and wig and sneaking his mare out of the stables. Arranging for him to string the treasury clerk along, then transferring the gold to Felix's saddlebags after staging the handover in a public enough place to ensure sufficient men of impec-cable standing and character were around to witness his treachery.

Because Felix had to stand trial for treason.

Revenge for his own filthy betrayal.

Claudia reached for her tunic and belted it tight. Which

meant, she thought, pushing tendrils of damp hair back from her face, Felix hadn't killed Lichas at all. Nor Tages. Felix wasn't a killer, and it wasn't Felix who'd sent thirteen-year-old Vorda to her death. It was Fufluns. She leaned against the idol to catch her breath. How did you do it, you bastard? The room's locked, Timi's outside standing guard like a dragon. How did you get in here?

She hurled the chafing pans on to the floor. That's why the little moons were so worldly. Alone and unchaperoned, they came in here, shut the door, then drank the drugged wine, which made them light-headed, and inhaled catnip and other concoctions, which induced hallucinations. And while they were confused and befuddled, you painted your skin red, put on a pair of ram's horns and then you bloody well raped them. *Worse, you told them it was the god's will.* She reeled at the very arrogance of a man raping these children time and again, whilst brainwashing the girls into believing it was their fault. It was the purpose of their dance, wasn't it? To arouse the god's passion? They had succeeded and so – her stomach lurched – pleasuring Fufluns was their reward!

She remembered the pride on some of the little moons' faces, girls now destined to grow up wild and promiscuous, but with no knowledge of why they'd been scarred. And she remembered, too, the awkwardness and despair that ran through the others; girls like Vorda, who hated the honour they'd been bestowed and would grow up frigid and frightened of men.

Something congealed under Claudia's ribcage. If he'd touched Flavia – so much as laid a hand on the girl . . .

Oh, Vorda! No wonder you were crying, you poor darling. Kol the goatherd saw you. He saw you scrubbing your skin until it was raw, ashamed and sickened and scared. It wasn't the dye you wanted to wash out of your shawl. It was contact with your rapist's skin.

With exaggerated care, Claudia felt her way once again round the walls. She imagined little Vorda skipping in here, Timi's star pupil, possibly even her successor. How proud and excited she must have been. Her big day's approaching. She drinks. The wine is better than anything her family can afford. The virgin bride drinks deeply for Fufluns. As she dances, her mind becomes fuddled. Her vision blurs. She loses her balance. Emerging from the smoke and the darkness is a figure. Red, proud and fiercely erect. He removes her tunic. Takes off her underclothes. Shows her how aroused she has made him. What a privilege to awaken the god's passion. Feel what an honour it is . . . She's repulsed, but he's *Fufluns*. He's a god. He's the idol-made-man. She cannot deny him. He takes her.

But how? How when there are no openings in this wall? No catches, no levers, no locks sticking out – and he could not have been waiting inside the chamber, or Timi would know. How the bloody hell could this pervert perpetrate his evil, when there was no other entrance?

Suddenly Claudia knew. She knew how he'd got in, how he'd got out – just as she knew the name of the red monster who preyed on small girls. She wondered why she wasn't surprised.

Thirty

Plucking a brand from the wall, Claudia picked her way down the stone steps. The plinth had moved easily, once she realized how the bastard had done it. The lever wasn't on any wall; it was by the floor, and like the pipes that had been installed in the villa, the mechanism that moved the statue aside had been expensive in the extreme. It had also been exceptionally well greased. Not a creak, not a groan, yet as she turned the handle, cogs moved the heavy stone plinth aside as though it was made out of cork.

At the foot of the steps, she followed the corridor. These Etruscans do like their underground chambers, she thought, passing row upon row of neat stone sarcophagi. They were not the oldest of tombs. Those had been tiny replica houses, but once the gods made it clear that the dead should be interred deep in the earth, as close to wolf-headed Aita's realm as they could manage, a complex array of passageways was excavated into the hillside, where the spirits of the rich had columns and courtyards to walk in and even the humblest had a niche. Her torch revealed joyous banquets on the walls, reflecting all the pleasures and enjoyment that the dead would delight in, and she tried not to picture the exultation in the rapist's heart as he strode smugly down this narrow corridor in the rock to take his own satisfaction.

Of course, it could have been any one of the three.

Drugs?

Terrence sedated his neurotic sister with opiates. Tarchis used drugs in the shrine, albeit benevolently, and had free access to the temple physician. Lars had worked at the hot springs as a masseur and fed his wife those lovely extra minerals.

The wherewithal to fit that pricey turning-device?
Terrence had inherited more money than he could ever spend. Tarchis was in the perfect position to siphon off temple funds. Lars had free access to Eunice's capital, since men automatically take control of their wives' finances.

Cochineal dye abounded, so Terrence could have picked it up from any one of a dozen places locally, while Tarchis and Lars painted themselves on a regular basis.

How about access to the god's chamber through this secret burial passage?
Well, that was the point. They weren't secret, these tombs. The hills all around were riddled with tunnels, a landscape Lars would know intimately, having been born here, plus Terrence owned the land and would know every well-surveyed feature, while all High Priests were aware of what was in and around their own temples.

And since rapists hate women, that didn't narrow the list.

Terrence was openly contemptuous of Thalia and had remained deviously single to maintain his playboy lifestyle. Tarchis had made it quite plain where a woman's place was: in the wrong. And if a thirty-seven-year-old masseur had married a woman twenty years his senior purely for money, charm would be his disguise.

But only one of those three possessed the core quality required to rape repeatedly and with no conscience. As Claudia followed the passageway through endlessly painted rock faces, so many things fell into place. Heaven knows, there were enough artisans in Mercurium with the talent to design a mechanism with the cogs and gears needed to swivel poor Fufluns aside. But how many of them were young enough not to question the customer's motives yet sufficiently indifferent to religion not to find the request sacrilegious? Moreover, an artisan bright enough to start his own business at the tender age of sixteen . . . Passing side chamber upon side chamber of sleeping Etruscans, she wondered how could this predator sleep? He slept, though, because he had no conscience. No remorse. He'd planned his campaign of rape with military precision, and of course it was not the hot springs that had been central to this story.

It was control. Rape was never about sex. It's always, *always*, about control . . .

The tunnel opened out into a large underground hall whose walls were lavishly decorated with figures and birds, animals and gods, and from which a flight of stone stairs swept upwards. But it was the wooden steps that caught Claudia's eye. New steps leading up to a door which, though locked, boasted a key on a hook on the wall. A spare. In case he somehow needed to make his escape via this route. Her lips pinched. Thought of everything, haven't you? Like the gears in Fufluns' chamber it turned silently. She was aware of her heart thumping against her ribcage as she eased open the door.

Straight into Terrence's bedroom.

'Claudia!'

The shock in his eyes was matched only by hers. Shit. She hadn't expected anything like this. She'd assumed the tunnel would exit into fresh air, but no. Terrence needed to extract every ounce of satisfaction from his abominable secret. Each time he looked at the wall, cunningly painted so the lock didn't show, he'd experience a ripple of pleasure and, of course, he'd been revelling all night like everyone else. Even fiends need their beauty sleep.

'This is an unexpected pleasure, I must say,' he said and she watched as surprise slowly changed to something she couldn't identify but which made her stomach turn over. Too late she realized it was cold calculation. Terrence had seen that she'd come here alone – and that she had no weapon, no bodyguard, nothing.

'You shouldn't have shown me that swivelling laurel. Without that, I would never have found the lever beneath the statue or made the connection between you and Lichas.'

What was it Orbilio said Hadrian had told him? *'Lichas said he loved me too much to let me waste my future on someone like him. He said I didn't know what he had done. I said I didn't care. He said I should, and when it got out my father would disown me.'* They'd assumed the toy-maker was referring to some sexual liaison, perhaps even a promis-

232

cuous past, when what he really meant was the contraption he'd designed on commission. *'I told him again I didn't care,'* Hadrian told Marcus, to which Lichas replied, *'That's what you say now, but what about when we're broke, when we're the scandal of the town and no one will talk to us, and when the luxury you've been used to and the family who raised you are cut off?'*

Rosenna got it wrong. Because her brother hadn't mentioned Terrence by name, she'd assumed the 'he' had meant Hadrian when Lichas told her he intended to go public. She was wrong. Lichas wasn't bothered by some trifling gossip concerning sex between two consenting adults! Still only seventeen, yet smart enough to have started his own business, admit his own sexuality . . . and follow his conscience.

'The clever part came from playing down the commission,' she told Terrence. 'Telling Lichas that you wanted the mechanism installed for . . . what? Using the chamber for private pagan worship?'

Terrence nodded.

'But paying no more than the going rate.'

As he climbed out of bed, naked and tousled, she saw the knife by his pillow. 'Too much money would have aroused his suspicions.' Green eyes smiled ingenuously. 'Couldn't have that.'

There must have been a veiled threat as well, she realized. 'I'm sure you reminded him that we all have our little secrets?'

'I saw no harm in reinforcing the close friendship I enjoy with his boyfriend's father.'

'Except trading Lichas's silence with exposure of his relationship with Hadrian only held good so long as Lichas didn't suspect any ulterior motive.'

What happened, she wondered? Had one of the little moons let something slip? She doubted they'd ever know, because if Lichas hadn't confided Terrence's secret to the people he loved best – Rosenna and his lover – he certainly wouldn't betray the trust of a rape victim! But somehow the toy-maker had discovered the real purpose behind the installation of his pivot and told Terrence that he intended to tell Tarchis.

'For a bright young artisan, you wouldn't credit the lad's naivety,' Terrence said. 'He actually suggested that out-of-the-way meeting place for *my* benefit. Discretion, can you believe that? I think he expected me to fall on my sword or something equally stupid.' His patrician smile was as cold as the Arctic. 'I guess he hadn't thought through the alternative.'

'And Tages witnessed the killing?'

'Dirty blackmailing creep. Came hurtling down the hill, saying if I gave him fifty gold pieces he'd keep his mouth shut. I ask you!' He sniffed in contempt. 'Another moron who didn't stop to use his brain.'

'But you obviously did, because you had the presence of mind to bury Tages, on the grounds that two corpses were bound to invite a murder enquiry.'

Claudia remembered her first meeting with Terrence and Thalia. *'Who'd want to stab him like that?'* Thalia asked, to which Terrence replied, *'I don't suppose anyone* wants *to stab anyone.'* Suddenly she saw a way to talk her way out.

'Look, Terrence, if it wasn't premeditated—'

'You know what I found most irritating? That bloody shirt-lifter washing up on my land. I thought he'd be miles away by the time he surfaced, but it just goes to show. Life's one long learning process, and really that's the beauty of it, don't you think?' There was just a fractional pause. 'Mistakes can be corrected.'

In an instant the knife was in his hand. Claudia turned and ran down the stairs.

'You're quite right. I *should* have taken you the long way out of the maze,' he called down quietly. 'But there's no way out of this labyrinth, Claudia.'

She heard the distinctive click of a lock behind him. Shit. She'd left the torch up there and now, as she plunged deeper into the darkness of the underground hall, she couldn't find the entrance to the tunnel. Terrence's feet echoed on the wooden stairs with inexorable slowness. With a knife in the one hand, the torch in the other, his expression made her blood run cold.

'Do you know what it's like to be a god, Claudia?'

She crouched as his flame made a sweep of the hall.

'When you're Fufluns, you can have any woman you want, and in whatever way takes your fancy.'

'They're not women, they're children,' she hissed back, crunching her shin on the ancient stone stairs. 'And you're not a god, either. You're a pitiful specimen of sub-human scum.'

His laugh echoed round the cavern. An echo of the laughter painted on the walls. The very echo of Hell. 'I like women who fight.'

'Thalia doesn't fight.' And where was that bloody tunnel?

'Wrong. Thalia stopped fighting back on her twelfth birthday when I showed her what men are for.'

Oh, god. His own sister. How could she not have seen through this monster? Right from the start, she'd been repulsed by the way he'd bullied Thalia, and now she saw it was the product of a lifetime spent undermining and demeaning her for no other reason than that she was female. Eunice had read him all wrong. He wasn't over-protective of her. He'd intentionally married her off to a man too old to make her happy and impossible to live with, because he enjoyed watching her suffer. Once she was widowed, he sought others way to torture her, and through opiates, turned Thalia into a rambling neurotic, feeding off his peers' irritation whilst tormenting her further by rubbing her nose into her past and dangling future husbands under her nose.

'Then why drug the girls?' *Where is it? Where is it? Where is the entrance?* 'Why induce hallucinations with catnip and that other foul stuff?'

'A chap needs variety in his diet.' His voice was pure honey as he swept the blackness with his torch. 'With those quivering virgins, the pleasure comes from making them do anything I want, simply by asking them nicely.' He chuckled softly. 'And Claudia, I do mean anything.'

Come on, come on, it must be close now!

'Have you any idea how it feels? Knowing that any time I choose – any bloody time – I can slip down here and get those little tame pussycats to do things even the most hardened whore draws the line at. But you, you're a fighter. You and I will enjoy a different kind of party.'

235

There! At long last, her hand found thin air.

'The hell we will!'

She ran, but he'd caught her shadow in a sweep of his torch and was loping behind down the tunnel.

'The only way you'll take me is by necrophilia, you pervert – or is that something you already enjoy?'

His only answer was laughter. It sounded unbearably confident, but that didn't matter. She was light, she was fast – but shit, he was faster. With the advantage of light and knowing his own territory, he was gaining. She'd never make the god's chamber in time! What now, what now? She ducked into a side chamber and flattened herself against the wall. Behind her, Terrence cursed as he lost sight of his quarry. She heard him slow down. Stop. Saw the patterns of light distort the paintings as he was forced to search each separate sepulchre. Claudia slid down on to her haunches and scrabbled around for a stone, an offering, anything that might serve as a weapon.

Nothing.

And she didn't even have a sandal to defend herself with, while he was armed with a knife, and there was no one to rescue her. Not down here. As far as Timi and Tarchis were concerned, Fufluns rested undisturbed on his plinth. Why would they open the door? They'd shut him away after the festival. It might be days before anyone entered. Orbilio had saved her neck in the past, but his own life swung in the balance. There was nobody left. Just her and her wits. And a desperate desire for justice . . .

Timing her move until he was inside a chamber, she slipped along the corridor one side room at a time. Three, four, five – sweet Juno, how many people were buried down here? But impatience only invites disaster. She forced herself not to think beyond the next chamber, then waited for the light to recede. Six, seven . . .

'I told you.' A strong hand clamped round her throat, pinning her tight to the wall. 'I like women who fight.'

Too late, she saw that he'd outwitted her. Realizing what was happening, he'd notched his torch in a holder in one of the tombs and played Claudia at her own game, grabbing her as she darted out.

'Kick and squirm away, my pretty one,' he crooned. 'But Uncle Terrence is a big man; he's strong and he's no novice at overpowering his struggling victims. In fact, he likes it.'

Dammit, the more she clawed and the harder she scratched, the more aroused he became until suddenly his mood changed. And dim as the light was in that corridor, it was more than adequate to see the knife point glinting an inch from her eye.

'Not so brave now, are we?' he whispered. As she froze, mesmerized by the tip, he pushed his thigh between her legs. 'Do you like that, my pretty one? Doesn't it make you feel good?'

First make them fight, so they can see how much more powerful you are than them. Then make them frightened, so they're ashamed of their cowardice.

'You call that little apology a penis?'

The grip on her throat tightened.

'Let me ask you again.' He thrust himself hard against her. 'Does it feel good?'

'Fuck you.'

Unhurriedly, the pressure on her windpipe increased until, gasping, gulping and choking, Claudia had no choice. 'Yes,' she gargled, and miracle of miracles, the grip lessened. 'Yes, it feels good.'

'How good?' Force was gently exerted on her throat again.

'Very good.'

'Then beg for it, you bitch.' The point of the knife moved half an inch closer. 'Pull down your tunic, tell me how much you want me, then take me inside you, like a good little bitch and maybe, just maybe, if you work really hard to pleasure me, *maybe* I won't have to blind you.'

He'd do it anyway. Terrence was a sadist through to his marrow. Claudia imagined the gratification he sustained from driving that blade into Lichas's stomach. Not his ribs. Not straight up and under into the heart, which, as a patrician who'd been taught military skills, he'd know would despatch a man swiftly. Terrence deliberately opted for slow. The most protracted and painful death he could inflict. Knowing the last thing Lichas would see was his pleasure.

237

'All right, all right,' Claudia whimpered. 'Please, Terrence. Not my sight. I'll do anything, anything you ask, I promise. Whatever you want.'

'Anything? Even . . .' He whispered things that made her gorge rise.

'Even that,' she whispered. Sick bastard.

'Then you'd better start begging, hadn't you, bitch? Take off your tunic and tell me how much you want all those things I've just said.'

Her trembling hands were not acting. As she fumbled to unfasten the brooch on her right shoulder, his gaze dropped to her exposed breast. Bunching her left hand into a fist, she jabbed her betrothal ring straight in his eye.

'Aaaargh!'

He reeled backwards, clutching his eye, but had enough composure to hang on to the knife.

'Bitch!' he roared. 'You're all bitches; I'll kill you for this!'

Claudia spun round and raced back up the corridor. Maddened by anger as much as the pain, Terrence was right behind, and as she swung into the chamber and grabbed for the torch, he punched out with his knife. But she was ready for this. She was diving downwards even as he lunged out, using the flaming brand as a weapon.

And there was only one part of his anatomy to aim for.

As he howled, writhed and roared, Claudia had the satisfaction of knowing Terrence would never rape another woman again.

Thirty-One

This time she wasn't waiting for anyone's sodding approval. This time, as she marched towards the infirmary, Claudia Seferius would not take no for an answer. Too much time had slipped past already.

Having left Terrence thrashing in agony (and pray Jupiter the pain never lessened), she'd raced back to the chamber as fast as she could, swivelled the plinth and jammed the lever with one of the bronze chafing pans. Not that he'd follow. He'd crawl back to his room, tend to his wounds, then try to find a way to talk himself out of it. Save it for the lions, she thought. The first thing she did was rush straight to Tarchis, who'd mustered the temple guard almost before she'd finishing spilling her story, and there was no question of not taking the bastard alive. Terrence was too arrogant to take his own life. In fact, he'd still be trying to worm his way out of it as they lugged him off in chains, and though it was too late for Lichas, Tages and especially Vorda, there was satisfaction in knowing he faced the grimmest of executions. For a patrician, the public humiliation would be as bad as the agony and she smiled. When it came to rapists, Rome did have a penchant for sending out a clear message!

The worst part was the impact this scandal would have on Mercurium. Terrence had supported the cult of Fufluns for his own vile ends, and discord was growing among the conquering Romans. They'd already vandalized the temple of Juno, trying to blame it on locals. Now they could argue there was no justification for maintaining these pagan practices. The high priest was a zealot, the chief sponsor a predator, and since they couldn't shape up, then ship out. Let's put paid to it once and for all. Claudia glanced at the vibrant scenes on the walls, listened to the music that offered calm in a world of worry – strings, flute and tambour. Lars was probably the only person involved enough and passionate enough to fight his god's cause, but would he want to?

There were times, she thought, when she couldn't see wood for trees. Jumped at every daft shadow. Lars wasn't after Eunice's money! The light in Eunice's eyes stood proof to that. The man idolized her! No conman would be so attentive, so loving, so passionate, so compassionate without letting his guard slip at least once. Claudia thought about the insight into Roman life that Eunice had offered him, how he'd reciprocated by inviting her into his world, then been overwhelmed that she'd embraced it. No doubt both believed that what they enjoyed was ephemeral – and when one doesn't expect something to last, that's the time it usually does. With Lars fighting his corner, Fufluns was looking at a good few Bridal Dances yet.

'Ah, there you are,' a velvet voice drawled, and it seemed right at home in this subterranean cavern. 'Amanda said she saw you riding off in this direction.'

'Does anything escape that little monster's notice?'

'With time on her hands and no one to play with, she's had nothing else to do, but that situation is set to change.' Candace smiled, and this time it lit up her eyes. 'I want to thank you. I want to thank you for giving me my daughter back, or perhaps more accurately not taking her away from me.' She paused. 'You could have denounced me as a conspirator in Felix's sabotage, but instead you showed me what I'd lost sight of, and for this I thank you. We are moving on. Naturally. But next time we will put down roots and Indigo will fade like frost in the sun.'

'I'm glad,' Claudia said. The child deserved it.

'Before we go.' Candace bit down on her plum-painted lip. 'You accused me of giving Larentia happy pills, but don't you see? Did you really not see why, no matter how much I forced her hand through those walks on the wind, your mother-in-law wouldn't set a date for the wedding?'

Well, I'll be damned. It had been staring Claudia in the

face all along! The old boot had nothing in common with Darius. He was too young for her for one thing, she'd never leave Tuscany for another, and it was far too hot in the south.

'Don't you think old people get consumed by the same urges as you youngsters? Course we do, and when you see my Darius, you'll understand why. Quite the stud, if you pardon the pun.'

The wicked old trout had been leading everyone on – including the man she believed was a wealthy horse-breeder. It was exhilaration that took ten years off her. To be courted and pampered by a much younger man turned other elderly widows green with envy, and she loved rubbing their noses in it.

'Did you see the way people looked at her?' Candace said. 'That was the drug, and that's why she kept stringing him along.'

Not just Darius, Claudia thought. Larentia had been laughing at her daughter-in-law all along. (And to think she'd actually felt sorry for the poisonous old bat!)

'Goodbye, Candace,' she said, wishing her luck. 'I think you and Amanda deserve it.'

'Actually,' a voice rumbled, 'there'll be three of us.'

Darius stepped out from behind a pillar, something he seemed very good at, and as much as Claudia wanted to remain cross with him, the fire had gone out of her belly.

'Claudia, I don't ever expect you to forgive me, but I do hope that one day you can understand.'

'I already do,' she said softly. 'Tortured by your family's deaths and the injustice of false accusation, on top of being consumed by a feeling that you'd failed everyone you ever loved, you truly believed in your heart that you owed them retribution.'

That gravel voice wasn't the rusty horse razor Orbilio imagined. It really had trod the path to Hell.

'I was wrong, though, that was the point. I brought vengeance on those who didn't deserve it, and . . . and I cannot ever put that right.'

'No, you can't,' she agreed crisply, 'but none of those

involved know that they've been set up, so I suggest you leave the rest of the silver for the families you've destroyed—'

'I can't,' he cut in. 'I've already spent it.'

On expensive renovations to Claudia's villa, among other things, she reflected, but when you're teetering on the edge of ruin yourself, this is no bad thing. Claudia Seferius had never had a problem with hypocrisy.

'Here.' Candace began to remove her welter of bangles and pendants. 'Like we said, my child, love is more precious than gold.' She handed Claudia her rings and anklets. 'I cannot carry Kush on my body, any more than I can carry Kush in my heart. I do not belong there, I have never belonged there. My homeland only brought me heartache and pain.'

'If you can both put the past behind you, you have every chance of success,' Claudia said. 'Once neither of you cared, and Darius, you were dead every bit as much as your father, your mother, Mariana and your child. But now you do care. You've begun to feel again, so for gods' sake don't waste it.'

Second chances are as precious as they are rare, but she couldn't linger with tearful goodbyes. The infirmary awaited and, funny, but inside this artificially lit subterránean warren, it was easy to lose track of time. So much had happened since dawn broke over that enormous pool of blood in the precinct that it was probably no later than midday – yet a lifetime could have passed since then.

Claudia closed her eyes and prayed to the Fates who measured the thread that that lifetime wasn't Orbilio's.

In the House of Shadows, where whispers flitted like gnats round the Runes of Adversity, the Goddess of Immortality lifted the veil from the Mirror of Life. In it, she saw spring blossoms ripen into rich autumn fruits. She saw seeds in the womb grow into man, then watched those same strong, knotted muscles turn scraggy and thin. Everything changed except Immortality herself. But all earthly things must come to an end.

As the last grain of sand trickled through the holed jug

that measured the span of human life, the Herald of Death slipped on his silent winged sandals.

'I don't care what the bloody priest says!' Claudia barged past the guard outside the infirmary and flung open the door. 'I have to see him. I have to talk to him. I have to tell him not to go yet.'

'Tell who not to go where?' a baritone drawled from the bed.

Claudia blinked. He was sitting up. Miracle of miracles, he was sitting up, with a bandage round his upper arm and he was smiling. Relief coursed through her veins, and for some stupid reason her legs had gone wobbly. Sitting up. Smiling. With a bandage round his . . .

Round his *upper arm*?

And what's this? It's not just one cot that's occupied, but *three* bloody beds. Orbilio, Orson and Rosenna, all pale, all sporting bandages . . .

'I'm sorry, milady, it is the Lord Tarchis' orders that no outsider be permitted in the infirmary without his authority.' The guard was one step away from breathing fire. 'I will have to ask you to leave.'

'Ask all you like,' the baritone rumbled. 'I've seen that look in her eye before.'

'What's the matter, guard?' A stocky individual with close-set eyes marched into the room, carrying a surgical box under his arm.

'I've tried to get her to leave, sir . . .'

'What for? Invalids need visitors.' He deposited the box at the foot of Orson's bed and flipped open the hinge. 'Cheers 'em up.'

'But Lord Tarchis—'

'Gave the order before he went to bed. It was an expedient way to keep order while people recovered from yesterday's revels.' He brought out a pair of sharp pointed scissors and cut through the stitch holding the bandage round Orson's shoulder. 'She can stay.'

'Will someone please tell me what's going on?' Claudia demanded. 'For gods' sakes, Orbilio, I thought you were at death's door!'

'I'm sorry if my good health disappoints you.'

'You do not enjoy good health, young man, so stop bragging.' The physician waved the scissors with uncompromising menace. 'If you must know,' he told Claudia, unwinding Orson's bloodied bandage, 'the only reason *that* little hothead,' he pointed to a contrite Rosenna, 'didn't do more damage was because *this* little hothead,' he tapped Orson's skull, 'got between them.'

No wonder there was so much blood in the precinct! It had spurted out from three different bodies.

'You'll need an abacus to keep count of the wounds,' he said, slapping a poultice on to a neatly stitched cut. 'Apparently, it was some struggle, our little wildcat none too eager to part with her skinning knife, but at a rough guess, our young hero sustained four, the wildcat sustained six – mostly slashes that cost them a lot of blood – while the braggart whose hand you seem to be crushing took a blow to the upper arm, two to the chest, and one in the side that was quite deep.'

Her stomach flipped over. Sweet Janus, if Marcus had done as she had asked, he would have been dead . . .

'Dammit, Orbilio, don't you ever do anything you're told?' It must be the stuff he'd put on that poultice, because her eyes had started to water. 'I specifically asked you to put Orson under arrest.'

'What for?' The boy's face twisted in puzzlement. 'Oi handed that jewel box in the minute Oi found it there under me bed! You can't go round arresting folks for being honest!'

Or giving civilians medals for being brave, she reflected. Looking at the expression that passed between Orson and Rosenna – a mix of complicity, affection and sorrow – it was obvious that, whether he'd seen her pocket the knife or had just been alarmed by her strange behaviour, Orson had shadowed her during the festival.

'Mind, Oi think you'll be happy with me news, marm.'

Claudia's stomach was still churning. 'Sorry, Orson, what did you say?'

'Oi said, your Flavia don't want me no more. Partly it were coz she thought it were boring, stupid and a complete waste of time, me making toys for them kiddies, but like I told her, if every man were a lord, where'd we be?'

There was merit to that, though Claudia preferred the alternative. 'I think I can guess the other part.'

'Aye.' He nodded glumly. 'It's coz Oi weren't there when she danced.'

That's Flavia for you! While Orson's saving Orbilio from death and Rosenna from herself, the little cow's bitching because her boyfriend wasn't watching her dance.

'You're lucky,' she told him, as the physician stitched up the fresh bandage. 'You escaped. I'm stuck with the wretched girl.'

It was good to see the ugly lug laugh.

'Right, Oi'm off then,' he told the doctor. 'Oi'm a working man, see, and me hands need to be busy.'

'As do mine, young man,' the physician replied sharply. 'Now lie still or I'll make you sew your wounds up yourself, and *you* can get back into bed, too, madam.'

Rosenna's lips pinched. 'Holy Nox, you don't seriously expect me to make a run for it in blooming bandages?'

Pushing her thick tangle of curls back from her face as the physician announced that she wouldn't be running anywhere with that amount of blood loss, young woman, and anyway, if the investigator intended to press charges, she'd be in the army's infirmary, not the temple's, Rosenna felt a rush of colour to her cheeks.

She glanced awkwardly at Orson, who beamed proudly back.

She twizzled a curl.

The colour of rosehips in autumn, eh?

Claudia watched the exchange and thought, *they'll be all right, her and Orson.* Both were fighters in their different ways, and though he was younger than her, just like her brother, he had a wise head on his shoulders, and Claudia envied the man who could truly be content with himself.

Yet something wasn't right. Although the infirmary was warm, goose pimples rose on her arm and the hair prickled on the back of her neck. It was as though the Herald of Death had just passed.

But if Terrence was in chains, Darius was innocent, Orbilio was alive . . . who was being summoned?

Aurelia stared at the goblet on the wooden table. Everyone said hemlock was painless, but no one she knew had first-hand experience. She wouldn't know for sure until she drank.

But there was nothing to live for. So long as Felix was suffering, she had been happy – if happy was the right word. She'd been able to wallow in her own cast-off misery, barren, unloved and empty. Her world had revolved solely round retribution, calling upon Veive for revenge. Veive had answered. He sent his arrows straight into Felix, and the winged avenger dipped them in poison for her without even asking.

She had watched impassively as the evidence mounted against him. The clerk testifying that it was Felix Musa who'd incited him to steal from the Treasury. The witnesses who'd seen Felix stash it away in his saddlebags. That actor had been worth every penny, she thought. The way he'd impersonated her ex-husband's walk, his dress, his every mannerism. Not that Aurelia attended the trial. She was supposed to be the tolerant ex, and of course she could have gone along to support him, but what if her emotions gave her away? She'd stayed in Cosa, content that he'd been found guilty, his assets stripped, his shame and humiliation made public – exactly like hers had been.

Fifteen years. Fifteen years she'd loved that man, and then what? He threw her away like an old sandal, and it wasn't her fault his father and mother were dead. They took their own lives. It was their decision, not hers, but oh how she rejoiced when Mariana had died giving birth. Now Felix would know what it was like not to have children. To be barren and sterile, like her.

And then Claudia brought her face to face with him again. Her Felix. Her very own Felix . . .

The love that she'd felt from the beginning welled up, but this time it came with an emptiness like she'd never known. He would not take her back. Not now, not ever; it was over. She'd hurt him too deeply for him to reciprocate, they couldn't even build again on a friendship, and now he was leaving with some coloured bitch and, worse, adopting her white bastard child.

As long as Aurelia had believed Felix dead she hadn't cared, but now, oh, the pain. The pain of seeing him, loving him, of being not only discarded for another woman a second time, but hated. Truly hated.

'Wolf-headed Aita is waiting,' the Herald of Death whispered softly.

Aurelia reached for the goblet. 'I'm ready,' she sighed.

In the House of Shadows, where no sunlight shines, the Seraph who measured the thread cut through cleanly.

Standing at the top of the steps, Claudia stared out across the landscape of Tuscany, over its vines and its olives, its sheep and its pastures all bathed in centuries-old sunlight. Down in the precinct, the water in the Pool of Plenty sparkled beneath the pomegranates, and it must have been a trick of the light, but she swore she saw one of the satyrs wink. A gentle warm breeze carried away the sacred incense that burned in the tripods – frankincense, cedar, cinnamon and juniper – and the ethereal music pulsed softly around her. Lyre, flute and tambour.

The gods had answered her prayers before she'd asked them, she thought. They'd given him life when she feared death, but the emptiness remained. He was leaving. Going back to Gaul to resume his post as Head of the Aquitanian Security Police, while she was returning to Rome.

'Don't suppose you know where a chap could find a crutch around here?' a baritone rumbled.

Claudia spun round. He'd managed to clamber into his long patrician tunic, but with his arm bandaged up, hadn't been able to belt it and was in danger of tripping himself up. Mindful of his wounds, she tied it gently and resisted the urge to push that ridiculous floppy fringe away from his forehead. As he leaned on her shoulder for support, she was sure she could smell sandalwood over the mouldy bread poultice they'd stuck on his wounds. Nonsense, of course. And besides, she was relieved he was leaving. Ever since that little white doughboy failed to win the effigy race, she'd been torn between fiddling her taxes (again), making a fraudulent claim for compensation (again), or watering the vintage (again). With the long arm of the law probing Gaul and not Rome, she was free to do all bloody three.

'Shouldn't you be in bed?' He was less than steady on his feet as she helped him down the steep steps.

'The doctor says providing I don't do anything stupid for a couple of days, I should be fine.'

'Liar. You didn't even ask the physician's permission, and that's stupid for a start. Did you see the way he punched Rosenna's pillow?'

'I was just too damn quick for him,' Marcus quipped, wincing as his side caught the handrail. 'Although I'll happily to go back to bed, if you'll come with me.'

'If we're playing doctors and nurses, you need to remember that I've already cauterised one patient this morning. And why didn't you have Rosenna arrested?'

'What, and rake the whole nasty business up even more? Right now the focus is firmly on Terrence, exactly where it belongs.'

Finally they reached the bottom, where the temple kittens found the hem of his tunic the perfect height to play catch.

'Yes, why *did* Rex try to cover up Lichas's murder, if he believed his son was innocent?' she asked, disentangling their sharp little claws.

'Because he was ashamed it would come out that Hadrian – his only son, and heir to his illustrious name – was running off with a commoner,' Orbilio said, puffing from the exertion. 'In dear old Uncle Rexie's book, that's worse than homosexuality, but put the two together and the disgrace it would bring if it became public was worth anything. Even covering up murder.'

Claudia distracted the kittens by trailing a herbal garland over the flagstones.

'So, er, you're not marrying Terrence, then?'

And who'd have thought that playing with a couple of cats would have made a grown man grin from ear to ear? Honestly, she'd never understand these patricians!